A GENTLE MURDERER

DOROTHY SALISBURY DAVIS

Edited, with an introduction and notes,

by Leslie S. Klinger

LIBRARY OF CONGRESS

Poisoned Pen PRESS

Copyright © 1951 by Dorothy Salisbury Davis
Introduction and notes © 2023 by Leslie S. Klinger
Cover and internal design © 2023 by Sourcebooks and Library of Congress
Cover design by Sourcebooks
Cover image: *Keep Your Fire Escapes Clear*. Federal Art Project,
1937. Work Projects Administration Poster Collection, Prints &
Photographs Division, Library of Congress, LC-DIG-ds-05007.

Published by Poisoned Pen Press, an imprint of Sourcebooks,
in association with the Library of Congress
P.O. Box 4410, Naperville, Illinois 60567-4410
(630) 961-3900
sourcebooks.com

This edition of *A Gentle Murderer* is based on the first edition in the Library of
Congress's collection, originally published in 1951 by Charles Scribner's Sons.

Cataloging-in-Publication Data is on file with the Library of Congress.

Printed and bound in the United States of America.
SB 10 9 8 7 6 5 4 3 2 1

CONTENTS

FOREWORD

Crime writing as we know it first appeared in 1841, with the publication of "The Murders in the Rue Morgue." Written by American author Edgar Allan Poe, the short story introduced C. Auguste Dupin, the world's first wholly fictional detective. Other American and British authors had begun working in the genre by the 1860s, and by the 1920s we had officially entered the golden age of detective fiction.

Throughout this short history, many authors who paved the way have been lost or forgotten. Library of Congress Crime Classics bring back into print some of the finest American crime writing from the 1860s to the 1960s, showcasing rare and lesser-known titles that represent a range of genres, from cozies to police procedurals. With cover designs inspired by images from the Library's collections, each book in this series includes the original text, reproduced faithfully from an early edition in the Library's collections and complete with strange spellings and unorthodox punctuation. Also included are a contextual introduction, a brief biography of the author, notes, recommendations for further reading, and suggested discussion questions. Our hope is for these books to start conversations, inspire further research, and bring obscure works to a new generation of readers.

Early American crime fiction is not only entertaining to read, but it also sheds light on the culture of its time. While many of the titles in this series include outmoded language and stereotypes now considered offensive, these books give readers the opportunity to reflect on how our society's perceptions of race, gender, ethnicity, and social standing have evolved over more than a century.

More dark secrets and bloody deeds lurk in the massive collections of the Library of Congress. I encourage you to explore these works for yourself, here in Washington, DC, or online at www.loc.gov.

—Carla D. Hayden, Librarian of Congress

INTRODUCTION

In Dorothy Salisbury Davis's *A Gentle Murderer*, a Catholic priest plays a vital role, working in parallel with the police to track a serial killer. Although the novel is noteworthy for the detailed study of the mind of the titular murderer, it is not the first crime fiction to bring psychology to bear, nor is it the first to involve clergy in the detection of crime. However, in its blending of the two elements, it is a masterpiece.

In her authoritative 1929 survey of the history of crime writing, *The Omnibus of Crime,* Dorothy L. Sayers suggested that two of the very earliest examples of crime fiction were the apocryphal tales of Bel and the Dragon and Susannah, both featuring the Jewish priest Daniel as the detective.[*] Bel and the Dragon was probably written about 100 BCE, and in it, Daniel solves the mystery of the disappearance of offerings to the idol Bel. Daniel anticipates modern police procedural techniques of fingerprinting and tire and foot plaster casting by using ashes to capture evidence of the theft. In Susannah, probably written one hundred years later, Daniel anticipates Perry Mason,

---

[*] Dorothy L. Sayers, ed., *The Omnibus of Crime* (New York: Payson & Clarke, 1929), 11.

taking on the role of defense attorney in a courtroom drama with all of the elements expected by the modern reader: accusation, trial, cross-examination, revelation of guilt of a previously unsuspected person, punishment of the guilty, and celebration of the defender.[*]

The first significant modern clerical detective is Father Brown, whose adventures G. K. Chesterton recorded in fifty short stories collected in five volumes, beginning in 1911.[†] Chesterton's character was widely admired, and Ellery Queen ranked Father Brown as the equal of Sherlock Holmes and C. Auguste Dupin, whom Queen considered the greatest of all detectives.[‡] There are many other examples of stories featuring clerics as sleuths, including such popular series as Harry Kemelman's Rabbi David Small, who appeared in a number of novels beginning with *Friday the Rabbi Slept Late* (1964), and the Father Roger Dowling stories by Ralph McInerny (starting with *Her Death of Cold* in 1977), which also became a successful television series. Philip Grosset—who is fascinated by stories about clerical detectives for what they tell us about "what really goes on behind the scenes" in their organizations and their personal lives—has created a website listing 380 clerical detectives.[§]

---

[*] Admittedly, in Susannah, Daniel is not identified as a priest, but there is no reason to doubt that this is the same Daniel as depicted in other biblical tales.

[†] There are two additional Father Brown stories that do not appear in the published collections, and possibly a third unpublished story. See *The Annotated Innocence of Father Brown* by G. K. Chesterton, edited by Martin Gardner (Oxford: Oxford University Press, 1987), 255. A "missionary" named Ben Baltic, who is also an investigator, actually preceded Father Brown, in Fergus Hume's *The Bishop's Secret* (1900), never to be heard of again. The first Father Brown story, "The Blue Cross," appeared in the September 1910 issue of *Storyteller* magazine, and *The Innocence of Father Brown* (London: Cassell, 1911) was the first collection of Father Brown stories.

[‡] See *Queen's Quorum* (Boston: Little, Brown, 1951), 60–61.

[§] "Clerical Detectives," https://www.detecs.org/intro.html.

Clerical sleuths have advantages over their secular counterparts, argues Rosemary Herbert in her *Oxford Companion to Crime and Mystery Writing*: "They are usually able to go everywhere, talk to everyone—no one so spans the social spectrum as the clergy—and take as much time as they need. Nor, as a rule, are they answerable to any worldly body for their actions."* This lack of official status leaves them free to poke into places where officialdom cannot go, but at the same time, it deprives the clerics of the resources of the police—and the strictures. A cleric may forgive a crime, while an official may not. And while a cleric may operate outside the rules, as recent scandals have revealed, the sanctity of religion and the presumption of morality may conceal wrongdoing behind the closed doors of places of worship.

In his 1989 book-length study titled *Mysterium and Mystery: The Clerical Crime Novel,*† Rev. William David Spencer delineates what he sees as common denominators of the clerical crime novel. These may be summed up as follows:

1. Things are not what they seem; matters are rarely what their surface appearance suggests. This is an inevitable result of the exposure of secrets to the clergy, whether in confessionals or otherwise, who must inescapably conclude that parishioners and others with whom they interact cannot be measured by their outward expressions but only by their actions.

2. Clerics themselves are regularly misjudged. There is an

---

* New York: Oxford University Press (1999), 76.

† Ann Arbor, MI: UMI Research Press (1989). Rev. Spencer did not include *A Gentle Murderer* in his study because, in an age before the internet, he simply was unaware of its existence (William David Spencer, email to the editor, April 22, 2022).

expectation that clerics are by definition saintly, but it is their very humanity that makes them such effective sleuths.

3. Murder is a sin against God. Not only is it an offense to society, but it is also an affront to the source of all life, and therefore it is imperative that God's agents take action.

4. In virtually all clerical detective stories, clerics must combat their own pride and are often obsessed with this character flaw.

5. Finally, no clerics are ashamed of their calling or vocation (though one or two may leave the clergy at the story's end). Rather, they are as firm in their beliefs as the secular persons they encounter may be confused about their own.[*]

Each of these elements may be found in *A Gentle Murderer*, and so it may be said that Davis's novel is part of a long tradition of clerical crime fiction. However, Davis only briefly develops the character of Father Duffy, her priest-detective, and the importance of Davis's work lies in broadening this subgenre by including the concept of criminal profiling.

The idea that understanding the mind of the criminal was an important tool of detection did not gain currency until the 1910s. Edwin Balmer and William MacHarg created the brilliant Luther Trant, who made scientific use of psychology in his investigations. These stories, collected as *The Achievements of Luther Trant*,[†] include the earliest fictional appearance of a lie

---

[*] Spencer, *Mysterium and Mystery*, 306–7.

[†] Edwin Balmer and William MacHarg, *The Achievements of Luther Trant* (Boston: Small, Maynard, 1910).

detector. Trant expresses his philosophy of detection simply: "[If any detective] has half the persistence in looking for the marks of crime on *men* that he had in tracing its marks on *things*, he can clear up half the cases that fill the jail in three days."* Trant was speaking primarily of using scientific instruments to measure the truth of the statements of witnesses and suspects, but his views opened the door to what would eventually become "criminal profiling," studies of the psychology of perpetrators.

The earliest "profiling" is usually identified as the work of Drs. Thomas Bond and George Phillips, who, in the fall of 1888, studied the evidence of the Jack the Ripper killings and offered conclusions about the personality of the serial killer.† Although many suggested that the Ripper had to be a medical man, based on the precision of the cuts inflicted by the killer, Dr. Bond disagreed, concluding that the gaping wounds inflicted by the Ripper were not consistent with the training of a medical expert or "even the technical knowledge of a butcher or horse slaughterer." In his opinion, the murderer must have been "a man subject to periodical attacks of Homicidal and erotic mania. The character of the mutilations indicate that the man may be in a condition sexually, that may be called satyriasis. It is of course possible that the Homicidal impulse may have developed from a revengeful or brooding condition of the mind, or that Religious Mania may have been the original disease, but I do not think either hypothesis is likely."‡

---

* Balmer and MacHarg, *The Achievements of Luther Trant*, 3. Of course, the idea of looking at "marks on things"—later codified as "Locard's exchange principle" (named after French criminologist Dr. Edmond Locard) and meaning that crimes leave trace physical evidence from contacts—was itself relatively new, its principal fictional proponent being Sherlock Holmes.

† Lea Winerman, "Criminal Profiling: The Reality behind the Myth," *Monitor on Psychology* 35, no. 7 (July–August 2004): 66–69.

‡ Expressed in a letter to Dr. Robert Anderson, the head of the London CID, in November 1888, quoted in *Criminal Shadows: Inside the Mind of the Serial Killer* by David Canter (New York: HarperCollins, 1994), 5–6.

Of course, because the Ripper was never apprehended, the veracity of Bond's observations was never tested. However, the idea of profiling caught on with law enforcement, and the Federal Bureau of Investigation (FBI) eventually created a team of investigators who applied their collective experience to studying serial killers. Notwithstanding the popular view of criminal profiling,* and no matter the official title of the Behavioral Sciences Unit of the FBI, profiling is rather less scientific than Luther Trant might have claimed. Instead, it consists of informed speculation about the likely psychology of a perpetrator, based on a deep knowledge of human nature.

Davis's Father Duffy and Sergeant Ben Goldsmith, the policeman who pursues the killer, derive their profiling skills from disparate backgrounds of religious training and police work. However, they both succeed in finding the killer, seemingly from opposite ends of his life. Ultimately, it is through combining their psychological insights with traditional police procedures, such as measuring distances, analyzing forensic evidence, and canvassing witnesses, that they are able to track him down. In pulling these elements together into a suspenseful tale, Davis constructs a brilliant novel unifying several different schools of crime fiction.

—Leslie S. Klinger

---

* Psychiatrists, psychologists, and criminal profilers make popular detectives. For an extensive but incomplete list, see Lucinda Surber and Stan Ulrich, "Stop, You're Killing Me," http://www.stopyourekillingme.com/JobCats/Psychiatrists.html.

1

"Bless me, Father, for I have sinned..."[*]

Father Duffy had heard the phrase over and over again that night, for it was Saturday and he was assistant pastor of St. Timothy's, one of the largest parishes in Manhattan.[†] He had heard small voices whisper of disobedience, untruths and petty thefts, older voices stumbling in their quest for delicate ways to phrase indelicate sins...lust, drunkenness, cruelty and sloth; and he had listened to the urgent rasp of the aged, repeating sins long since forgiven but well remembered by the sinner whose each accounting might be his last. Some had come on tiptoe, some in bold clicking heels and some in measured shuffling from the last pew in the church, where even now they would be sitting like Lazarus,[‡] repeating their unworthiness.

It was after nine o'clock and neither side of the confessional was occupied. The priest sat in the semi-darkness, his body stiff

---

[*] Though not prescribed in the Bible, these are the traditional words preceding a confession by a Catholic penitent.

[†] A fictional parish.

[‡] Lazarus was famously resurrected from death by Jesus (John 11:1–44), so this metaphor suggests that the people in the last pew are sitting deadly still until they are returned to life to walk to the confessional.

and aching, with his hand on his breviary.* He was waiting for perhaps one tardy penitent, as a child watches for one last drop from a turned-off faucet. He smiled at himself for the stubbornness that kept him waiting there, sweat-soaked, for just one more. That was greed of a sort. Through the open window above him the August heat rolled in like a fat old man, and settled with him in the cubicle. It brought the smell of dust, bus exhaust, frankfurters and tobacco smoke. He would have liked a cigarette… ten minutes more. He held his watch to the dim, curtained light: nine twenty-three. In a brief hush in the flow of traffic down Ninth Avenue someone called: "Good night, Father."

That would be to Father Gonzales, another assistant. His stole laid away for the night, Gonzales would be standing a moment on the church steps before going around to the rectory for sandwiches and a cold drink. A wave of street traffic muffled the voices. Father Duffy felt the ribbon in his breviary and opened the book, still without turning on the light although he had yet a half-hour's reading to finish his office of the day.

Why should he wait like this? Why should he wait in the darkness? A thousand priests had confessed a hundred thousand sinners that night, and in the morning as many more as needed would be confessed. And even now, for as many as confessed…he heard a roar of drunken laughter somewhere, a woman's giggle, a police siren, the smashing of a bottle…

"Father…"

He was startled at the voice, having heard no sound near him, nor noticed any light as the curtain parted. He glanced at the face beyond the screen, thinking he might have imagined the voice, weary as he was. He averted his eyes immediately. But in the darkness beneath him he could still see the outline

---

* A book containing the services for each day.

of the face. As his imagination held it, the facial contours were like the negative of a film in which the lines are so exaggerated as to suggest great suffering. And yet the wide eyes were full of calm, he thought. The penitent was there, having won a great struggle with himself. He was a young man, and the small, worn face reminded Father Duffy of pictures of St. Francis.* He was reminded also of boys he had seen in the war after their first experience under fire…boys no longer…all this in the instant while he drew the panel across the empty section and made the sign of the cross.

"Father, I think I've done a terrible thing. I always wanted to do something good in my life, always, and it's never worked out that way. I wanted to be a priest. I didn't want to and I did want to…my mother saved and saved…"

He spoke a little above a whisper, calmly for the first few words and then with mounting excitement. Father Duffy did not look up. He nodded his head slowly to quiet and encourage the distraught man.

"Father, I think I've killed someone. I wanted to die myself. But I committed murder instead. I wanted to do some good. I tried. I went up there—Father, are you listening?"

Again he nodded, trying to do it more slowly, no more than halftime to his heartbeat. Without articulating the prayer, the priest craved wisdom from heaven.

"I was always welcome up there, Father. All I had to do was let her know I was there if she was home. She was kind to me. Now I think she tried. I took a hammer with me. My mother gave me a hammer for my tenth birthday. It was the only present

---

* Saint Francis, the patron saint of Italy, venerated poverty and emulated the life of Christ. He was the founder of the Franciscan Order and a great lover of nature.

she ever gave me. St. Joseph was a carpenter,* she said. I had the hammer, and when she said 'why?' I couldn't remember why. That's something I always wanted to know myself. Why? Why couldn't I? Why didn't anyone care? Why didn't anybody pay attention? Why? why? They could have. I didn't run away. Now I remember why I took the hammer—her windows always stuck this time of year. It's so hot... You don't believe me, do you, Father? No. I can see you don't..."

From a humble, pathetic outpouring, the tone was changing to something close to abuse. "If you don't believe me..." the voice hesitated again.

Out of an inspired discretion, Father Duffy said almost matter-of-factly, "How long is it since your last confession?"

There was a long moment's silence and Father Duffy anchored his chin upon his breast that his reflexes might not betray him into a sudden startling move.

"Oh Father, when I was a child...Father McGohey gave me a prayerbook for my first Communion. Then he took it away because I was fighting, he said. But I'll tell you the truth, Father. I always knew he didn't take it away because I was fighting. He took it away because I lost the fight. Then my mother gave me the hammer. I wanted one with claws. She knew it. She had to give me one with two heads. I couldn't take out nails if I made a mistake. I had to smash things...full of blood and hair. I washed it in the sink. The funny thing then, Father—I felt clean then, too. I never felt so clean before. I walked out without even looking back to see her..."

Somewhere nearby a siren sounded...police, fire,

---

* That is Joseph, the father of Jesus. Jesus is referred to in Matthew 13:55 as "the carpenter's son," though scholars point out that the Greek term really means no more than an artisan in wood, iron, or stone. There is no reference in the Bible to Joseph owning a hammer.

ambulance… Father Duffy could not tell. The man beside him heard it, too. The priest could hear him suck in his breath through his teeth.

"They're coming for me, Father. Only I don't want them to come for me. It's not that I'm afraid. I just want to walk in to them myself. I want to hang on just once. I want to be clean just once. I dreamt I was right up to my neck in slime once. It was all stinking and I kept trying to keep my mouth clean but it kept sucking me in. That's what the world's like if you let yourself get dirty once…"

The breviary slipped from the priest's sweating hand. He let it go. Gratefully he felt it fall on his leg and slide down his cassock noiselessly.

"I thought if I could just keep my mouth clean I wouldn't dirty anything kissing it. But I couldn't even kiss the crucifix. I knew I couldn't ever touch anything again without getting the slime all over it…"

The sirened car roared past the church, its wail sloughing off. Again the man's voice changed, calmer now.

"I can make it now, Father. There's still time. How much time we're given in this world and how little to do with it that we really have to do! I had to commit murder to finally have something important to do with this half-hour. Sometimes I watch people with brief cases and suitcases fighting for taxis. That's a sin, too. How jealous I am of them—only I'm not jealous of them for taking taxis. It's just being important, having to be some place in such a hurry and somebody waiting for them. Father, absolve me, please, and let me hurry. Bless me, Father, for I have sinned. I confess to Almighty God, and to you, Father, that I have sinned…"

He had begun the routine of confession as he had learned it

from the catechism as a boy. While the words of the confiteor*
flowed out by rote, Father Duffy strove in his own mind for the
words that he would say to this man. How often he had striven
to give each penitent a bit of guidance that would be especially
his, that would give him hope and confidence that he could go
and sin no more… To say to this man, "Go and sin no more…"

"…May the almighty and merciful God grant me pardon,
absolution and full remission of my sins. Amen."

Father Duffy moistened his lips. "There is penance you
will do according to the laws of society beyond any I should
give you," he said slowly, sickening at his own inadequacy—
the pompous, hollow words…"You are going to the police
now?"

When he received no answer, he glanced at the man to see
him nodding that he would. His eyes were streaming with tears.
If he was sane, his soul was racked with remorse, the priest
thought. Sane or insane, he was suffering and had suffered. But
so also had his victim…

"God give you courage," the priest said, "and me wisdom. I
know you are aware how grave your sin is. You are truly sorry
before God?"

"Father, I'm sorry that she suffered, that I made her suffer.
I'm not sorry she died. There's nothing dies but something
lives. Don't you see, I'm confessing everything that made me do
this…"

"But you have blamed yourself for murder…"

"You're mixed up, Father, and I haven't got time to straighten
you out…"

"There is time."

"No. There isn't. Just this once there isn't. If you'd asked me

---

* A Latin prayer confessing sins, at the beginning of the sacrament.

yesterday, I'd have explained it all to you. Father, bless me. I'm going now."

"God give you courage," the priest repeated, for the man was already on his feet, his hands on the ledge of the window between them. "If you want me to, I'll go with you, and you can explain it on the way."

"You'd spoil everything by coming with me. Don't you see? I've got to walk in there and say: 'Here I am.' Have you given me absolution, Father?"

"I'll give you conditional absolution. I'll visit you."

The man had the curtain parted now. The pale light from one high chandelier silhouetted his frail shape, and for an instant Father Duff saw something else: he was still carrying the hammer.

"I'll offer my Mass in the morning..." the priest called out.

"You wouldn't even tell me to go in peace. And you were right, Father. It wouldn't do any good. There isn't any peace on earth. Especially for men of good will, there's no, peace."

When the curtain dropped from the man's hand, it left the priest in darkness. And he had never known a darkness more profound.

2

When Father Duffy left the confessional, only two people remained in the church, one of whom he knew to be blind, Mrs. Callahan. Every Saturday night she was the last one out of the church. Her son guided her to the next to the last pew early in the evening and then went down to O'Reilly's Bar and Grill to pass the time until she was ready to go home. More than once Father Duffy had guided her along Sixty-third Street himself, and then up four flights to the small apartment she kept as neat as a match box, for all her blindness.

"Mind, it's not that he forgets me, Father," she would say. "It's just that he forgets the time."

The other occupant of the church was a younger woman who, as the priest went down the aisle, got up, genuflected and left. He did not recognize her and decided she had probably been walking down Ninth Avenue, and, passing the church, stopped in for a visit. As he heard the great door swing closed behind her, he stopped. Somewhere not far from there was the man with the hammer. The priest looked at his watch. It was ten minutes to ten. At most the man was no more than a few minutes away. Suppose he had lost his resolve to go to the police? By now he might be afraid of betrayal. Suppose she had looked up at him, or that he had thought she had looked up at him? Father Duffy lifted his cassock in his haste to follow her into the street. He slowed his pace on the church steps. The girl was talking with a young man who had obviously waited outside the church for her. They walked off, arm in arm.

"Well, Father, do you think the old lady's got enough of them out of purgatory to suit her for one night?"

It was Mrs. Callahan's son. The smell of beer was heavy on him. "Well, she's got you out of O'Reilly's at least," the priest said. "Good night, Tom."

Inside the church again, he walked its length uneasily. Had he left the confessional at the same time Father Gonzales had left his, where would the man have gone? Directly to the police? Had he picked the church at random? Had he done his terrible deed in the vicinity? The priest laid his stole away and extinguished the church lights. He knelt a moment at the altar and then went down the darkened aisle and locked the doors. It was after ten when he set the lock in the side door by the sacristy and let it slide closed behind him.

A heavy breeze seeped up from the south, dank with the smell of fish and the sea. What oppressed him most was the conviction that the man was sincere in his confession, or at least in his intention—that he was aware of guilt and the need for retribution. It placed the priest under the seal of confession. He could not break it before his conscience. Nor was he expected under law to divulge his information—not even if justice or a human life depended on it. Whatever anxiety tortured the little man who trudged the streets of New York with a hammer in his hand at that hour, it was no greater than the burden of it he had placed on Father Duffy.

In his room he finished reading his office distractedly.

He was sensitive to every sound of the city—the screeching brakes, running feet, a shout, a crying child, the rectory doorbell, Father Gonzales' footsteps on the stair and past his door, Monsignor Brady's door opening and closing at the front of the hall. In his shirtsleeves, he turned on the radio—music...hillbilly, jive and "music to read by." Music to sweat by, he thought, plucking the shirt from where it clung to his back. He rubbed the aching muscles.

The minute-hand on his alarm clock lumbered toward eleven. It reached it simultaneously with the time signal on the radio. The newscaster began as he did every other night of the year. He numbered the global tragedies, fears and fiascoes, and finished off his reports with the metropolitan roundup—robbery and rescue, pathos and nonsense. Murder in New York was not among them. Nor the word mentioned in the five-minute summary at midnight.

As he turned off the radio he remembered the man's last words: "No peace on earth, especially for men of good will."

3

There was a party going on that night when Tim Brandon returned to the boarding house on Twelfth Street. There was generally a party on Saturday night. He could hear it half a block away. But then there were parties in most of the houses in the block, and with the windows open, the songs of one reached out to join the laughter of another. But Tim recognized Mrs. Galli's voice. The laughter rolled up in her, shaking one layer in her buxom figure after another, and then exploded into the faces of those around her. They invariably rocked with it as though the whole room were shaking, even if they didn't know what she was laughing at. Whatever Mrs. Galli did, the world did with her.

She had been calling up the stairs to him all night, Tim thought. The more wine she had, the more people she thought of to call into the party, and she would want him, especially him.

Her son's concertina started as Tim went up the outside steps. He paused a moment and looked in through the limp curtains. "When I was a fisherman there by the shore..." Johnny Galli sang. He was a baker and the son of a baker, and if ever he had caught a fish he had trapped it in his mother's goldfish bowl, Tim thought. He thought about goldfish and bowls for a moment, and how much like them people were, except that most of them didn't know they were in the bowl. He knew it. It was why he liked the darkness and preferred to see a party from where he watched now. The chorus of Johnny's song was picked up in Italian. The singers swayed with the music and closed their eyes, remembering the shore they sang about, the long white beach and the blue Mediterranean and the great gulls flying...

Tim was more weary than he could remember ever having been before. He entered the house and went upstairs unnoticed. In five minutes he was sprawled on his bed, clothes and shoes still on, and asleep.

He awoke suddenly to the sound of his name. He looked about the dark room frantically, trying to get his bearings, for he had been torn out of a wild and terrible dream.

"Tim, Tim, are you in there?"

He heard music now behind the voice and the knocking, and fumbled his hands over the bed. The tufted quilt was familiar. He turned his head and felt the coolness where the air sluiced his wet neck and forehead. He moistened his lips and breathed deeply. The knocking persisted.

"What is it?" he called out.

"It's me, Katie, Tim. Mama thought you'd be sorry if you didn't come down."

"Just a minute, Katie."

He groped for the light cord above his head and pulled it. Sitting up, he shook off sleep and the dream. "Come in if you want to."

A slim, dark girl opened the door a few inches at a time.

"I didn't want to bother you, Tim. But you know how mama is when there's a party."

"It's all right, Katie. I'm just groggy with sleep. The light hurt my eyes." He swung his feet to the floor.

She moved a pile of books from the one rocker in the room and sat on the edge of it tentatively.

"How do you feel, Tim?"

"How do I feel?"

"You had a headache this afternoon."

"Oh. It's all gone. I needed sleep. That's all."

"Wasn't it hard?"

He felt a constriction in his breath as though a hand were at his throat. The dream seemed to be creeping up on him again. He fastened his eyes upon her to keep from being dragged back into it.

"Don't look at me so funny, Tim," the girl said. "I don't see how anybody could fall asleep with all the racket downstairs."

"Oh." He sat a moment with his face in his hands.

"I'd better go downstairs."

"Don't go yet, Katie," he said, making an effort to be congenial then. "Let me get awake. I'll go down with you." He got up and went to the window. He caught her reflection in it. She was watching him, unaware that he could see her. Her eyes asked him frankly to come downstairs for her sake, just to be in the room with her, like a protector. She had come eagerly on her mother's errand. Something hurt him in the thought of it. It was too soon after the dream, gnawing as it was at his consciousness. He flung the window to its limits and leaned out.

"Look at the stars up there," he said over his shoulder. "Like you could step from one to another of them and never stop going."

"I'd like that," she said, when he pulled back into the room.

He turned and looked at her. "Would you, Katie?" He answered himself, seeing the response in her eyes. "I believe you would. Just think. If we were doing that, we could reach down and pick up the earth and just toss it like a snowball."

She giggled at the picture. "Where would you throw it?"

He thought about that a moment. "I'd smash it right in the face of the sun, I think. It would go f-f-ft and that's all there'd be to it. You know that's what's going to happen some day. That's how important the earth is really, Katie. A lot of people know that."

"It's more important to God," she said. "You shouldn't say things like that, Tim."

"How can it be so important to God if it means so little to men? He's got lots of worlds, and they've got only one."

"I don't know what you mean."

"Good. I hope you never learn it."

"I'll learn it," she said proudly, "if it's something to learn."

He nodded. "Maybe. But I won't be the one to teach you."

"You'd better comb your hair. It's all messed up."

He went over to her then and brushed his hand against her cheek. "Poor little Katie. You don't like to hear me talk like that."

"Your hand smells funny."

"Does it?" He drew it away and looked at it, turning it over slowly. "Have you ever thought about all the things a hand does, Katie? Without hands, how lost we would be! How would your brother make his bread? How would I repair things?..."

The girl got up from the chair and shook her hair out from where it clung to the back of her neck. Out of the habit of household chores, she straightened the spread on the bed.

"What were you doing with the hammer, Tim?" she asked, picking it up from where it lay with his jacket at the foot of the bed.

He did not seem to hear her, absorbed now in his own words. This was not unusual. She was accustomed to his ramblings, sometimes directed at her, but as often spoken as though she were not there at all. She liked it a little better when he was not speaking directly to her, in fact. Although she could not explain it, those times seemed to include her more than when he did talk with her. No one she had ever known talked like Tim. The boys she knew talked baseball, cars, hot bands and getting into the big time. When they stopped talking and looked at her, every fiber in her body tightened to its defense. First the eyes and then the hands. She was drawn to it and frightened of it, hating herself. It was like Tim was saying now...

"'...And if thy right eye scandalize thee, pluck it out and cast it from thee... And if thy right hand scandalize thee cut it off, and cast it from thee; for it is expedient for thee that one of thy members should perish, rather than that thy whole body go into hell.' What is hell like, Katie? What is it like when cutting off our hand is nothing compared to it?"

She was startled by his appearance when she turned to look at him. There were great hollows under his eyes and his whole face looked gray, almost green, slimy, swimming as it was in sweat.

"You better go to bed, Tim. I'll tell mama. It's after midnight, anyway."

"No," he said harshly. "I've got to have some music. I've got to sing. When I can't work I've got to sing."

He pushed the rocker out of his way and got a towel from where it hung at the side of his dresser. He looked at himself in the mirror and brushed the sweat away with the back of his hand. He caught her reflection in the glass...

---

* Tim combines Matthew 5:29–30. The Douay-Rheims Version of the Bible reads, "And if thy right eye scandalize thee, pluck it out and cast it from thee. For it is expedient for thee that one of thy members should perish, rather than that thy whole body be cast into hell. And if thy right hand scandalize thee, cut it off, and cast it from thee: for it is expedient for thee that one of thy members should perish, rather than that thy whole body be cast into hell."

"I frightened you, Katie. I frightened the little bird."

"I'm not a little bird."

"Oh? Have you grown into an eagle all of a sudden?" He smiled at her and picked up his toothbrush and soap.

The whole room changed when he smiled. "I'm a skylark," she said, lifting her chin.

"Ah, that's it. A little pilgrim of the sky." He went to the door. "Don't fly away until I come back. I can't fly alone, you know."

"Katerina!" The rich full voice of her mother boomed up the stairs.

Tim went to the head of them. "She's talked me into coming down, Mrs. Galli. As soon as I wash my face."

"Before you come down it will be already time to go up. The wine will be gone."

"Then save a song for me."

"Send her down, Tim. Maybe if she runs down to Krepic's before he closes..."

"Not alone!" Tim shouted.

"Then I'll go out myself," she said petulantly, her chubby, jeweled hand not moving from the railing.

Tim could feel a knot of revulsion rising in him. He shook his head and shivered. Easy, easy, he told himself. This always passes.

"Don't you care whether I go or not?"

Go to hell and good riddance, swiller of wine and men, he thought. He choked out the words: "Send Johnny."

"You'll hurry before he comes back?" Her hand slid down the railing with a slow sensuousness.

He plunged toward the bathroom without answering.

In his room, the door open, Katie pulled his tool kit from beneath the bed and laid the hammer away in it, refastening the strap around the canvas. She took a shirt from the hanger on the pole that was stretched between the walls in the corner of the room. The other of the two shirts she had ironed for him that day was hanging there, as was his other pair of army suntans[*]—his complete wardrobe. It was then that she wondered what he had done with his third shirt, the clean one that he had put on that afternoon. He was wearing a tee shirt now, and that so soaked with sweat it might have been wrung out in the sink and put back on without looking any different. Her thoughts drifted from it to the shirt she now laid out on the bed for him. She unbuttoned it and smoothed it out, feeling of the kind cleanliness of it, and relishing it as she so relished the same virtue in Tim. He was the one clean thing, she thought, in a world very much in need of scrubbing.

She went to the mirror and pushed up the waves in her black hair. She touched her lipstick on her lips with her little finger, spreading it where a little had congealed in the corner of her mouth. There was a faint scent to her hand, the same as she had noticed on Tim's hand... Putty, she thought, or some such pungent stuff as would cling to the hammer from his work. She lifted her hand again and smelled it, and then put it from her, lest straining for the association she lose it altogether. Humming "When I Was a Fisherman,"[†] she left the room and went downstairs.

---

[*] Canvas shirts issued by the military as part of a soldier's uniform. Was Tim in the army?

[†] Apparently a traditional song.

4

Father Duffy had the six o'clock Mass that Sunday. He had no more than fallen into a sodden sleep when the alarm clock wakened him. He was conscious several seconds before he could identify the sound. Whatever his dream, his first waking thought was that he was lying on the sidewalk somewhere, unable to move for a weight that was holding him down. He recognized the ringing then and was completely awake. Before he reached it, the alarm had rung out.

Raising the window shade he looked out on the deserted street, the night's debris its only ornament. In another hour or so, the kids would gather up the beer cans and build skyscrapers with them, and they would harvest the bottle caps and count them into imaginary cash registers.

A police prowl car drove up to the call box on the corner, and Father Duffy permitted himself his first fully formed thought of the man with the hammer: where was he at that moment? He shaved, showered and dressed, forcing the thought from his mind, calling on God and all His saints for help. He tried to fill his mind with prayers, and, in final desperation, repeated aloud to himself the prayers he had learned in childhood, pausing with each phrase to evoke from it an image. It was like thumbing through a box of old holy pictures, and he found himself hastening from one to the next without prayer, only with curiosity. It became a child's game, and his mind sought then for a child's saint, and he was again with the gentle St. Francis…and the gentle murderer.

At the altar, each time he turned upon the worshipers he scanned their faces, hoping fervently to find among them the man he had likened to St. Francis. He was sure now that he had not gone to the police. Sure? Fearful that he had not. Again and again, he strove to put the torment from him.

The Mass finished and his thanksgiving said, the priest abandoned himself to his troubled curiosity. He walked to the corner and bought a newspaper. He returned with it to the rectory, and in the study paged through it. Murder, rape and assault were not nearly so remote as he had thought. They were almost as conventional to Sunday breakfast as the comics. They were even conventional to some of the comics. But none suited the description of the one confessed to him.

Monsignor Brady looked in on him, frowned, bade him a curt greeting and moved on. He turned back then and told him that his nephew, who was also a priest, was visiting with them, and asked if Father Duffy minded giving up his nine o'clock Mass to him. The young priest agreed. When his superior left, he lit a cigarette. A few minutes later the housekeeper, as though she had smelled the cigarette smoke, brought him breakfast on a tray. Once more he turned on a radio and waited for the news. It was actually less than twelve hours since he had heard the confession. He seemed to have carried the burden much longer, so much longer, in fact, that for a few seconds he permitted himself to wonder if it had really happened at all, if he had not imagined it. But the face as he remembered it was real, and the words began to sound again in his mind. His mother had given him a hammer…St. Joseph was a carpenter…the only thing she had ever given him…his first confession…Father McGohey… McGohey, MacGoughy, McGooey…he had lost a fight…

Father Duffy emptied his coffee cup and got up. He turned the radio up only to find music still playing and then down again to a volume that only he might hear. He had been assuming that the man had come to the confessional almost directly from the murder—that was because he was carrying the hammer. Perhaps the man was carrying it as a symbol of his guilt: something to strengthen his resolve, something to show to the police. The murder might have been committed long ago…

Something else occurred to him then: the whole thing might be a horrible hoax. There might have been no murder at all. The supposed penitent might have been someone under the influence of God knows what, carrying on a private and deranged grudge against the priesthood. Things as fantastic had happened before.

Murder, he thought grimly as he glanced down at the paper, was far less fantastic. He turned up the radio as the hour signal sounded. Nothing for him.

"Nothing for me," he repeated when it was over.

What *was* for him, then? He could find out from some source or other what murder might have been committed with a hammer that was unsolved, or perhaps wrongly solved. And if there had been a murder last night, as yet undiscovered, he would learn of it soon. There was obvious haste in reporting such news. But in either instance, what *was* there for him? His vows prevented him from going to the police. And could he go, what could he tell? That a man unknown to him confessed the murder? Beyond an imagined likeness to the holy picture concept of St. Francis, how could he describe the man? Walking down Ninth Avenue to Forty-second Street and across to Broadway, would he not see a hundred faces whose emaciation and aged youth likened them to that same concept?

There were other ways of identifying a man. The top comic sheet taught even children that police did not rely on faces to identify criminals.* They looked for fingerprints. Among the hundreds on the little ledge in the confessional box, uppermost were those of the man with the hammer.

He left the newspaper on the tray for the housekeeper, and hastened to the rectory basement. There he got a screwdriver, and, during the eight o'clock Mass, he slipped into the confessional and removed the small board. At the other side of the church, Father Gonzales was hearing confessions. There had been no one on Father Duffy's side since the last penitent of the night before. Careful not to touch the upper portion of the board, he tucked it into the folds of his cassock and carried it to his room.

---

* The popular comic strip *Dick Tracy* by Chester Gould featured weekly a frame depicting a page from the "Crimestopper's Textbook," instructional material for the amateur detective.

5

The east sixties are almost another world from the west sixties in New York. More than Central Park divides them, although less than a five-minute bus ride spans the geographic difference. That morning Norah Flaherty brushed her six oldest children out of St. Timothy's after the seven o'clock Mass. She bought them a Sunday paper, forbade them the funnies until they were home, arbitrated the order in which they were to see them, and herded them along to Sixty-fourth Street two abreast and up the walk-up single file.

She sipped a cup of warmed-over coffee while she cautioned the oldest girl on the do's and do-not's of the day, the most important of which was that they might play in the bathtub provided they put on their bathing suits, and provided the baby was not left in it alone. Also, they were not to waken their father. He needed his sleep, working on the nightshift. She hurried out of the house then, hairpins in her mouth which she fastened one by one into her tawny hair as she went down the steps. She caught the crosstown bus and five minutes later had crossed into that other world. Invariably she got out at the front of the bus and thanked the driver.

His answer varied as little as her exits: "Take it easy."

She hesitated on the curb to figure the ways of the traffic light. The bus driver waited, too, watching her. She drew a few deep breaths.

"My, it's cooler over here," she said up to him. "Sometimes I wish I could bring the kids."

He nodded and waved her across the street. She went in the service entrance of a large apartment hotel, getting a hat-tip from the doorman as he caught sight of her from his station at the guest entrance.

She spent the first two hours in the building counting the linen for which she was responsible, sorting and mending it. Actually this was not Sunday work, but she was very sensitive about disturbing people, and besides, doing it on Sundays saved a couple of hours for her family shopping during the week. Mrs. Flaherty considered it indecent for anyone to sleep beyond ten o'clock, however. Accordingly, she began her rounds at that hour, a great ring of keys in one hand and a bucket in the other, her arm stacked with towels.

At half-past twelve she knocked at 4-B, leaned back to select the key in the light, and then slid it into the door and let herself in. The blinds in the apartment were still drawn, and she clucked her disapproval as she switched on the light in the foyer. Having used almost every moment and motion of her life to advantage, Mrs. Flaherty humped the towels on the table, took the damp rag from her bucket while she lifted it over the threshold, and without wasting a step, wiped the smudge marks from the brass doorknob and its fittings, inside and out, and then from the panel at the light switch. She was meticulous in her work and proud of her short-cuts. She gathered the bucket, two towels, and went directly into the bathroom which lay between the living room and the bedroom with an entrance off the foyer as well as the one off the bedroom.

She sang tunelessly that she might not take Miss Gebhardt unawares. The door between bath and bedroom was almost closed, but not quite. The slippered feet of Miss Gebhardt were visible to Mrs. Flaherty just off the bed.

There was nothing gentle in the way she closed the door between them. She had no use for women who fell across their beds at night unable to take their shoes off, and in her weeks of cleaning she had formed a very low opinion of Miss Gebhardt and the rowdy company she found evidences of. Nor did she like people who had no regard for those working for them—"no more than they were dogs." The bathroom was a mess, an empty soap powder packet on the floor and part of the powder spilled, wet towels lying in the tub, rusty-looking at that. An altogether distasteful job lay ahead of her. She clattered about it noisily, and thought of the things she would say to Miss Gebhardt if "that one" were to come to and complain of the racket.

The devil himself could not waken Miss Gebhardt apparently, and Mrs. Flaherty finished the bathroom and moved into the foyer once more. She had wrung out the towels and carted them now to the laundry chute. She caught one of the porters rolling the refuse barrels to the elevator and dumped the waste into it.

When she returned to the apartment and got as far as the kitchen the telephone rang. She wished that she were done now, that she might slip out without meeting Miss Gebhardt. It occurred to her that if she hurried she might make it. Having an extension phone by her bed, "that one" would lie there a half-hour talking into it. But the phone continued to ring.

Mrs. Flaherty grabbed her rag from the bucket and wiped the dust from the window sill and the door. She gave the fixtures a quick polish. If the one in there could stand the phone ringing, she could. She wasn't going to touch the sink, she decided, seeing the array of bottles and glasses. Nobody said she had to do their dirty dishes after them. The phone persisted. The gorge rose in her as she often said of irritations, and she stomped out of the kitchen and down the three steps into the living room. She caught the phone as though she would choke it.

"Hello?"

"Dolly?" The man's voice was impatient.

And well it might be, she thought. "This is not Dolly. It's the maid."

"Then be so kind, please, as to ask Miss Gebhardt to take the phone."

"If she isn't taking it after all this time, I don't think she wants it."

"Will you ask her, please?"

"I'll ask her," Mrs. Flaherty said after an instant. I'll ask her all right, she thought. She was becoming curious about Miss Gebhardt. She wanted to see how anyone could lie next to a wailing telephone and do nothing about it. She was up the steps when she thought of something and went down them again. "Who do you want me to tell her is calling?"

She received no answer. "Hello there?" And after a moment: "Are you still not there?"

"I still am here and expect to be until four o'clock. What do you want, Mrs. Flaherty?"

"Is it the desk? There was a man on here asking for Miss Gebhardt."

"I know. He must have hung up. He said she's a heavy sleeper." The clerk giggled.

"I'm hanging up," Mrs. Flaherty said and did so, resolving to never again pick up a telephone where she was working.

She drew the blinds in the living room, thinking about the incident. The clerk was on to Miss Gebhardt. She probably slipped him a dollar now and then. She was generous. That much you had to say for her. By the clerk's tone, he recognized the caller. She had excuse enough to go in and rouse the sleeper, she reasoned, or to pretend to that intention. The clerk could tell who it was that called, she might say, and it sounded terrible important.

With that resolve she went to the bedroom door and knocked, softly at first, and then with deliberation. Slowly, from things she had read in the papers, she began to think of sleeping powders. Panic rose as she pounded on the door.

She flung it open then and saw again the slippered feet, glittering in the half-light as though there were more life in the shoes than in the feet which still lay stiffly as she had first seen them from the bathroom door. There was a sickening odor to the room, partly perfume and partly an acrid dankness. Mrs. Flaherty tiptoed a few steps toward the bed. It seemed at first that Miss Gebhardt's auburn hair was flung all over the pillow and that she was lying face down. But her toes were pointing upward.

Mrs. Flaherty's knees betrayed her in the instant she realized that she had seen all there was left of Miss Gebhardt's face. She crawled from the room, moaning hoarsely. It was not until she reached the foyer that she found her legs and her voice. Then she ran screaming into the hall.

6

Waiting until her mother left for church, Katerina Galli went upstairs to change her dress. It was late morning and Tim had not come down yet. But with her ear tuned to every sound from his room she was aware that he had been up for some time. The other boarders were unwilling to miss a meal even on Sunday. At nine o'clock they sat down to bacon and eggs, and now, nearly two hours later, the smell of the bacon had seeped through the whole house. There was not enough air stirring to carry it outdoors.

Before dressing, Katie made her own bed and then her mother's in the front room. For an instant there, folding the spread over the huge bed, she remembered the times she had climbed into it beside her father when she was a little girl. She could even remember the smell of sleep about him, although she could no longer remember his face except as it smiled at her from the picture on the dresser. He had died when she was eight years old. Looking on the smooth bed now and seeing the two hollows in it, one much deeper than the other, she wondered what her mother thought about as she lay there night after night. What was remembering like when you could remember a lifetime?

What was it like sleeping alone in the bed, waking up at night and putting your hand to the empty place?

A sound from the end of the hall hastened her from the room. Outside it, she slackened her pace so as not to be caught in her haste to see him. He was halfway down the stairs when she reached the railing.

"Good morning, Tim," she called.

He turned and smiled up at her. "Hello, Katie."

"There's coffee all made on the stove if you want me to warm it up."

"Thanks. I'll do it."

She wanted very much to do it for him, to be invited to have a cup with him, but she was too proud to admit it. He had waited until everyone was gone from the house except her. He might have waited a few minutes longer and she would have been gone too. It was enough for her that he was content in that. She dressed, listening on her way between her room and the bathroom to know if he was still in the kitchen. In spite of her pride she timed herself to go downstairs as he was coming from the kitchen.

"Going to church?" she asked.

"Yes."

"Me too."

"Then we can go together," he said matter-of-factly. He held the door for her.

She had forgotten her missal and beads, but she would pray on her fingers rather than go back for them now. She lifted her head and walked down the street beside him in proud self-consciousness. Throughout the service she was aware only of being beside him. She could hear his breathing and smell his shaving soap. Her head bowed, her lips forming prayers without thought, she contemplated his hands folded before him, clean, gentle hands that she had never touched except when he had brushed her cheek the night before. She listened to his voice only in response to the prayers at the end, and for an instant, concentrated on her own prayer, offering it for some vague communion between them. Preceding him out of the church, she sensed an electric pleasure when touching fingers with him at the holy water font.

He removed his coat when they were on the street and folded it over his arm. He looked at her, seeming to see her for the first time that day. He did not look her up and down. It was just that he was aware of her although his eyes were not on hers. And she was not embarrassed.

"Do you have to go right home, Katie?"

"I don't think so." She was grateful then that they had not met her mother. No matter where she went she always got the warning from her mother to come right home. It was no more than habit with her mother, the warning. As often, she would chide her for staying around the house too much.

"Then what do you say to a bus ride?" Tim asked.

"I'd like that, thank you."

They walked to Fourteenth Street, where without seeming to deliberate their course, he selected a crosstown bus. Riding it to the end of the line, they got out and walked along the East River. From there they could see the United Nations building, a glistening shield in the sun.

"The parliament of the world," Tim said, pointing to it. "The last great hope of man*...if that were only so."

---

* In his 1862 Annual Message to Congress, Abraham Lincoln called American democracy "the last best hope of earth." During the 1940s, politically liberal Americans frequently referred to the United Nations as "the world's last great hope for peace," to the point that, as one conservative scholar writes, "It became a shibboleth and an article of faith." John P. Rossi, "Winston Churchill's 'Iron Curtain' Speech," *The Imaginative Conservative*, May 6, 2014, https://theimaginativeconservative.org/2014/05/winston-churchill-iron-curtain-speech-john-p-rossi.html.

"If what were so, Tim?"

"If they really hoped in it."

"I think they do."

"What makes you think so?" His tolerance was in his voice.

She thought a moment. "If they didn't believe it, they wouldn't be there at all."

"You're very wise, Katie. But then when I was seventeen I was that wise, too."

"You make yourself sound as old as Santa Claus. How old are you, Tim?"

"As old as Santa Claus."

"Really how old are you?"

"Thirty-four, I think. Now, doesn't that sound very old to you?"

"No," she lied. She didn't care how old he was. Lots of women married men twice their age. Then she thought of how old he was when she was born. Seventeen. That was different, somehow. "What were you like when you were seventeen, Tim?"

"When I was seventeen," he repeated thoughtfully as though that were an answer in itself.

"Did you still want to be a priest?"

He stopped walking and looked at her. "How did you know I wanted to be a priest?"

"Mother told me. You must have told her once."

"Maybe I did."

"Did you still want to?"

"Why do you harp on that, Katie?"

She sensed his sudden irritation. "I don't know. I suppose because I wanted to be a nun once. I was fifteen then."

"What made you change your mind?"

"I don't know. Growing up, I guess." But the color in her face betrayed her. "You could still be a priest, you know," she added to cover her embarrassment.

"Couldn't you be a nun? Is there any reason why you couldn't be a nun?"

"I guess I could if I still wanted to." She was further confused at the sound of accusation in his voice. "It's just that now I feel different about it. I'd like to get married...some time."

"Let's talk about something else," he said.

"Is there something wrong with me wanting to get married?" she persisted.

"Will you stop it, Katie, or else go home? How do I know what's wrong with it?"

"I'll go home if you want me to."

He touched her arm, leading her forward. "No, of course not. I don't want you to go home. I'm sorry I said that, Katie. I wouldn't hurt you for the world."

She moved along with him in silence.

"Marriage was spoiled for me. Everything was spoiled for me. Or maybe it's the other way around. I've spoiled everything."

She knew better than to ask him what he meant although the sudden thought that he might have been married hurt terribly. He walked along, looking at the ground. Suddenly he caught her wrist. He held it so tightly that it hurt.

"But the world's not going to be spoiled for you, Katie. And don't let it spoil you. It's going to try. But don't let it, ever."

She rubbed her wrist where he had released it.

"Let's get on another bus, and try starting over," he said.

She wanted that very much. Something had happened between them that had never happened before. But then she had never been further from the house with him than the church at the end of the block.

"Let's," she said. "I do love starting over."

"So do I." He drew a dollar bill and some change from his

pocket and counted it. "Do you know what we'll do? We'll take the Madison bus and get off where we can walk to the park."

"What park?"

"Central Park, foolish girl. Haven't you ever been there?"

"A couple of times. We went to the zoo when I was in grade school."

He looked at her. "When you were in grade school—you're a child."

"I'm not. You said something like that to me last night."

They were in the bus before he spoke again. "What else did I say last night, Katie?"

"Don't you remember? You weren't drinking or anything."

"If I remembered I wouldn't ask you," he said, rubbing his fingers over his eyes and forehead. "It seems like years ago... when I was seventeen maybe, and I already knew too much of the world and myself to be a priest."

"Priests know a good deal about the world. They have to."

"They learn it out of books," he said curtly.

She looked out of the bus window, pondering his words. They stung less in their curtness than in what they told her of him. They implied that his knowledge had come from experience. In her mind she linked that with marriage having been spoiled for him. How quickly her prayer had been denied, she thought bitterly. But he had not actually said that he was married. If he had been, her mother would have found it out. She found things like that out in no time at all. More cheerful herself, Katie tried to think of something to say that would please him.

"Are you working, Tim?"

"An odd job here and there. Why?"

"I didn't mean that. I meant writing."

"No. But I think I'm going to be able to start again soon. Maybe today even."

"Did something happen? Did you get some money?"

"Yes and no," he said. "And in that order."

"Will you tell me about it in the park?"

He smiled. "No."

"Will you let me read some of it when it's written, then?"

"Possibly."

She smiled and settled back in her seat, spreading the creases from her dress.

"You didn't tell me what I said last night," he reminded her.

"You didn't say anything much. You just sat there grinning like a cat. You made Johnny play every Irish song he knew. And some he didn't know, you hummed the tunes for him till he picked them up. And every one, you'd say, 'My mother liked that' or 'that was one of my mother's favorites.'"

"My mother was Irish," he said, as though in explanation.

"Your mother's dead?" the girl asked.

"Yes. Many times." He glanced out of the window to see where they were.

They heard then the gradual rise of police sirens behind them. The bus slowed down and pulled to a stop as two police cars and a police technical truck roared past them. The cortege turned left a few blocks ahead and the sirens stopped.

"And once she died in bed," he added, getting up. "Let's walk from here."

7

"Now, Mrs. Flaherty, try and compose yourself. You'd be surprised at the number of violent deaths that occur in New York every day."

"But the terrible things I was thinking about the poor woman, and her lying in there dead all the time."

Lieutenant Holden leaned forward. "What kind of things?"

Mrs. Flaherty looked into his eyes and also leaned forward. She whispered confidentially, "I thought she was drunk."

Detective Sergeant Goldsmith, examining the contents of a table drawer behind them, stopped to listen.

Holden straightened up. "Had you ever seen Miss Gebhardt drunk, Mrs. Flaherty?"

"No. But I cleaned up the kitchen often enough. The number of bottles there you'd of thought it was the Union League Club.* My nephew's a bartender there."

Holden nodded. Only the phone call had prevented her from cleaning up the kitchen thoroughly before the body was discovered. Goldsmith turned from where he was working.

---

* A private social club founded in 1863, on East Thirty-Seventh Street.

"You're sure you didn't touch anything in this room, lady?"

"I am. Only the telephone. I never do a lick without raising the blinds to see what I'm doing, and I didn't touch them till I was off the phone. Then I went in to her."

Goldsmith went back to work without comment.

"Mrs. Flaherty, you've worked for Miss Gebhardt six months?" Holden continued.

"I've worked for the management six months, since my husband, Billy, went on the nightshift. I work where they send me."

"But you've attended this apartment for six months?"

"I have."

"Did you see Miss Gebhardt often?"

"Often enough. She was always saying to come back later, the way you'd think I had nothing better to do than pop in here when she felt like having me."

"Did you have any idea why she didn't want you to come in at your convenience?"

"I had the notion she was entertaining company."

"Only the notion?"

"Well, I never seen her with all her clothes on, if you know what I mean, your honor, and that's no way to be receiving company, I thought, so I'd argue with myself over the notion."

"I'm not sure I do know what you mean, Mrs. Flaherty. She would come to the door when you knocked. Just what was she wearing on those occasions?"

"Them negligee things."

He nodded. "But from the door there, you could see into the living room. Did she have company?"

"Not in the living room, your honor."

"I see."

"But many's the time I heard tinkling and rattling in the kitchen."

"Mrs. Flaherty, did you ever see anyone in this house besides Miss Gebhardt?"

"Yes," she said after a moment, "there was once last month she let me in when a man was here. He was sitting there where you are in his shirtsleeves, a nice-looking little man. I felt a bit different about her after that."

"Why?"

"Well, it's kind of hard to explain, your honor. He was nice to me in no special way at all. It was just that he'd get out of my way. There's some wouldn't budge if you had to crawl under their legs with the vacuum cleaner."

"Did you talk to him?"

"No more than thank you. Oh, and I remember him saying, 'You're Irish, aren't you?' 'County Mayo,' says I. 'My mother came from the old country too,' he says. Then she called him out to the kitchen to fix something or other she'd broken, a light switch, I think. 'I'm the handy one to have around the house,' he says, going out. And he excused himself. To me, mind you. If you want to know what I think about that, I'll tell you."

"Please do," Holden said.

Sergeant Goldsmith had finished his search of the desk. He sat with his back to them, listening.

"Well, I have the notion with her living here in a place like this—the rent is enormous, you know—and the way she talked and all—oh darling this and darling that—she come up in the world all of a sudden. And him I took to be a poor brother or something like that."

Holden smiled a little. "Maybe. You might be right. But all you have to go on is the good impression he made on you, isn't it, Mrs. Flaherty?"

"Are you going on anything better?"

"No. I'm not. That's a fact," he said easily.

"Besides," she added, appeased by his humility, "that was one of the few times I ever seen her with a dress on."

"You don't miss much, do you?"

"Not if I can take it in, going by."

"Do you remember if she called him by name?"

She thought for a moment. "No. There's none comes back to me now."

"And yet she probably did call him by name. There were two of you in the living room. How did she speak to you?"

"Darling," she said promptly. "And if she darling'd from the kitchen that day to the two of us, you can be sure I was the last one to answer her."

"I guess that answers that," Holden said. "Can you give me any sort of description of the man?" He turned to Goldsmith. "Will you ask Wilson to come in and take this, Sergeant?"

"I'll do it." Goldsmith took a notebook and pen from his pocket.

Mrs. Flaherty rocked in the chair, trying to remember. "How do you describe just nobody?" she said finally. "That's what he looked like. Nobody at all, or anybody you'd meet on the street."

"You're tired," Holden said. "We've asked you a lot of questions. I'll have someone drive you home soon."

"The kids'll have the house in a shambles, and their father wouldn't say a word to them lying in the middle of it."

"Just a few minutes more, Mrs. Flaherty. How old do you think the man was?"

"Maybe twenty-five. Maybe thirty-five. It was that kind of a face. Kind of sad and quiet-looking. Except when he smiled he looked different. Kind of holy-looking. Big eyes. Brown, I'd say, but I'm not sure, and they were awful big. He was no more than a couple of inches taller than me. He had nice hands. I remember looking at them on the arm of the chair."

"Any rings?"

"None," she said. "Not even dirt rings under his fingernails. But all the same I took him for a working man."

"By that you mean manual labor?"

"I do." Obviously she had a low opinion of any other work.

"How much would you guess his weight to be?"

"No more than my Billy. A hundred and thirty-four at his best weight."

"Hair?"

"A fair share of it." Then she added: "Flat and loose-like, it was, and the color of a mouse."

"Would you say the call this afternoon was from him?"

"I would not. There was the difference of night and day in their voices."

"And he was the only guest you ever saw in the house?"

"The only one I saw. But I'm sure as I'm sitting here, there was others. And not the brotherly kind, if you know what I mean."

"I see. Now, Mrs. Flaherty, when did you last give the apartment a thorough cleaning?"

She puckered her face in concentration. "I did all the woodwork Friday afternoon, and the floors Saturday. I polished the furniture Wednesday, so I gave it a lick with the duster Saturday."

"Do you do dishes?"

"I do not."

"And the bedlinen—how often is that changed?"

"Every other day. Yesterday I did that. Towels every day."

"What time were you in here yesterday?"

"It was the last stop. I came in about four and left at five-thirty."

"Was Miss Gebhardt here?"

"She came in about five. 'I'm exhausted,' she says, 'and I have to dress. It's such a trial—shopping these days.' I says to myself: If that's all that's exhausting you, you're fortunate."

Holden rubbed his chin. "When you let yourself in today, Mrs. Flaherty, the place was in darkness?"

"It was. I lit the light in the foyer myself."

"What made you decide to polish the fixtures and the door-knobs right then?"

"I didn't know you'd be needing them," she snapped. "I like to save myself steps."

"There were no smudges or spots that drew your attention to them?"

"Not as I think on it, your honor."

"Now the matter of the telephone," Holden said. "Did it often ring while you were here?"

"I wouldn't say often. I never answered it before. They'd take the message downstairs after a few rings. But this afternoon you'd of thought it was possessed."

"Getting back to the gentleman you met here, did he have any sort of an accent, anything in his voice you'd recognize if you heard it again?"

"He was just quiet-spoken. Kind of like you, your honor."

"I'm a police lieutenant, Mrs. Flaherty. Lieutenant Holden, assigned to homicide."

"I always thought lieutenants were young men."

"Well, it doesn't always hold in the police department," he said, getting up. "And I'm not exactly senile."

"Excuse me, Lieutenant. But you are middle-aged."

"Lieutenants get middle-aged very quickly, unless they get to be captains first. Thanks for your patience, Mrs. Flaherty. That's all for now, unless the sergeant has any questions."

She looked at Goldsmith appraisingly.

"And if you've got the idea all sergeants are hard-boiled," Holden added, "you'll find him the exception. As gentle as Miss Gebhardt's visitor. He'll see that someone takes you home." He slumped back in the chair while Goldsmith escorted her up the steps. He nodded when she turned and bade him goodbye again.

"The poor man's tired," she said to Goldsmith.

"It's the feeling you get coming up against something like this. Now, when we open the door here, Mrs. Flaherty..."

She interrupted. "What do you mean, the feeling you get? Isn't this your job?"

Goldsmith smiled. "It's our job, but we don't always relish it. How did you feel when you tackled that bathroom this morning?"

"Ah, now I get you," she said, wagging her head. "The world's full of terrible people, isn't it?"

"Well, it's full of people who do terrible things," he said. "Now, when you get into the hall, don't be alarmed if a lot of lights flash in your face. The newspapers. It might be as well if you don't stop to talk to them now."

"If the devil spoke to me first I wouldn't answer him till I've a cup of tea."

"Good. You'll be home soon."

She allowed herself to be led to the door and then drew back again. She looked the detective squarely in the eye. "You're a quiet sort for a policeman. What's your name?"

"Goldsmith. Sergeant Ben Goldsmith."

"Do you happen to know a patrolman named Alec Donovan?"

"I'm afraid I don't."

"Well," she said, "you're not missing much. I'm glad to see they've the responsible ones handling murder."

8

Holden leaped to his feet the instant the door closed on Mrs. Flaherty. He was moving back and forth across the room when Goldsmith returned.

"The others are waiting downstairs," the sergeant said. "Do you want them up here?"

"I don't want anyone in here. Not till we're through. There's no reason those fellows can't wait in the lobby, too." He indicated the newspapermen crowding the hall.

"The management, Lieutenant."

"Then let the management find a place for them. What's the story on fingerprints?"

"The place is lousy with them, big prints, little prints, thumbs, elbows..."

Holden cut him off. "How many people?"

"Five so far."

"Take out hers and Flaherty's, that leaves three. Where are they?"

"In the bedroom mostly. There's some in the kitchen."

Holden grunted. "None in the bath?"

"Mrs. Flaherty is a thorough woman."

"The towels?"

"We've got them. But I think they're a washout."

Holden glanced up. Goldsmith's pun was unintended. "The soap box?"

"A lot of people threw out soap boxes today. The lab's working on it."

"I don't want any prints missed. Have them spray the walls, the woodwork, the light fixtures, especially that one in the kitchen...every bottle in that cupboard."

"Right."

"And the bed, the linen on the bed. It's good grade stuff?"

"Not as special as some she's got in the closet, but the boys'll bring out anything on it."

Holden lit a cigarette and went to the window. Looking down, he saw the crowd milling about, stretching, straining, striking up a camaraderie they never found except in disaster. He closed his eyes and thought about Dolly Gebhardt. The medical examiner placed her death between eight o'clock and ten Saturday night. She was wearing evening clothes. She probably had not eaten dinner. The autopsy now in progress would determine that, also the probable weapon with which she had been murdered.

Holden dragged deeply on his cigarette. There was always a lag at this stage of investigation that put him on edge. Laboratory reports incomplete, witnesses not immediate...all the important routine work to be done and yet the pressure for haste upon him...the possibility that a murderer was throwing up his camouflage, burning bridges, making time.

He turned from the window as Goldsmith came back from the bedroom. He watched him move about the room, studying the pictures on the walls, the books, magazines. The sergeant might be there on a visit by the looks of him—a young doctor, a teacher maybe. Probably a teacher: patient, inquisitive, but rather off-hand about it. A small man nobody would take for a detective, there was a warmth in him that had not yet burned out in the coldblooded business of criminal investigation. That was his great value: his human understanding. It brought him to the most unlikely criminal. No fingerprints and weapons man, he always started by studying the victim. The apparent leisure with which he could approach it grated on Holden at moments like these however.

"You've had the afternoon in the boudoir and lounge, Goldie. Just who was Dolly Gebhardt?"

Goldsmith was accustomed to his superior's sarcasm at this junction. "She was born Doris Arleen Gebhardt in 1910 at Spring Falls, Minnesota. She was in the chorus line a good many years ago, but I'd say she fell by the wayside early."

"Don't be so damned poetic. Give me the facts."

"She was a call girl, a high-class prostitute."

9

The early edition of the tabloids carried the story...not much story but plenty of bold print. They described Dolly Gebhardt as an attractive redhead and former show girl, they called the murder brutal, and they mentioned Mrs. Flaherty. Father Duffy read the piece through, his heart pounding. For the load he had borne by knowing that murder had been committed, he now picked up one twice its weight. The penitent had not gone to the police, and with each hour that he remained unapprehended, the weight would be that much more unbearable.

He laid the paper away and put on his coat. Downstairs he looked up the Flaherty address in the parish record. He walked the distance briskly, not knowing what he might say or ask. There was something vaguely comforting in the fact that out of all the people in New York who might have discovered the crime, one of his parishioners had...comforting and frightening. The largest city in the world was very small to a man in flight. It was large only to his pursuers.

He nodded absently to those who greeted him. Half the neighborhood seemed to have gathered on the steps of the tenement building where the Flahertys lived. Word of his coming flew up the stairs ahead of him, and Flaherty came down with his lunch box as the priest rounded the second floor railing.

"Hello, Billy."

"Good evening, Father. Are you here about the murder?"

"I thought there might be something I could do."

"There is something, Father. You can talk sense into Norah's head. She's past listening to me for many a year. I'm all the time telling her if I don't bring home enough we can go without. Not to be hiring herself out, and the kids running round like wild geese. Now look what she's brought us. What do the likes of us want meddling in a murder?"

Or the likes of me, Father Duffy thought.

"I'll see what I can do, Billy."

"You can tell her to stop pleasuring in it. Isn't that some kind of sin, Father?"

"It's very human, Billy," the priest said.

Flaherty grunted. "Well, I never knew a humaner woman than Norah. I have to hurry, Father, or I'll be late on the job. It's the fourth floor but you'll hear it from the landing."

Indeed he could hear it from where he stood when Flaherty left him, the great spiraling "oh" that from many years of association with Irish women he knew to be the climax of a shocking story. As though timed with his reaching the floor, however, the laughter and talk subsided. When he reached the open kitchen door off the hallway three women were sitting at the table, watching for him. They stood up in unison. He waved them back into their seats.

"You're come about the murder, Father," Mrs. Flaherty started. "Lord, how news travels. Will you have a cup of tea if I put up the kettle?"

"Thank you, no, Mrs. Flaherty. I just thought I'd stop up in case there was any advice or help I could give you."

"That was real thoughtful, Father. You know Mrs. Healy and Mrs. Hernandez?"

He nodded to the neighbors. "You must have had quite a day, Mrs. Flaherty."

"I'll be a long time forgetting it. My heart's just beginning to settle… Get back in your bed there, Sally! Shame on you, coming out before the priest like that."

Father Duffy nodded at Sally, an eight-year-old in a cotton nightgown she had outgrown at six. The girl ducked back into the bedroom.

"We could go into the parlor, Father, but we'd have to move Michael and Donel…"

"No, no, no. I've spent half my life in the kitchen, and I'll only be able to stay for a few minutes."

"It was me found the poor woman, you know, Father, and me in the house an hour not knowing…and handling them towels myself. As I was telling the girls…" She turned to her neighbors. "You won't mind hearing it again?"

They shook their heads that they would not. They would hear it many times.

"It eases me some to tell it, Father, and it's a terrible strain holding it."

He nodded and settled in a chair by the sink, hearing the full story without prodding or subtlety. His tension mounted when she told of her interview with Lieutenant Holden. The priest recognized the visitor she had described.

"You've never seen the man around St. Timothy's, have you?" the priest asked, trying to be casual.

"What would he be doing here?"

What indeed, he thought. "I don't know. Things like that happen."

"You don't think he's in the neighborhood, Father?" Mrs. Healy asked.

"No. Of course not."

He had been and gone, the priest thought. He had groped his way across the park in whatever darkness had overcome him last night, and he had found St. Timothy a momentary refuge. There he had taken brief courage, and lost it once on the streets of New York again.

"He don't sound like a murderer to me," Mrs. Hernandez put in then.

"Where did you get the notion he was?" Mrs. Flaherty demanded. "It's the furthest thing from my mind. And I made a point of it to the police, too. That kind had all manner of men hanging on her. Take the one on the phone. 'Be so kind, please, as to ask Miss Gebhardt to take the phone.'" She mimicked his tones. "That gentleman is used to giving orders. I'll wager a day's pay...excuse me, Father... I'll take my oath—he has a valet, a butler and a cook." She rolled her eyes to the ceiling. "And it's a terrible thing to say, but it wouldn't surprise me if he had a wife. I ask you, what good is he up to, calling one like that, and calling her 'Dolly,' mind you, when I picked up the phone?"

"I have a sister called Dolly," Mrs. Healy said with some indignity.

"That's not my meaning at all. I worked for a woman once had one of them Mexican hairlesses*—excuse me, Mrs. Hernandez—and called it Dolly. The point I'm making is he was on intimate terms with her."

"Couldn't that be your imagination, Mrs. Flaherty?" the priest asked. He had begun to sense Miss Gebhardt's position and the suspects it would suggest to the police. But he had to be

---

* The Xoloitzcuintle breed of dog, also known as perro pelón mexicano or Mexican hairless; it ranges from eight to fifty-five pounds in weight.

careful. He must not again say anything that might throw suspicion on the man who had confessed to him.

"Well, if it's imagination, Father, the police have a share of it, too. If I was to nominate a candidate out of my acquaintance in the house, it'd be him. Didn't he keep the phone ringing till it near put me off my nut? Didn't he make sure I was going to call her, and how else would I call her if I didn't go in where she was? Then didn't he hang up the minute I laid down the phone?"

"I'm beginning to see what you're getting at, Norah," Mrs. Healy said. "You'd make a wonderful detective. He couldn't stand waiting for her to be found, so he calls up and makes a fuss till you go and find her. Then he hangs up quick before anyone gets on to him. I heard the very likes of it on the radio the other night. The husband..."

"That's my exact meaning," Mrs. Flaherty interrupted.

"Wasn't he the cagy one?" Mrs. Healy clapped her hands in admiration.

There was one question Father Duffy longed to ask, but the one he had asked earlier forestalled him. A few minutes later it was answered in the conversation, Mrs. Flaherty directing her words at him.

"And it wasn't the little man I saw there called up. I'd take my oath on it. And I told that to the lieutenant."

10

As soon as Father Duffy left them, the three women swung about the table and relaxed.

"There! Wasn't I telling you only yesterday," Mrs. Healy said, "the clergy are into everything."

Mrs. Flaherty drew herself up. "Who has a better right?"

Mrs. Healy made a noise of disgruntlement.

"On the contrary," Mrs. Flaherty followed up, "I think it was decent of him to come climbing up here and sit down in the kitchen. There's some I know wouldn't come till you're wanting Extreme Unction,* and maybe getting here late for that."

"All right, all right. I was only thinking on the queer tight way he was watching you tell the story."

"It's just the way of the man. He's awful serious-minded nowadays. It wouldn't surprise me if he was going on a crusade against that sort of woman."

"I've seen a few on the corner I'd like to give him the names of, then," Mrs. Healy said. "Standing there as bold as morning within a stone's throw of the church."

---

* The Catholic sacrament for anointing of the sick or dying.

"What awful bad things they must think of," said Mrs. Hernandez.

"It'd poison a pup, I daresay," Mrs. Flaherty put in. "What gets me is wondering the kind of men taking up with them."

"Them coming off the boats," Mrs. Healy said. "They say during the war the soldiers were terrible..."

"That's it then!"

"What's it?"

"Father Duffy. That's what he's after. He was a chaplain in the army, you know. They say he hated it and he won't join any of their organizations. That's what it is. I've often thought to myself when some of them conventioneers are in town what they do to a decent woman on the street would turn your stomach. So what'd they do with one like that meeting her?"

Mrs. Hernandez shook her head. "They're not all like that. My oldest son is a veteran."

"Your boy could go through hell without getting singed," Mrs. Flaherty said. "Oh, we're going to get a fine sermon Sunday at the eight o'clock." She rocked back and forth, thinking about it.

"The Monsignor won't let him," said Mrs. Healy.

"Then we'll get it by the innuendo. You'll see. And he's the one to do it. The men will take it from him. They say when he was in the army the boys thought the world of him. He'd go through the barracks of a Sunday morning shouting: 'Come on, you bloody heathens, get the hell out of your beds and into the chapel!'" She gave a great thump with her hand on the table.

"You'll wake up the kids," Mrs. Hernandez said.

"The kids? She'll be waking the dead," said Mrs. Healy.

"There's one I won't waken," Mrs. Flaherty said in sudden sobriety. "But I'll never forget the feeling—standing there at her door trying... And then when I went into the room..."

She was off on the story again from the beginning.

11

At eight o'clock that night Lieutenant Holden returned to headquarters after a tardy dinner. Goldsmith arranged a series of reports before him, the autopsy findings on top, while the lieutenant called the chief inspector. Hanging up the phone he wiped the sweat from his chin.

"That's so the old boy can stick his feet back up on the railing and enjoy the sea-breeze. What a great night for something like this."

"The only comfortable place I've been to today was the morgue," Goldsmith said. "Which is a nice thought for Sunday. Want to go over the autopsy?"

The lieutenant picked up the report and read it through, now and then repeating a section aloud. Goldsmith was lining up photographs.

"Last meal about two o'clock," Holden commented, "salad, greens…"

"A vegetarian, no doubt," Goldsmith said.

"Some alcohol. Probably a cocktail or two. No more." Holden looked up. "Would you say she was the kind to drink alone?"

"I doubt it. McCormick's checking that. Also her shopping tour."

"Sunday's a tough night for that."

"We'd like to find out if anyone was with her yesterday. There's a set of fingerprints on her wardrobe door. It looks as though she'd taken somebody there to show him what she had in it, or maybe what she didn't have. According to Flaherty's cleaning schedule, those prints got there after Friday afternoon."

Holden returned to the autopsy report. "The blunt instrument," he murmured. "Hammer, butt of a gun…"

"If you'll look at these pictures, Lieutenant, I think we can eliminate the gun. The depth of the wounds indicates more leverage than a gun would allow."

Holden went to the wall board where Goldsmith had lined up the pictures. The sergeant traced the areas he wanted to call particular attention to. Holden nodded while he listened to Goldsmith's theory. He returned to his desk.

"That would mean a mechanic's hammer. Is that your idea?"

"It is. The medical examiner corroborates."

"That would suggest someone who drives a car, maybe his own, maybe not. All it really suggests is someone who has access to a mechanic's hammer. I suppose practically all the men she entertained owned their own cars?"

Goldsmith sat down on the corner of the desk. "We don't know all of them yet. And I don't think she entertained many of them at home. She went out on her important calls, though she may have had a regular or two. Before we get to the suspects I'd like to go over what we can of her activities Saturday."

Holden agreed and Goldsmith lit a cigarette. "We know that she went shopping in the afternoon. I think she bought, or at least shopped for, something in fur. There was a newspaper in the living room opened to an ad for furs—Friday's paper, by the way. Saturday she came home tired about five o'clock. She wasn't feeling very well. As you can see in the report, she had a bad stomach. But she had a dinner appointment important enough to keep anyway..."

Holden lit a cigarette from Goldsmith's. He had learned most of this during the afternoon's questionings, this and a lot of things that were no doubt extraneous. He noticed that some of them were missing from Goldsmith's recapitulation. He had pared off the non-essentials.

"Her date must have been for an early dinner," the sergeant continued. "That inclines me to the opinion that her client might be an out-of-towner. I don't think she rested at all then. She probably showered and dressed as soon as Flaherty left. I think she expected someone—but not her date. Whoever she expected was keeping her late. She smoked two cigarettes in the living room. The lipstick matches what she was wearing when she died. She wouldn't wear that shade in the afternoon. I think she waited there in the living room as long as she dared without chancing to stand up her date...all dressed to go out, and carrying in her evening bag over two hundred dollars."

Goldsmith flicked the ash from his cigarette into the wastebasket.

"That's a lot of money to start an evening with," Holden said.

"And to finish it with," the sergeant added. "It was still in her purse and the purse was open on the bed. But we'll come to that presently. By a few minutes to seven she could wait no longer. She went out without leaving a message at the desk. In a way, that throws off my theory that she was waiting for someone but I think she was, nevertheless.

"Outdoors, the doorman tried to get a cab for her, but she flagged a cruiser herself on the corner of Madison. Unfortunate. It may take a while to turn up the cabbie. She was gone no more than a half-hour when she returned, the cabbie helping her out of the car and upstairs. She had a shock, or else she really got sick. Probably that. The hotel employees tell this story. That would be a few minutes after seven. The doorman rolled the cab down the street away from the front door when the driver didn't return quick enough to suit him. In fact, he doesn't know when the driver returned. He didn't think of him again till we started questioning.

"The cabbie didn't take the elevator downstairs. The operator remembers a persistent ringing on the fourth floor a few minutes after they had gone up, but when he got down, there was no one there. It's probable that the man was worried about his cab and ran down the stairs when the elevator was so slow. The stairs are clearly marked in the hall. And something we know now: the murderer used them."

Holden looked at him.

"We've got the shirt he wore. It's in the lab. A couple of hours ago one of the men picked it up behind some ashcans at the service entrance."

"He didn't pick up the murder weapon, too?"

"Just the shirt. Rolled up in a ball. Washed and rolled up in a ball. He must have gone out of here in his undershirt."

"Or naked," Holden said. "I think he could have gone out naked for all the notice there was taken of him."

Goldsmith smiled. "Possibly. The funny thing is, I don't think he was trying to avoid attention particularly. I think a lot of things fell his way."

"Then why didn't he take the shirt with him?"

"That I don't know."

"I see you've eliminated the cab driver," Holden said.

"I don't eliminate him. He's the best suspect we have at the moment. He might have returned…"

"Why not have killed her then?"

Goldsmith thumbed through the reports.

"There was a phone call to her apartment about eight-thirty. She was alive then. Alive and able to answer it. That's all we know about the call."

Holden drummed on his desk. "You don't like the cabbie because of motive. Is that it?"

"Mostly. There's no indication that the murderer was interested in her physically—at that moment. And there's the money untouched."

"At that moment?" Holden picked up.

"At that moment," Goldsmith repeated. He rummaged through the photographs. "She was on the bed, not in it, fully dressed, as you can see here. There is every indication that she was murdered there. Apparently there was no struggle. It's just possible that she was asleep. If she was, it means that after the cabbie left someone came whom she trusted. Maybe the person she expected earlier."

"What was wrong with her?" Holden asked.

"An ulcerous stomach."

"Nothing worse? Or nothing she could have thought was worse?"

"We'll have to check her doctors for that."

"You see what I'm driving at, don't you? The possibility of a mercy killing?"

"If it was, it was done the most unmerciful way in history. I don't think so, Lieutenant. It looks more emotional than calculated."

"How about her date? Could he have come up there jealous?"

"I doubt it. Remember the shirt. But a lot of things are possible. I've no doubt you're going to turn out some very fine gentlemen with those prints and that little book of hers."

"But you don't buy any of them, is that it, Goldie?"

Goldsmith shrugged. "Maybe, maybe not." He picked up

a match from the floor and examined it almost as though it were a clue to the matter at hand. "Take the shirt the guy was wearing—cheap, worn, but there'd been starch in the collar. No laundry marks." He looked up at the lieutenant. "Somebody was taking awfully good care of that guy. I wouldn't be surprised if poor old Dolly tried it, too, in her own fashion. But she wasn't the kind to dip his collars in starch. I wonder who is."

"What size collar?"

"Fourteen and a half. A little man."

"A little man scorned…"

"I wonder," Goldsmith said.

"Is he the fellow Mrs. Flaherty described?"

"That's quite possible, and to quote her on it, he was one man she entertained in street clothes. A brother to her."

Holden got up and gathered the reports. "He's your kind of guy, isn't he, Goldie?"

"I think so."

"Okay. I'll put McCormick on the others. Unless they counter me from upstairs, he's yours."

"Thanks, Lieutenant."

"Just keep in touch. That's all. No secrets. Keep me posted."

"Every step of the way."

12

In the big kitchen of the house on West Twelfth Street, Lenore Galli sat beside the open window. A pile of socks and her sewing-basket were on the table. She had not touched them. Upstairs a chair scraped across the floor and Tim's footsteps began again, back and forth across the room, forth and back. Then quiet. She counted on her fingers the hours he had been working. It was ten o'clock now. Six hours.

She unfolded a pair of socks and used one of them as a fan. A cat whined somewhere not far from the window. The snarl spiraled into screeching that sent a bolt of pain to her head. The pain eased off. She sighed and listened to the scratchy flight of one cat up the withered catalpa tree near the window. Her body tensed as she waited for the sound of pursuit. The roughness of her fingers caught a few threads of the sock. She looked at her hands. Rummaging in the sewing-basket she found scissors and cut away the hangnails and with the point cleaned beneath her nails. The screaming of the cats started again. Someone next door flung up his window and shouted out. There was a moment's silence, then a low, persistent snarl. A few seconds later she heard a splash of water and the scurried flight of the animals.

She got up then and went to the kitchen sink, where she soaped and soaked her hands, all the while examining her face this way and that in the mirror above the sink. She sniffed about herself for any smell of perspiration, and after she had dried her hands, dabbed herself with cologne. She combed her hair, straightening the part in the middle and then turned to look at herself with the hair flowing down her back. It was still a deep brown, although a few threads of gray shivered through it. After a moment of reflection on the way it failed to cover her thickening shoulders, she braided it up again. She rubbed her face in the towel and fluffed powder on it. There were no lines yet except the laughing kind, and her eyes were rich, shining limpidly back at her from the mirror.

She tidied the sink and went to the refrigerator. Taking a leg of chicken from it, tomatoes and preserves, she fixed a tray and took it upstairs. In the upstairs hall, she set the tray down for a moment on a little table. Katerina's door was partly open. Her mother tiptoed to it and looked in. The girl was asleep, her light on, a book lying on the floor where it had fallen from her hand. Moving very softly, Mrs. Galli put out the light and drew the door closed.

Taking the tray, she went on to Tim's room at the back of the house and knocked gently. "I've brought you up something to eat, Tim," she said, opening the door before he answered her knock. "You need nourishment for all that work."

He whirled around from the card table where he was working. The table and floor were littered with papers. "I don't want anything, thank you, Mrs. Galli."

"Mrs. Galli," she chided him. "I thought you were going to call me Lenore."

"Lenore," he repeated tentatively, his hands against the table as though he had retreated into it although he had not risen from the chair. He could smell the cologne on her as she advanced into the room ponderously.

"That's better," she purred. She set the tray on the bureau. "Too much work and no play... You didn't come down for supper and you missed your dinner. There's not much of you to begin with. But I never liked big men. l always liked that about you. You think less of your stomach than up here." She motioned to her head with a jeweled finger. She rolled to the door and closed it, staying in the room. "You like to keep the door closed. I don't blame you. I should get you a key. The palookas going up and down here wouldn't understand the kind of work you do."

All the while she spoke Tim cringed against the table. With the door closed she seemed to overflow the room like a genie rising from a bottle.

"Go away," he whispered to himself. "Please God, make her go."

She stood at the tray now, opening a cola bottle and pouring the liquid into a glass. Twice herself she was, reflected in the mirror. Looking at him through it, she smiled.

"I have a key for my room. It's the only room in the house with a lock to it." She turned and advanced with the glass in her hand. "Here, Tim. This will make you feel better. 'Pepsi-Cola hits the spot, twelve ounce bottle, that's a lot...'" she sang the jingle, the richness of her voice like the velvet color of the drink.

He leaped to his feet, his hip catching the fragile table and careening it over on two legs, the papers tumbling among the discarded sheets already on the floor. He went down on his hands and knees to gather them, eager to escape the sight of her for those few blurred seconds at least. His sweat dripped on the pages in his hand.

She set the glass on the dresser and squatted down in front of him to help, her dress a taut line across her knees. Tim spun away from the sight and sprang to his feet. "Sweet Jesus," he muttered hoarsely. His face was gray-white, the blue veins standing out on his forehead.

"Will you get up from there and leave me alone? Please…"

She leaned on the bed and hoisted herself up. She flung the handful of papers on the bed. Her smile was gone and some of the hair had straggled from the pins.

"What's the matter with you? Am I so ugly? Am I so old?"

He shook his head. "No, Mrs. Galli, no, no, no." He motioned desperately toward the tray. "Thank you for bringing that to me."

"Mrs. Galli, Mrs. Galli! There's more man in that cat scratching up the tree out there than there is in you."

"Please," he said, thumping the fat of his hand against the chair.

"Please," she mimicked again. "It was please before and thank you after. I could take you in from the street all shaking like you had palsy. I could knit you sweaters and socks and darn them for you. I could put food in your belly and a blanket around you at night. It was please and thank you for all of that. Wasn't it?"

"Yes, it was," he said more quietly. His pressure was easing off as her anger mounted. Her anger was easier on him than her affection.

"You liked my arm around you then. You let me take your hand. Put it where it's warm. 'Envelop me,' you said. 'Envelop me.' I never forgot the word. I looked it up. A hundred times I looked it up."

Her anger was easier on him, but not her memories. Tim moistened his lips and reached for the cola she had poured for him. She slashed out with her fist and spilled the dark stuff to the floor and over his manuscript.

"That kind of refreshment I can give you, can I? Well, I'm telling you you won't have it. You can lick it up from the floor.

That's what you can do. Get down and lick it up like a dog. Then get out of my house. Go and do your begging on somebody else's doorstep. All your life you beg, don't you, beggar-boy?"

She watched him gather the pages and wipe the cola from them with his sleeve. Her anger snapped the instant she spilled over the glass. She turned from him, trying to hold a part of it to hide her rising shame. Catching her reflection in the mirror, she saw the red splotches on her face and the ugly sweat seeping through them. Her heavy breathing hissed through her teeth. Her mind churned wildly as she sought for words, for issues on which to abuse him.

"You think I don't know what's changed you. I seen you looking at her and her looking at you, and neither one of you looking at the same time."

That thought seemed to revive her anger. She swung around and pulled him to his feet, forcing him to look at her. "She's my daughter. Flesh of my flesh."

"I know," he said helplessly. "I know."

"You want her, do you?"

His head shot up and he wrenched free of her grasp. He looked at her, and through her.

"I don't want her. Before I would lay a hand on Katie I would cut it off."

"I don't believe it. You think she didn't tell me. My Katerina don't keep secrets from her mother. You think I didn't see you coming out of the church with her. I did. I seen you get on the bus together. Coming home at three o'clock. Leaving me to stand over the stove. And I told her something, too. Letting me get old-looking when I'm not over forty-one. 'Oh, mama,' she says, 'why do you care how you look?' There. That's your fine young Katie for you. I'd like to see if she looks as good as me at forty. What were you doing in the park?"

"Talking," Tim said. "Talking and walking, and then we ate a hot dog and came home."

"You didn't hold hands even, I suppose?"

"No," he said, and then added wistfully, "We didn't even hold hands."

She believed him, and believing him, had nothing left for which to abuse him. Her anger was all spent even as her other emotion was spent in the anger.

"Is that poem about her?" she asked sullenly.

"In a way." He laid the pages together on the card table as he righted it.

"Am I in it?"

"Yes. In a way you're in it, too."

She fussed about the dresser a moment, setting the glass upright. "It's awful stuffy in here. I'll open the door." Her movements to the door and back were awkward. She fumbled with the dresser scarf, painfully aware now of her own awkwardness, her bulk. She was tired, conscious of the weight of her body in each part of it separately. "There's some coke left in the bottle. I'm sorry I spilled it over your poem, Tim."

He permitted her to give him the glass. He drained it in one swallow.

"It's the heat," she said. "If it would just let up for a couple of days things wouldn't choke up inside us. You need clean curtains. New York's awful dirty in summer."

"Thank you," he said, giving the glass back to her.

"There's more in the icebox. I'll go down and bring you a bottle. Eat something here while I'm gone. Don't leave it for the flies." He did not protest.

At the door she turned. "Tim, don't put me in the poem like I was just now. It was the heat—and things."

13

By Monday morning conspiracies and taxes had crowded the murder into the small sub-heads of the tabloid front pages: CABBIE SOUGHT IN SLAYING. On page three, however, the caption read: FATHER REFUSES BODY OF MURDERED REDHEAD. Only in the final paragraph was the theme of the front page explained: the cab driver was expected to throw some light on Miss Gebhardt's activities on the evening of her death.

Father Duffy read the story through... Reached at his home in Little Falls, Minnesota, Albert J. Gebhardt, an iron-ore miner, commented on his daughter's death, "I'm surprised it didn't happen sooner." Dolly's life was no secret to her father or to any of the other five hundred souls in Little Falls. Someone had visited her in New York and taken home a righteous story of her career. Since then, Albert Gebhardt did public penance for the sins of his daughter over a thousand miles away.

It was an odd twist on the biblical prophecy of the visitation of one generation's sins upon the other, Father Duffy thought. He dropped the paper in the waste basket and went to his desk. There he composed a letter to the parish priest at Little Falls, acting on a hunch and inquiring if there had ever been a Father McGohey serving there. He gave the possible variations of the spelling as they came to him.

The letter sealed, he drew another piece of paper from the drawer and tried to recompose the distraught confession of the murderer…the hammer, his mother had given him one because St. Joseph was a carpenter…he wanted to be a priest…a prayerbook for his first Communion…the hammer…her windows always stuck this time of year…dirty again…the dream of slime…if I could just keep my mouth clean…

Bit by bit, the fragments came back to him, and he refashioned the story in all its incoherence. In a way it took on a strange logic of its own, the priest thought, especially in the association of his crime with early guilts in his life, early guilts and sufferings. He read through his notes and then juxtaposed the phrases to bring them as exactly as he could into the order he had heard them. He rewrote the confession and read it a few times, committing it to memory. Then he tore the papers into small pieces and burned them a few at a time in the ashtray.

He closed his eyes and remembered again the feeling about him in the confessional that night, the ache and heat and someone calling good night to Father Gonzales. For a moment he caught the outline of the man's face as it was when he had first looked up to see if there were someone really there. He remembered his association of the face with St. Francis, and then with the faces of boys he had seen returning from their first experience under fire during the war.

Two thoughts out of the whole pattern seemed to converge for Father Duffy then. They had no right to come together because only one of them came out of the confession at all. The other was out of himself, his own character, prejudices, experience. But wherever the conviction came from, he was virtually certain in that instant that Father McGohey had at some time in his life been an army or navy chaplain, and probably in the first world war.

14

"Look, I was cruising down Madison. I was thinking to myself if the damn buses wasn't lined up like a string of elephants I'd have a chance of picking up a fare. Then I sees her standing there, waving this fancy pocketbook. Like crazy she was waving it. 'Break it up, boys,' I says. 'I'm coming through.' But like I said, she could of got a dozen other cabs."

"I understand that," Lieutenant Holden said, having combed the drivers of the city. "But she did get you."

"Yeah. She got me," the cabbie said dismally.

"Do you carry a tool kit or tools of any sort?"

"Not me. When anything goes wrong I just sit till they come and get me. I ain't mechanical on eight bucks a day. No sir."

"Then you don't have a hammer in the cab?"

"Look, Lieutenant, I wouldn't be in here on my own accord like this if I had the hammer you're looking for."

A police stenographer in the back of the room changed pencils.

"Just answer my question," Holden said. "Do you have a hammer?"

"Yeah. I have one. I keep it on the seat beside me. I got mugged once. Want to see it?"

"I think that would be advisable," Holden said quietly. He motioned to a uniformed policeman standing at the door.

The cabbie looked around to see him depart. "You don't waste no time, do you?"

"We try not to," Holden said. "Now I'd like to hear the details of what happened from the moment you picked her up."

The cabbie sat back in his chair and crossed his legs. He accepted the cigarette Holden offered him. "She jumped in. Didn't waste no time," he started. "Gave the door a good whack shut. I don't get one out of ten can get that door closed themselves. Some day I'm gonna get a new hack. In the neck I'm gonna get it. Five thousand bucks. Anyway, 'I'm late,' she says. 'Fifth Avenue and Tenth Street. Try and get there in a hurry.' 'I don't aim going in second, lady,' I says, 'but we ain't going to set any records this time of day...'"

Holden made a note of the address while the cabbie talked. So did Goldsmith, who sat at his desk throughout the questioning, listening although apparently absorbed in work of his own. Now he drew a map from his drawer and opened it.

"Well, I get all the way down to Twenty-third Street. I'm beginning to make time then and she leans up to me. 'Driver, you'll have to take me back.' 'Forget something?' I says. But I take one look at her and I could tell she didn't forget nothing she wanted to remember. That dame was sick. She looked good when she got in but right then that makeup on her face was like something stuck on, something that was going to fall off any minute. I made a U-turn and stepped on it. I don't like people getting sick on me. If they're real sick they can't think about the fare, and I ain't got what it takes to ask 'em for it. One time I damn near got a baby. You think that's funny. Happens in the newspaper maybe, but let me tell you..."

"We'd better wait for that," Holden said. "It took you

about a half-hour to get to Twenty-third Street and back. Then what?"

"I pulled up in front of her apartment—almost in front, that is, I thought the doorman would come and get her. Maybe she don't want him. Maybe she figured she can't wait. He was putting somebody in a private car. Anyway, she asks me to help her upstairs. Says she'll make it worth my while. That suits me. I take the key out of the car, go around and give her an arm. She leaned hard and she wasn't no lightweight. We goes in through the lobby. A couple of people look round at us. Maybe they think she's drunk. I don't know. The guy at the desk looks up. Says 'good evening' just like it was one. She don't say a word. The elevator's there. The operator says 'good evening' the same way. I think maybe she'll let go of me then. No sir. If I'd tried to get away I'd had to leave her my right arm. Right to the door. She leans on the wall while she gets out the key. I take it from her and open the door. Then she grabs my arm again and says, 'Help me into the bedroom, please.' I don't like that much, but I figure she's got to sit down before she pays me…"

"Were there any lights on in the apartment?" Holden interrupted.

The cabbie thought about it. "Yeah. There was one on down there in the living room. We went through that hall there and she says the bedroom switch is on the wall. I turned it on."

"Did you close the door to the apartment before helping her into the bedroom?"

The cab driver rubbed the back of his neck. "I just don't remember that. It was closed when I went to go out again—I know that…"

"All right," Holden said. "Take that when you get there. You helped her into the bedroom and lit the light. Then what?"

"She sits down on the bed and pulls off her earrings. I'm

standing there waiting for my money. I don't like asking her for it just like that, so I asks her if I can get her anything, maybe call up a doctor for her. 'I'll be all right,' she says. 'Just open that window for me.' If I'd had a block and tackle I don't think I could of opened it. I pulled and I pushed and the sweat rolled down my back. I couldn't open it. 'Let it go,' she says. 'Please give me my purse.' I gave her that in a hurry."

"Where was it?"

"Down at the bottom of the bed."

"Open."

"Not when I gave it to her. She fumbled inside it and pulled out five dollars. Looked hard to make sure what it was. Whatever was the matter with her, I don't think she was seeing so good. 'Is this all right?' she says. 'Want change?' says I. 'No.' 'That's swell,' I says. 'You better call a doctor, lady.' I figured she had advice coming, anyway."

"What did she do with the purse then?" Holden asked.

"She tossed it over on the dressing table. It didn't make it. Fell on the floor. I picked it up and laid it on the table for her."

"Did you look around the room at all?"

"Just while I was waiting. It was kind of messed up"

"As though someone had been through it?"

"Naw. Like she just threw things around getting dressed. Underwear and stuff."

"Did you leave then?"

"Just about. I was just going when she says, 'There's something I wish you'd do for me.' 'What?' 'Go into the kitchen and make sure the latch is off the hall door there.' 'No ma'am,' I says, 'I don't like to do that. I'll stop by the desk and ask 'em to send up the janitor...' 'Never mind,' she says. 'I'll manage.' I beat it then. Boy, did I beat it. There was something about the whole business I didn't like. As soon as I got out in the hall, I felt like

I'd been in there a week maybe. I poked and poked at the elevator bell. The chains were going up and down but no cage. Then I saw the stairs sign and I ran down them. I was right by the service door when I reached the first floor so I scrammed out that way. Somebody pushed my cab down a ways. I just hopped into it and beat it. I picked up a fare on Fifth Avenue going to Riverside Drive and Ninety-sixth Street. That's all." He put his cigarette out beneath his foot.

"And after the Ninety-sixth Street fare?"

"I hopped over to West End. I cruised down there to about Seventy-fourth. I got a couple of dames there going to the Alvin Theatre."

"And then?"

"I stopped over at Kavanaugh's on Eighth Avenue for a corned beef sandwich."

"Keep going," Holden said.

The cabbie drew his record book from his pocket. "Yeah," he said after a moment. "A couple of sailors. Frenchies. I took 'em to Pier Sixteen. That's around Fulton. I headed back up through Chinatown. Figured I might get some slummers.* No soap.† I didn't get nothing till I was up around Washington Square. That was ten o'clock..."

"Okay," Holden said. "That'll do it." He swung around to Goldsmith. "Any questions, Sergeant?"

Goldsmith got up from his desk and went over to the cabbie. "You didn't by any chance go into the kitchen to make sure that door was locked?"

---

* That is to say, non-Chinese Americans visiting the "slum" of Chinatown.

† The earliest appearance of this slang phrase in print, according to the *Oxford English Dictionary*, is the 1926 *Wise-Crack Dictionary* compiled by George H. Maines and Bruce Grant (New York: Spot News Service), in which it is defined as "can't talk business." The equivalent is "nothing doing" or "it's not going to happen."

The driver smirked nervously. "No sir. What I did do: going round to the stairs when the elevator didn't pick me up, I tried that door just to make sure it was locked."

"Or to make sure it wasn't locked?" Holden snapped.

"No sir. If it wasn't locked I was going right straight to the desk and tell 'em. Like I told you, I felt funny about being in that place. And I felt like I'd been in there a hell of a long time."

"That often happens," Goldsmith said easily. "Our imagination distorts time on us under some conditions."

"Yeah, don't it?" said the driver.

"Did you see anyone when you left by the back entrance of the building?" Holden asked.

"Not a soul. I waved at the doorman when I was going round the hack. I figured he moved it. But I don't think he saw me."

"If you'll wait in the room out there," Holden said, "the stenographer will type up your story. I'd like you to sign it."

"Sure."

The cabbie was at the door when Goldsmith called to him. "You said you did not get the window open. Is that right?"

"Right. I couldn't budge it."

Goldsmith nodded his thanks and the stenographer followed the driver out.

Goldsmith returned to his desk. "There's a lush private club down in the neighborhood she was heading for. I wonder if she didn't have a date there."

"What kind of club?" Holden asked.

"Where the rich and the famous relax in private. The girls sing, dance a little maybe on order. It's a very tête à tête* sort of place."

"Her kind of girl?"

---

* Literally, head-to-head, meaning face-to-face or intimate.

"Nope. She'd be there on invitation, the invitation of her escort. Then afterwards..." Goldsmith shrugged.

"Where would the escort have met her?"

"That's something else again."

"If she had to stand him up there," Holden said, "you'd think she would have called the club. You don't disappoint people in her business. Not if you want a second call."

"It may be that she just had the name of her host and the address. Her phone isn't listed. I'd guess it that way and put somebody with a delicate touch on it. With the right approach you might get the name of her host."

"You're too busy, I take it," Holden said with slight sarcasm.

"I'll take it if you say so, but I don't think I'm going in that direction otherwise."

"We've got a few other delicate guys on the force."

"Good. I'll be up at Dolly's place for a while if you're looking for me."

Holden picked up the inter-office phone. "You and Dolly," he said to Goldsmith as the sergeant reached the door, "a couple of free-lancers."

Goldsmith tipped his hat.

15

The sergeant had the apartment to himself for the first time. It looked well-beaten, he thought, as he closed the door behind him. There was not a pin in it unaccounted for. As he stood in the foyer, taking in the place generally, it occurred to him that somebody was going to get a very nice apartment one day soon—the sunken living room, the large bedroom, a kitchen large enough for table and chairs, a foyer that could be used for dinner when there was company. The right size for him and his wife. A convenient neighborhood, too. He threw his hat on the table. An inconvenient rental. Very inconvenient.

He looked at the door. One of the things he wondered about was why, with a kitchen entrance to the place, Mrs. Flaherty used this one. He went into the kitchen and examined that door. It was double-locked, the chain bolt now on. There was no such fixture on the front door. That accounted for Mrs. Flaherty's using it. There she could let herself in and out.

Dolly Gebhardt had expected someone the night she was murdered, and she expected him to come in the back door. The inside lock was to be left off for him. It was therefore logical to suppose that he had a key to the other lock. It might also be assumed that he had used it before, indeed often enough to have his own key. Since none of the staff recalled a frequent visitor, he probably used the back stairs, as had the taxi driver. Why?

Goldsmith refined the possibilities to two: the visitor was someone of such renown that he would be recognized in the lobby, or his person was so disreputable that he would be conspicuous and not especially welcome. Goldsmith favored the latter possibility since the subject fit the shirt collar.

There was some pattern, too, in the sort of visitors Dolly brought home with her. Very few visitors came that she did not accompany. Except for one "gentleman" who called every week or so, most of her visitors were young men. In their twenties, the clerk suggested, and presentable if not distinguished-looking. Very shy. Embarrassed. There were not many of them, and he had not recalled seeing any one of them twice.

The detective tried to open the kitchen window. With much pounding it yielded. He thumped it down again and moved into the bedroom. The window was still closed. Nor could he make it yield. He tried the living room windows then. Only one of them opened, and that after he was sweating for his efforts. However, he found what he had hoped for: several small circular marks at the top of the frame at the side. Someone had taken a hammer to loosen it. He stepped back with some satisfaction and wiped his hands and face in his handkerchief.

The phone rang behind him. He reached around and picked it up.

"Send it up," he said after hearing the message.

A few minutes later the fur piece Miss Gebhardt had purchased on the day of her death was delivered. The delivery man watched with fascination while the detective signed for it.

Inside Goldsmith opened the box and examined the fur. "Not such a much," he said aloud, picking it up. He doubted that his wife would wear its sort. But she wasn't keen on furs of any sort. He called headquarters and reported its arrival to Holden.

"How much?" the lieutenant asked.

"Reduced. Two hundred and seventy-nine dollars cash."

Holden named a furrier. "Is that the place?"

"That's it," Goldsmith said, looking at the box.

"She was alone when she bought it, Goldie."

"I kind of figured that. She wasn't going to show papa the price-tag. Just the fur. Then she'd say: 'Only four hundred eighty-nine dollars. Want your change?'"

"Sounds reasonable."

"A bargain at half the price. How I'd love to deliver this box to his castle—wherever it is. I bet his wife would love it. I'll see you, chief."

He hung up and took the box to the bedroom, flinging it on the pile of clothes already heaped there in inventory. He returned to the living room and pulled a footstool up to the one bookcase in the room. It had been obvious from the stack of magazines that Dolly liked light reading. That was why two volumes of poetry were so conspicuous among the Cinderella fiction, mystery and adventure. They were old books, the products of bargain stalls, one a student's edition of Shelley* and the other a cheap copy of the complete poems of Francis Thompson.† It was too much to hope that they might be inscribed, Goldsmith thought, examining the front pages. There were only the price

---

* Percy Bysshe Shelley (1792–1822), one of the leading Romantic poets of England.

† Francis Thompson (1859–1907) was an English poet and Catholic mystic. His most famous work was "The Hound of Heaven," called by *Boston Globe* literary columnist Katherine A. Powers "perhaps the most beloved and ubiquitously taught poem among American Catholics for over half a century" ("Poet du jour," *Boston College Magazine* [Summer 2002], https://bcm.bc.edu/issues/summer_2002 /ll_poet.html). J. R. R. Tolkien cited Thompson's work as an important early influence on his writing (Christopher Tolkien, ed., *The Book of Lost Tales* [Boston: Houghton Mifflin, 1984], 29n).

marks on them. If there were a clue to murder in them, it was in their contents and in the sort of person associated with Dolly Gebhardt who would be interested in them.

Taking them with him, he went out and locked the door.

16

It rained that afternoon, a great burst of it at first that presently spread into a steady, gentle fall. Of all the people who welcomed it, none was more grateful than Tim Brandon. He had been sitting in a little park when it started, aware of everyone else who was sitting there listlessly, and thinking that everyone was aware of him. When the rain came, he felt it like a curtain about him, through which he could peek at others, safe himself from their prying eyes.

He watched the puddles form in the pavement, and remembered the patches of ice he had run and slid upon as a child. The little air bubbles in them had looked like nickels and quarters. He turned over the money in his pocket now, a crumpled dollar bill, a fifty-cent piece and four pennies. It was every cent he had to his name. He got up and shook the rain from his hair. He began to walk, holding between his shirt and his skin, under his arm, a wad of damp papers.

Street after street he walked, gradually corralling his thoughts from Mrs. Galli, his finances and Katie. More and more he had been thinking of Katie these last couple of days, but she, too, had to be banished now. By late afternoon he was on the lower East Side, his mind charging ahead of him with the lines he wanted to put on paper. The pushcarts were covered with swatches of canvas and people huddled in doorways cursing and blessing the weather in one breath. Kids were damming the flow of rain in the gutters with broken plates, tin cans and bits of boxes, they were sailing match packets, the slime of the street oozing through their toes. The sight fascinated him. It drew him out of his concentration, and he stood on the curb, watching the muddy water play around their feet. Instinctively he drew the back of his hand across his mouth, wiping saliva and the rain from it. He knew in an instant the association it had for him and shuddered. He hastened on but felt the drag of his waterlogged shoes. The slippery feel of them revolted him. He thought he was going to be ill and leaned a moment against a lamp post, tilting his face into the rain.

The blessed rain was clean and fresh from heaven. It cleansed his mind and face. He watched a boy come out of the shop beside him taking great bites out of a frankfurter. His sickness was no more than hunger, he decided. He went into the shop and asked for one.

"Mustard?" the woman asked, holding the stick with a big blob of it dribbling off.

"Don't!" He turned his head away quickly.

The woman shrugged. "If that's the kind of stomach you got, I give you some advice. Don't eat frankfurters. Ten cents, please." He gave her the fifty-cent piece and got his change. Taking the sandwich out with him, he walked another block and then crossed the street. There, in the shelter of the Williamsburg Bridge, he sat down on a pile of old sewer tiles and ate it.

He felt better then. He listened to the tumble and humping of traffic on the bridge above him, and glanced up at the giant frame of the structure. There was a wonderful grace and sweep to the arches that supported it. Closing his eyes and opening them again, he could imagine the colors of cathedral windows in the veils of rain. Gradually he once more composed his thoughts, and marshaled back before him the lines of the poem he had been pursuing. He drew the moist papers from beneath his shirt and a stub of pencil, sharpened at both ends, from his pocket. The blank pages he had folded into the middle were dry. He put them on top now, and began to write, using the top of a fruit box across his knees as a table.

As darkness drew upon the city, he bent closer to his words. Now and then he paused to scrape the pencil sharp on the rim of a pipe. His only interruption came from a bum who must have felt a kinship, for he started: "Excuse me, brother..." Tim gave him a quarter and kept on working. Finally he had no paper left. He whistled softly while he folded the sheets and tucked them away under his shirt once more.

Walking westward, he decided that he didn't care if Mrs. Galli were home. In fact, if she were, so much the better. She would feed him and rub his hair with a towel. He would stay downstairs until after midnight, until she had gone to bed. If he could keep her from coming into his room, everything would be all right. Indeed, it was comforting to think of her warm hands on his chilled back, of the hug she might give him. Then he drew for himself the picture of Katie, her solemn eyes watching him. He imagined himself looking up at her and catching a flood of color in her face. All day, he realized, he had been waiting for the indulgence of this moment—when he would permit himself long thoughts of Katie. He quickened his steps. In a flash of memory, he watched her go down the aisle to communion that morning and recaptured her radiance on her return from the altar and the sense of exaltation that surged up in him with his awareness then of her presence and the Lord's beside him.

He could not regain the thrill of memory but that once, try as he might. Its fading depressed him a little. He blamed himself for his failure of concentration. All his life, he had failed in that. If his will had been equal to his wish, the world would have been shot through with his poetry even as the heavens were shot through with stars. And that thought was a diversion...a diversion of a diversion. Thoughts sifted through his mind like sand through a child's fingers. He remembered lines from Poe: "Is all that we see or seem but a dream within a dream?"*

By the time he turned into Twelfth Street his spirits were as heavy as his shoes.

There was a low light in the living room from the lamp in the corner by the piano. The outside door was open. A light was on in the hall, also, but the kitchen was darkened, a bit of linoleum shining a reflection of the hall light. Mama Galli was not home. Tim paused at the foot of the staircase. The sliding door to the living room was open. He caught the pale reflection of himself in the mirror over the fireplace. He caught some other movement also, movement within the room on the sofa which crowded against the wall, its arm by the door. The light was insufficient to define it. He was about to go upstairs, his hand already on the railing when he heard giggling. It was Katie.

He returned to the door and looked in. He could scarcely see the girl for the bulk and position of the boy holding her. Katie looked at him over the boy's shoulder, and while he stood there without the power of speech or movement, she pushed the boy from her and got up. The boy whirled around, saw him, and scrambled to his feet.

Katie threw her hair back and smoothed her dress. "Hello, Tim."

---

* From "A Dream within a Dream," first published in the March 31, 1849, issue of *The Flag of Our Union*.

He did not speak, looking from one to the other of them.

"This is Tom Crosetti, Tim. We graduated from high school together."

Crosetti stuck a big hand at Tim, hiding his embarrassment as best he could.

Without a word Tim wheeled away from them. Katie caught his arm. In almost the same motion he turned to her, he slapped her hard across the face. The girl stumbled back from the blow.

"You little bastard..." The boy started for him.

"Don't touch him, Tom!" Katie regained her balance and grabbed his arm. "And keep your filthy tongue still."

"What is he, your father or something? What's the matter with you?"

Tim groped his way out of the room and up the stairs, the words a whorl of color and sound in his brain following and surrounding him so that he could not escape them...

"Shut up, Tom! Go. Shut up and go home."

"Look, little girl, you were asking for it, asking for it, asking..."

"Go..."

"Tiger cat, tease, tiger, tease..."

Tim swung his door closed on the sound and leaned against it in the darkness. He fumbled inside his shirt and drew out the manuscript. He flung it toward the dresser, neither knowing nor caring whether it landed there. The numbness was going, everything inside him becoming an ache, the slow hard ache of grief that can't be rubbed away. He made his way to the bed and sat down there, aware only of loss and pain.

Katie found him there when she knocked on his door, and, getting no answer, opened it. The light from the hall shone in on him. Without speaking, the girl went into the room and lit the lamp over his bed. She drew his hands away from his face and saw that he was crying, and then herself began to cry.

"Tim, don't say anything. Just listen to me." She turned her back on him. "It's hard for me to say this. I wish you could help me. I know you don't want to. I wish you did. I never let a boy touch me before. Not since I was a little girl. I didn't then, but it happened. I never let it happen again till tonight. I didn't really want it tonight. I hate him. I hate myself more. I waited all day for you to come home. I was thinking about you. I thought maybe it was you when he came. Then when mama went out he stayed. He put his arm around me once. I didn't want it, but I thought I heard something. I thought maybe it was you again. I thought if you saw it... I don't know what I thought, Tim. I just know I was thinking of you. All the time." She swung around. "Why do you make me say these things?"

He got to his feet wearily. "You know I'd never touch you like that, Katie."

"I know. That's why it makes me feel so rotten inside. So dirty."

"Poor little Katie. I've made you miserable, too."

"No. I've done it myself. I had to spoil things. I'm no good. I've never been as happy with anyone as I am with you. But I had to spoil it."

"It's me that spoils it, Katie. You'll know that some day. Don't cry anymore. Your face is red where I slapped you. Don't you hate me for that?"

"I couldn't ever hate you, Tim."

"Thank you," he said very humbly.

"Tim, you won't hate me for what you saw tonight? You won't shut me out of you for what I did?"

He smiled. "My dear, you are the light I live by. My life would be nothing but darkness if it weren't for you."

Her face was suddenly radiant, all purity, all youth, all beauty flooding it before him. He felt like flinging himself down in adoration before her, but he felt also that he must hold the vision before his eyes that he might take his share of it then to cherish forever.

"Tim, will you kiss me...just once?"

Their lips met gently, as soft a benediction upon each other as the rain that night upon the city.

17

Goldsmith waited at headquarters for Holden to come out of conference with the chief inspector. While he waited, he went over the file on Dolly Gebhardt—statements of witnesses, scientific reports, the summary of the medical examiner. His own contribution was negligible, he thought. That was probably the reason Holden had called him in. He could imagine the lieutenant's reaction if he were to tell him he had been reading poetry. Holden came finally, whistling.

"I thought maybe they were putting the heat on," Goldsmith said.

"For Gebhardt? You know better than that, Goldie. The old boy's happy with our handling of it."

Goldsmith grunted. "It doesn't take much to make him happy."

"That's my feeling," Holden said. "I'm not as easily contented. How are you coming?"

"Something. Nothing. I finally got a line on a girlfriend of Dolly's."

"Good. McCormick got a line on a boyfriend. That's why I called you in."

"I was noticing him in the files—her host Saturday night, T. C. Loring, manufacturer of bedsprings. That's a nice touch."

"It's not Loring I'm talking about," Holden said. "He never met her. A blind date. Didn't even have her phone number. He waited until eight o'clock, had his dinner alone—at your club—and then presumably found other entertainment. When he saw the paper Sunday night, he took the first train home to Toledo."

"I don't see where we'd get very far seeing him," Goldsmith said.

"I agree. Even if we scared him into telling us where he got lined up with her, I think we'd find two or three go-betweens. We'd lose the trail before we got to the source."

Holden looked at his watch. "The gentleman due here right now is Edgar G. Winters. He's the unhappy owner of several sets of fingerprints in Miss Gebhardt's apartment. The elevator operator recalls a gentleman of his proportions calling there Friday night, several Friday nights, in fact. His secretary also recalls taking six hundred dollars from the office safe for him Saturday. He called this morning and asked to see us. That's the picture."

"It's a great omen, him wanting to see us."

"Don't be ungrateful, Goldie. He could clean this all up for us with a confession. Maybe he was jealous."

"That naïve he can't be."

Within five minutes Mr. Winters arrived, white-haired, portly and very nervous. Holden waved him into a chair and rang for the stenographer.

"This is a terrible business, officer, a shocking thing," Winters started.

"Hold it a minute," Holden said. "We need routine information first. Then, you understand, Mr. Winters, your statement will be taken down and you'll be expected to sign it."

"Will it go into the newspapers?"

"It might. That depends on a lot of things."

"It will kill my wife."

"Miss Gebhardt is already dead," Holden said coldly. He motioned to the stenographer and began questions on age, occupation, previous arrests... Then he asked abruptly: "Where did you meet Miss Gebhardt?"

"At a party," Winters blurted. "Yes, at a benefit party."

"For whose benefit?"

"I don't know that. I'm invited to so many. My wife rarely goes. She is something of a recluse. Indeed, that's why..."

Holden interrupted. "When was the party you met her at?"

"Two years ago. Yes, two years ago. It was a Christmas party."

"This is August. Christmas came early that year?"

"More or less. I mean it was two years ago, more or less."

"Obviously. Pin it down for us."

"See here, officer. Be so kind as not to fluster me. I came in of my own volition, you know."

"Be so kind..." Goldsmith thought. The phrase had occurred in Mrs. Flaherty's testimony. "Be so kind as to ask her to take the phone..."

"A lot of people come in of their own volition, Mr. Winters," Holden said. "Some of them confess to murder."

"I certainly didn't come here for that. I'm sorry I came at all if that's what you expect."

"Be glad you came, Mr. Winters. How often did you see Miss Gebhardt?"

"Once a week we met."

"You met? Where?"

"At her apartment."

"Intimate?"

"Rather," Winters said miserably.

"Did your wife know of the relationship?"

"Certainly not. Miss Gebhardt did know of my wife, however."

"Is that a fact?" Holden said with great sarcasm.

"The truth is she threatened to call my wife Friday night."

"What would she want to do that for?"

"Money. I mean that's what she wanted for not calling. It was a great shock to me that she would stoop to that. Miss Gebhardt seemed different."

"What do you mean?"

"Different, that's all. She didn't seem that kind of a girl."

"What you really mean, Mr. Winters, is that she seemed different from the others you've known, isn't it?"

The big man squirmed in his chair. "I wish you wouldn't twist my words, sir. I'm trying to tell you this in the easiest manner possible."

"I'm not particular whether it's easy for you or not, Mr. Winters. As far as we're concerned, we've heard dirty stories before. The fact is I'd like to get the information out of you the hard way. What was Gebhardt's price for not calling your wife?"

"Five hundred dollars."

"Did she tell you what she wanted it for?"

"Only when I insisted. It turned out to be something as ridiculous as a fur sale."

"And then you made up?"

"After a fashion."

"You had lunch with her Saturday?"

"Yes."

"Did you go shopping with her?"

"No. I didn't."

"Of course not. You wouldn't want to be seen..."

"You're quite wrong, sir," Winters interrupted. "As a matter of fact, I offered to go with her. It was she who discouraged it."

"Do you know why, Mr. Winters?"

"She said she wanted to surprise me."

"Cute," Holden said. "You must have had quite a making-up party. That's a far cry from the blackmail approach she tried the night before."

"Dolly was quick-tempered. Sometimes she blurted out things she did not mean at all."

That was one thing she hadn't meant, Goldsmith thought, not for a measly five hundred if she intended to stay in business. He made his first note of the interview—on Dolly's temperament.

"Gebhardt actually paid two hundred and seventy-nine dollars for the fur," Holden said. "When you called her Saturday night, did she mention the bargain?"

"I intended to tell you about that call," Winters said. "No. She didn't mention the fur till I prompted her. As a matter of fact, she said she wasn't feeling well." He shuddered.

"You were the last known person to speak to her," Holden said. "I'd like you to repeat the phone conversation as exactly as you can."

"May I smoke?"

Holden's package was lying on the desk, but he did not offer it. "Smoke if you like."

Finally, when Winters' hand shook trying to light the cigarette he had taken from his pocket, the lieutenant struck a match for him. "The telephone conversation," he prompted.

"When I returned home Saturday afternoon, I learned that my wife had gone to the country. I'd been urging her to do that all summer. We have a place only the caretaker gets the benefit of. At any rate, I had dinner alone Saturday night, and it occurred to me that if Dolly, Miss Gebhardt, were not engaged, we might spend the evening together. Ordinarily I saw her Friday evenings only. I called. It was several moments before she answered her phone. I asked her if she had found a fur piece to her liking.

"'Yes,' she said. Now that I recall, she did not use my name during our whole conversation. In fact, the conversation was rather strained. But, at the time, I laid it to the fact that she was not well."

"Did it occur to you that there might have been another man there?"

"Well…yes, after a bit, it did occur to me."

"Go on with the conversation."

"I said something about how I thought she might look in the fur. Foolish, sentimental stuff. She said it was too hot to think about it."

Goldsmith closed his eyes an instant and tried to imagine how that would sound to someone hearing only her part of the conversation.

"I asked her if she had an engagement for the evening," Winters continued. "She told me then that she was not feeling well. I suggested that I might come up and do something for her. 'Not tonight,' she said. She sounded a little desperate. It was then that it occurred to me that someone might be with her. 'Tomorrow?' I asked. 'Call me,' she said. I went on to tell her that Ida, my wife, had gone to the country, and that we might go away ourselves somewhere for the weekend if she felt up to it."

He paused to take a deep pull at his cigarette. Holden did not take his eyes from his face. The only sound in the room was the stroke of the stenographer's pencil.

"A peculiar thing she asked me then—'How old are you?' I thought it was her way of telling me to act my age."

"Did you tell her?"

"I made some flippant remark, something like 'over twenty-one.'"

"Then what?"

"I had the strange feeling then," Winters went on, "that she wasn't listening to me at all. 'Dolly?' I said. It was a second or two before she answered. I asked her outright then if there were someone with her. Until then, I'd never really thought very much about Dolly's other engagements, you see. I hadn't permitted myself to...I..." He floundered miserably.

"I know," Holden said, "your high sense of morals. What did she say when you asked if there was someone with her?"

"'I just don't feel well,' she said. 'Call me tomorrow.' And without another word, she hung up."

"At the time you felt that she wasn't listening to you," Holden said, "was there any other noise on the wire, as though, for example, someone might have taken the phone from her?"

"There was no noise distinguishable in itself. But she sounded as though she were coming on the phone when she spoke again."

Holden nodded. "What time did you call her?"

"I had dinner at seven-thirty. It was no more than an hour later."

"Where did you spend the rest of the evening?"

"Home. I did not go out at all. I rang the kitchen for ice at perhaps nine o'clock. I spoke to my man when he was going out for the evening. I thought it was rather late he was getting through. That was a quarter to ten."

"And the next day?" Holden asked.

"I called about noon. I happened to make the call from the vestibule of my home. One of the hotel employees answered, a woman with an Irish accent. I asked her to look in on Miss Gebhardt when there was such a delay in the answering of the phone. I was worried, you see. Unfortunately at that moment I heard someone at the door. The servants were out. I had to answer it, so I hung up the phone."

"You thought it might have been your wife at the door?"

"It was my wife. At the first opportunity, I called back but the line was busy. That was probably an hour later. I didn't have a chance to call again until late evening. By then I had seen the newspapers."

"Why didn't you come to us then?"

"The shock was considerable. Then when I got thinking about it in some order, I felt there were certain things I should take care of first. I didn't know what this visit with you might involve."

"What sort of things had to be taken care of?"

"On some pretense, I wanted to get Ida out of town. She has a heart condition. It's a source of great worry to me."

Holden looked at him. "You might as well feel sorry for yourself, Mr. Winters. I can't think of anybody else in the world who will. Wait in the other room till the statement's ready for you to sign. Read it first."

Winters got up with as much dignity as he could muster. "I'm not a suspect in her murder, am I, sir?"

Holden smiled contemptuously. "Your kind of murder isn't that clean. On your way."

When he and the lieutenant were alone, Goldsmith got up and helped himself to one of Holden's cigarettes.

"Worth coming in for, Goldie?"

"I'd like to have seen him squirm some more, but I'll take that for a down payment."

"Look, Goldie, the town is crawling with his kind. We put on the heat, he puts it on. He knows a lot of firemen. See what I mean? This way you get the leisure to read poetry." He grinned when Goldsmith's eyes met his over the cigarette. "I presume that's what you're doing with the two books you signed out on the inventory?"

Goldsmith took the cigarette from his mouth and looked at it. "Funny thing about one of those poets—Francis Thompson. When he was down and out a prostitute took him home with her and kept him. That's when he started writing poetry."

18

Day by day, the Gebhardt murder story moved further back in the newspapers. When, toward the end of the week, it disappeared altogether for a day, Father Duffy decided that he could wait no longer. He had received an answer to his letter to Little Falls. No one there remembered a Father McGohey. By the time it came, it no longer mattered. He had located a Reverend Walter A. McGohey, a captain in the United States Army during World War I. In 1919 he had returned to his parish in Marion City, Pennsylvania.

Friday afternoon Father Duffy stepped off the train in Marion City. He had one week's vacation coming, and as it turned out, the Monsignor was glad to have him take it while his nephew was in New York. Less than a week before Father Duffy had planned his vacation in Canada. He had thought about the long days fishing, and nights so quiet that he could hear a bird stirring in its nest. A week ago? Much longer it seemed, and unimportant, anyway. And of the choice between tramping the thousand dusty streets of New York and the one dusty lane which was the whole of Marion City, he still felt that he had chosen the more direct way to his quarry.

The priest checked his bag at the station and inquired the direction to St. Teresa's rectory.

"You can't miss it for the cemetery," the station master told him, pointing through the town. "We're more dead than alive here." He chuckled at his own joke.

Walking through the town, Father Duffy decided there was more truth in the jest than the jester had intended. Marion City had been a mining center at one time, but the coal veins had dried up, and the only business left was in the stores which served the few farmers in the area. Most of the buildings were in need of paint, including St. Teresa's church and parish house.

An arthritic looking old woman came to the door in answer to his knock. "Father McGohey?" she said to his inquiry. "He's out yonder." She motioned to the cemetery. "He's been dead fifteen—sixteen years. Do you want to see his grave, Father? We've a terrible time keeping them up."

"Presently," he said. "Did you keep house for Father McGohey?"

"I did. And Father Blake before him, and Father Hanrahan before him, God rest his soul. He was my brother." She opened the door a few inches wider but kept herself squarely between him and the house's hospitality. "Is it about the missions you've come, Father? You can see we're a poor parish. The church roof is leaking in three places and a lump of plaster fell on Mrs. Cartright's head last Sunday. She said it was enough to make a Lutheran of her. All the farmers hereabouts is Lutherans and they have all the money."

She had the poor mouth* as his mother would have said, Father Duffy thought, and the melancholy was in her bones. "I'm not looking for a donation, Mrs.—"

---

* Slang: to make the worst of things.

"Miss Hanrahan." It was only then that she opened the door its full width. "Will you come in and sit down, Father? I've nothing but a bit of bread and tea in the house, but I'll put on the kettle." She led him into a parlor that matched the tale she told.

"Don't trouble, Miss Hanrahan. I had lunch a short time ago."

"I hope it was tasty," she said, sitting on the edge of an old wicker chair. "I've no taste for food myself no more. And fortunate that is, the poor share of it we get from charity. Are you related to Father McGohey?"

"No. As a matter of fact, I never met him. But I heard about him." He was not sure how he hoped she might construe that, but it started her talking, as almost anything would in her loneliness. And that was what he wanted. If there were information for him in Marion City, he had come first to its best source.

She screwed her mouth into a sort of smile. "There's more people heard of Father McGohey than ever saw him, I dare say. He was a hard man to work for, plagued as he was with the bad temper. But he made up for it in his own fashion. It was like the devil was plaguing him but the Lord won him."

She nodded approval of her own summary, and then looked up at him. "You never heard him preach? No, you said you didn't meet him. He'd start a sermon and all you'd know was the first word and the last till you got on to his way of talking. He'd string all his words into a jumble and be started and finished before you knew whether it was Advent or Pentecost. They say he got that way during the war. He was an army man, and do you know, I think he was sorry having to come home? He was real military in his way of doing things. He trained his altar boys like little soldiers, and he had enough of them to attend a cathedral. But here I'm chattering. You've no notion how lonesome it gets, Father."

Father Duffy looked at his hands. Somehow he had known

this of Father McGohey. He felt very humble in having followed this instinct.

"Would you like to wash, Father? Are you off a train? Father Mullens is at a diocesan meeting. He won't be home till supper."

"No thanks, Miss Hanrahan. You've been here a long time?"

"Fifty-five years. This was my brother's first parish. He died here of pneumonia."

"I'm sorry," the priest said.

"He would of died some place else. He was always too delicate for a priest."

"Is there a parochial school?"

"There was till ten years ago. My brother laid the cornerstone and never lived to see it up, and me living to see it burned to the ground. There was more children in the town then. There was coal mines and plenty of work for them able to do it. Now the children get their instructions Tuesday and Friday afternoons and go to the public school. I don't see as they're so much worse off."

Father Duffy smiled. "Father McGohey's altar boys," he said, "they interest me, Miss Hanrahan."

"Were you in the army?"

"Yes. But I wasn't quite as fond of it as Father McGohey apparently was."

"Oh, there's many of your opinion." She leaned forward confidentially. "For them as likes a parade, it was all right. But for them as likes to pray to themselves, it was a terrible distraction."

"Father McGohey was of the old school," he said, putting together the best story he could of it. "He liked efficiency, he liked sportsmanship, but, like most military men, he liked a winner."

"Oh, you've got him down to a T."

"Did he fix up a gymnasium for the boys?"

"He did. And he led them in calisthenics himself. A great place this for gymnastics, with them going out from it to do the work of grown men."

"I suppose he had boxing," the priest suggested.

"There was some of that till the mothers wanted a stop to it. The men were all for him, of course. But the women—some took it and some didn't. Finally somebody got word to the bishop and there was a letter from him though it never came out and I shouldn't be telling it of the dead. But after that there was no more fighting that he refereed them in. You know, I'll say this, there was never so much going on around here since Father McGohey passed on, and it's kind of nice thinking about it."

"Would you happen to remember any of the boys involved, Miss Hanrahan, maybe a little fellow who happened to get badly beaten?"

"That's twenty-five years ago and there was a few of them got bloodied up. Do you know the boy's name, Father?"

If I knew his name…the priest thought. "The name escapes me, Miss Hanrahan. But he probably wasn't as big as the rest of the boys. It was about the time of his first Communion, and he got a prayerbook for the occasion. It might even have been around the time of the bishop's letter. He lost the prayerbook because he was fighting. Then later, his mother wanted him to be a priest…"

"Wanted him to be!" Miss Hanrahan interrupted. "She sent him away to be one. Mary Brandon. I can see her as clear as if she was sitting there where you are this minute."

Which, Father Duffy realized, was clearer than he could see Miss Hanrahan for that instant. It could be all wrong, of course, but he prayed that it was not.

"Mary Brandon. God knows what ever became of the poor woman. She had but the one son and a man for a husband I wouldn't wish on the devil for company in hell. Father, I know of nothing filthier in this world than a drunken man when he's filthy. That was Big Tim Brandon. There wasn't a clean word came out of his mouth when he was drunk, nor a kind one when he was sober. He worked in the railroad yards in them days. And every time he got paid he headed out into the hills and filled up on the bootleg stuff. It was prohibition then. And Mary was as gentle a soul as you ever met. She did beautiful sewing. It was her kept the boy and herself alive. I'm sure he never gave her a cent. He wrote to her folks in Ireland, you know, when she was a slip of a girl, and she came over a greenhorn and married him. I'll say this for Mary, there was never a word of complaint on her lips. And the things they say he used to do to her. I wouldn't repeat them to a priest."

"The boy," Father Duffy said quietly. "What became of him?"

"Well, the time you were thinking about, him getting beat up? God knows, the both of them were beat up by the father often enough and never a word, but when Father McGohey took the prayerbook away from Little Tim—Big Tim and Little Tim we called them—when he took the prayerbook, Mary came up here and gave him a tongue-lashing to do him the rest of his days, priest or no priest. It was my notion afterwards that Mary herself went to the bishop but I never let on. What's the use making more trouble when there's trouble enough already. Do you see, Father?"

"I see," Father Duffy said, seeing only that here was a beginning for a hard and bitter life for a boy when his mother came to his defense among competitive youngsters.

"Little Tim was a bright little thing, awful bookish we used to say, and he was terrible religious. He was never an altar boy, his mother feeling that way about Father McGohey, but there wasn't a morning him and her didn't come to Mass, except when the father was home. The boy'd come alone then. And after church them days, if there wasn't school, he'd go off wandering in the hills. He didn't want to be home when the father was there, you see, and the other kids didn't care much for him.

"When he got older, fourteen or fifteen maybe, Mary was all the time writing to one order after another to see if they'd take him in to study for the priesthood. She wouldn't ask Father McGohey. But what she doesn't know to this day, if she's alive—it was Father McGohey wrote to a seminary out in Indiana some place and got them to write to her saying if her boy had a vocation they'd be glad to have him. All they wanted was the recommendation of the parish priest. She came up then and asked. Father McGohey never let on, and he wrote a fine letter. I remember the boy going off on the bus. He had the look of the angels about him."

"How old was he then?"

"No more than fifteen. And we never saw sign of him since to know whether or not he was ordained."

"That would have been about 1932 or '33, wouldn't it?"

"It was the depression, I know that. Oh, and I know prohibition was over. Big Tim was drunk at the Sunshine Inn the very day his boy left. When the bus drove by there he threw his glass through the window."

Father Duffy sighed. It was small wonder the old woman remembered the Brandons. He had expected a rotten story. Now he began to wonder about Big Tim. He doubted that he would get that part of it from Miss Hanrahan. But a man didn't debase himself like that with no reason at all.

"What happened to the parents, Miss Hanrahan?"

"The funny thing, Father. Big Tim seemed to pull himself together for a while after the boy was gone. He'd even come to church with her of a Sunday. But he was too far gone. He took to drink again and he was all the time drooling tobacco juice down the sides of his mouth. Terrible it looked. Disgusting..."

"...If I could only keep my mouth clean..." Father Duffy remembered the words in the confessional, the description of the dream.

"And Mary got kind of queer and strait-laced. Wouldn't wear anything but black. To make an end of the story, Big Tim was lying drunk on the tracks one night and a train went over him. Killed him dead. The boy never came home for the funeral. And it wasn't long after that Mary went out to live with her sister in Chicago. Maybe a year or so later it was, I got a queer letter from her. She said she wanted to give me her address in case Little Tim was ever looking for her. Wasn't that a strange thing, Father, and him in Indiana, the next state to Chicago?"

Father Duffy nodded. "Do you have the address?"

"I think I can find it for you, Father. It came right when Father McGohey died and I put it with the parish records he left. But the boy never came back."

19

It was late afternoon when Father Duffy left Miss Hanrahan. He had tea after all and hot soda biscuits. He visited the church and Father McGohey's grave, and then Tim Brandon's who died June 5, 1934. All the while he turned over in his mind what he had learned of the Brandons. Was it enough to return to New York with the name, Tim Brandon? Knowing his name, could he find him? He envisioned himself asking after him from one street corner to the next. And finding him, what could he say to move him? What did he know of Tim Brandon except as a child and then as a frenzied man who committed a murder he had not intended? In confiding his sin to him, he confided his life. What did he know of that life? And what, as a priest, was his first obligation? To see that the murderer surrendered to civil authority? No. His first obligation was to help a penitent save his immortal soul, to account before God for his life.

Leaving the cemetery and waving goodbye to Miss Hanrahan, who watched him forlornly from the window, Father Duffy returned to the railroad station. He learned that a west-bound train would leave between six and seven. It would connect with a Chicago train at midnight in Pittsburgh. He bought his ticket and walked through the town again. Several men lounged on the porch of a general store. Some of them tipped their hats. They watched him enter the store, and one among them bade him time of day.

In the store he bought a postcard and addressed it to Father Gonzales. He wrote: "Greetings! Seeing America. See you next week." Reading it, he wondered if it sounded as hollow as he felt it did. His intention was to suggest that he was enjoying his vacation. Outdoors again, he inquired the direction to the post office.

"I'll be going up by there on my way home, Father," one of the men said. "I'll be glad to take it."

"I've got an hour or two to kill, thanks. I'll walk it up."

The man shrugged. "If you got nothing better to do, come on back and jaw with us for a while."

He mailed the card and accepted the invitation. One of the men started to get up to give him a chair. He waved him back to his place and sat down on the steps. There were four men there, two of them old-timers, and the others of no particular age under forty. A shaggy Airedale roused himself and came over to sniff at his shoes.

"That dog likes the smell of traveling feet," one of the men said. "He don't travel much himself no more but he still likes the notion of it."

"I kind of feel that way about it myself," the priest said.

"Missionary?"

"No. I'm just on vacation."

One of the men offered him a cigarette. He accepted.

"The Evangelicals had a missionary in here Saturday night," the man said. "We used to have a lot of 'em come round in the old days. They don't have the same fire no more, either. I guess they figure what's left here ain't worth striking the match to."

One of the old-timers took his pipe from his mouth. "You and Pete wouldn't remember it," he said, motioning to the younger man, "but there was a gal used to come in here every summer. They'd pitch her a platform up on Chisholm's Corner. A disciple of Aimee McPherson* I think she was. I never heard so many ways to perdition as she could reel off."

"The Bible's full of them," Father Duffy said.

"She had some that weren't in the Bible. I'll take my oath on that. And you can't tell me she'd been saved from all of them. Why, she wasn't nineteen years old…"

The conversation drifted from one evangelist to another, the roads leading to salvation, and those away from it. It was some minutes later that the priest brought them around to talk about temperance preachers.

"You a temperance man, Father?" one of the men asked.

"I take a drink now and then if there's no one around that's going to be scandalized at it. In moderation it's all right. But I've known a lot of homes where drinking brought nothing but misery."

"Yea, that's a fact," one of the young men said.

"I've known men who could drink their paycheck in one night," the priest said.

"And borrow on their next," someone added.

Once more the old-timer took his pipe from his mouth. "You young ones wouldn't remember him, but I don't think there ever was a man could drink like Big Tim Brandon. I seen that man

---

* Aimee Semple McPherson (1890–1944) was a famous Canadian Pentecostal evangelist. She founded the Foursquare Church in Los Angeles and attracted many wealthy and famous people to the movement. In 2021, the movement claimed almost nine million adherents.

stand in the Sunshine and drink down a quart bottle without moving excepting maybe one foot so he wouldn't spit tobacco on it."

"I remember him," a younger one said. "I was in school just ahead of his kid. He went off to be a priest. That was the day..."

"Am I telling the story or you?" the old man interrupted. "I was in the Sunshine that day, standing elbow to elbow with Big Tim. The Sunshine's the tavern, Father." He nodded, apparently in its direction. "Tim stood there waiting for that kid to leave town, just waiting. And when he saw the bus pull out of the station he said a terrible thing. I ain't ever repeated it and I don't aim to now. Big Tim's dead and the kid ain't showed up since. As far as I'm concerned I think he had reason for his drinking, but I ain't going to argue it with no one."

"You didn't tell the most important part, Andy. He picked up a bottle from the bar and pitched it through the plate glass window when the bus passed."

"As far as I'm concerned that ain't the most important part." Andy leaned over the porch and spat in the dust.

There were a few seconds of silence while, the priest thought, each of them went over in his mind what he remembered of the Brandons.

Finally the other of the old men explained, "The mother was awful fond of the boy, Father. The two of them went to church a lot. I don't mean that's bad. Hell, I don't know exactly what I do mean. She just wasn't the right woman for Tim Brandon. How did we get talking about Tim, anyway?"

"I mentioned drinking," Father Duffy said.

Andy tilted his chair onto an even keel and got up. "I ain't saying Tim Brandon was a good man. He wasn't. But he was just a lot of man. He should of bred fifteen kids, not just one scrawny runt. Now I'm going up to my supper. Good day to you, Father."

They watched him shuffle up the dusty street. The other man of his age nodded after him. "Andy laid out fifty dollars of his own money for Big Tim's coffin. His old lady didn't speak to him for a month. Women just don't see things that way."

20

Sergeant Goldsmith lingered a moment on the street outside a Greenwich Village night club. He didn't look like a patron, he thought, and he felt less like one. He had not been home since nine o'clock that morning. A few minutes earlier he had called his wife and half-heartedly suggested that she meet him. He was grateful when she decided that he would get through earlier without her. He pushed through the swinging door and went downstairs.

It was a small basement club with the tables close together, the music hot, and the air-conditioning sharp. The patrons had a hearty camaraderie with one another, even the out-of-towners who had been tipped off that this was the place to look for many a star-in-the-making.

Goldsmith checked his hat and pushed his way to the bar. He ordered a drink and watched the patrons through the mirror. He wondered if some of them ever saw the light of day.

"What time does the show come on?" he asked the bartender.

"Any time now. Any time at all."

A lugubrious patron on the next bar stool eyed the detective. "You from out of town?"

"Nope. Born and raised here." Goldsmith sipped his drink. He could have done nicely without conversation.

"Then how come you don't know when the floor show starts?"

"They neglected that in my education."

"Ha!" the man said, shoving his glass to the bartender. He turned to Goldsmith. "Did you go to college?"

"Nope."

"Ah," the drunk said wisely, "that accounts for it. The only damn thing I learned there—never miss a floor show. But they also taught me to be careful I wasn't the one who gave the floor show." He weighed each word carefully. "Made a solitary drinker of me." Suddenly he grabbed Goldsmith's arm. "Hey, get a load of that flaxen doll. Oh hell, she's gone."

Even as the man was speaking, Goldsmith caught sight of the woman before she ducked back behind the drapes. "You'll see her," he said. "That's Liza Tracy."

"The one in the picture upstairs? Naw. The picture's a kid."

"Retouching," Goldsmith said.

"Little Liza looks like she's had all the retouching she can stand. Don't they have any fresh ones in New York?"

Goldsmith sighed. He was very tired. "The shipment was late this week."

The head waiter herded the patrons back against the walls, and the orchestra leader took the microphone to the center of the floor. A spotlight picked him up, and tried out a variety of color gelatins on him. Meanwhile the pianist improvised sweet and melancholy tunes, the themes of each reaching farther back through the years.

The drunk chuckled. He held his hands out and moved them slowly together. "He makes me feel just like Alice in Wonderland."

Goldsmith laughed. As the drunk described it, he understood the feeling perfectly. The varying lights heightened the illusion. "He's setting the mood for Liza. You're supposed to be getting nostalgic."

"If he doesn't stop soon, I won't be here. I was in short pants when that tune was popular. Was Liza around then?"

"She was probably getting her first big break—in some speakeasy."

"Holy mother. I take back what I said about the retouching. When I get to be her age, I want to go to her barber."

Stories and imitations from the master of ceremonies began the show. He warmed up the crowd and then introduced in turn a folk singer on a high stool, three Calypso singers, a boy who made baby-talk on the harmonica. The floor was completely darkened then. A trombone sounded mournfully, its cry heightening as a blue spotlight shivered across the floor and trembled on the drapes. Liza Tracy slid from behind the black curtain and made her sequined entrance on a high note. The applause rippled while she held it. She rolled the blues and her hips from one table to the next. There was gravel in her low notes and the brittleness of ice in the high ones. She worked hard. So did the audience, never quite with her for all their heartiness. When she was done they applauded a beautiful memory, and if it wasn't quite the memory of Liza Tracy, it was one of someone like her. As soon as she was off they clamored for a quick round of drinks.

"That's something that was and ain't no more," the drunk said profoundly. "They should have left it in the picture frame. Excuse me." He made his way to the rest room.

Goldsmith waited until the dance floor was crowded. Then he pushed through to the m.c. "I'd like to see Miss Tracy," he said. "Where's her dressing room?"

"Why don't you set her up to a drink? I tell you, boss, she'd love it. Not too many. She's got to go on again. But a couple of drinks, you know. Morale. Right out where people can see she's human. They're scared of her."

"I'd rather talk to her first in her dressing room."

"Okay, boss. But you'll find it chummy back there."

It was chummy. She shared one small room with the Calypso trio. She came to the door when the m.c. called her.

"Thanks," Goldsmith said. He waited until the m.c. left. "I'd like to buy you a drink, Miss Tracy. Up the street."

"How far up the street?"

"You can name it."

She weighed the offer for a few seconds. "Give me ten minutes."

The detective collected his hat and waited for her at the entrance. He waved at the drunk who had returned to the bar, and wondered what he would think seeing them leave together. If he ever met the guy again he thought it would be fun to tell him Liza was his sister.

Miss Tracy came and Goldsmith tipped his hat to the drunk and opened the door for Liza. Her high heels clacked up the steps ahead of him. She had nice legs, he noticed.

Not until they were settled in the booth of a nearby tavern did she say a word except "Scotch" to the bartender as they passed. She downed the drink as soon as it was served. Goldsmith made a remark about the show having been an experience. She gave him a dirty look. When he poured his drink into her glass she accepted it.

"You wouldn't believe it," she said then, "I've been playing that hole for a week and there wasn't a bastard in the place offered to buy me a drink."

"I'm buying you a drink," Goldsmith said, motioning the waiter to serve them again.

"Did I say you were a bastard?"

"No. But I'm expecting it."

She stroked her flaxen hair. The drunk had been right. She was wearing all the makeup she could take.

"You a cop?"

"Yes."

"I figured that." She picked up the fresh drink. "Here's to the taxpayers. I hope they're buying."

"So do I," Goldsmith said. "When was the last time you saw Dolly Gebhardt, Miss Tracy?"

There was not even an extra flutter to her eyelashes. "How'd you find me?"

"It wasn't easy."

"What did you do, find my old number in her place?"

"A very old one."

"I move a lot. Restless."

He nodded. "You were the only woman in her book except a masseuse."

"A masseuse," she repeated, turning the empty glass around in her fingers. A masseuse was not the kind of luxury she could afford. Goldsmith figured she was weighing Dolly's career against her own.

"When did you get to know her?" he tried gently.

"We were both in the line in one of the Scandals,"* she said then. "That was the end of the '20s. 1930 maybe. She was fresh from the sticks. Isn't her old man a son-of-a-bitch?"

"Her father? Maybe it's harder on him this way."

"Like hell. With the crust he's got he could sit on a hot stove. I'll tell you one thing, mister—there was none of him in Dolly.

---

* *George White's Scandals* was a Broadway musical revue that ran annually from 1919 through 1926 and then was revived in 1928, 1929, 1931, 1936, and 1939. Dolly and Liza were in the chorus line.

She had a heart the size of a battleship." She pointed a green fingernail at him. "And don't ever let 'em tell you she made her money easy. She made it hard and spent it easy."

"I've just about reached that conclusion myself," Goldsmith prompted.

Miss Tracy nodded, her mouth bitter.

"I imagine a lot of kids down on their luck got a lift from her," he tried again.

"A lot more than showed up for her funeral. Looking for an angle on one of them?"

"Maybe." Goldsmith offered her a cigarette and lit it for her. "But not necessarily. You see, Miss Tracy..."

"Liza," she interrupted. "Tracy's not my own name anyway."

"You see, Liza, when it comes to murder, or any other crime for that matter, there are two people involved: the murderer and his victim. In a way, the victim has to cooperate with the murderer..."

"I get you," Liza said. "You want to get out of me who she was cooperating with."

Goldsmith smiled. "Well, I'd listen to any ideas you have. But what I thought we might talk about is Dolly. I'd like to know something about her—the kind of stuff a friend could tell me."

"I didn't see her much. We weren't the visiting kind. She wasn't, anyway. The truth is I didn't see her for maybe fifteen years after the Scandals closed that year. I got out to Hollywood myself. Remember the Follies of 1932? I guess you wouldn't. How old were you then?"

"Second year of high school. I remember them."

"I was in that. Not much, but it got me seen. I was in the

Broadway Review of 1936, too. In the picture, that is.* Broadway wasn't reviewing nothing then, unless breadlines maybe."

"Where was Dolly then?"

"I don't know. Trying to make a buck. We wrote letters for a while, kidding one another. In the big time. The letters petered out when we lost our starch. During the war I got into a camp show. I pulled a dirty trick. I got so homesick when I saw New York, I cut the show. I got some work then. I took up singing. At that date, I took up singing. The way I come up since—Eighth Avenue. I'll be back there. You don't come up that way. You go down there. Easy and down. I'll be home for Christmas, like they say. A drunken agent thought up this stunt. Not bad. But you got stones in your head if you think you're going uptown with what I got. There's a lot of things wrong with me, but stones in my head I don't have. Can the city stand another drink?"

"I think so." He emptied his own glass and reordered. "Where did you meet up with Dolly again?"

"In front of the Astor Hotel. Just walking by like that. We did a double-take and fell all over each other. You know, long lost buddies."

"I know."

"Then I was up there at her place a few times, every day almost for a couple of weeks, and we cooled off again. Some dump she had. Steps down into the living room, a marble bathroom..."

"I've gotten to know it pretty well," Goldsmith said.

She looked at him as though she realized for the first time who he was. "You would, wouldn't you? I mean, her getting killed like that." She shuddered.

"I would. Did you ever happen to meet any of her friends during your visits?"

---

* These are fictional films.

"A couple. Nice guys. I don't remember them much. I haven't been near there in maybe a year."

"Young fellows, weren't they?"

"Kind of. Not kids if that's what you're getting at. Dolly wasn't taking…"

"I didn't mean that," he interrupted. "You wouldn't remember their names?"

"No. I got no memory at all for names."

"Would you remember their faces again if you saw them?"

"Maybe. No guarantees."

"Did she tell you about any of them?"

"Why should she?"

Goldsmith shrugged. "You had to talk about something. They'd be natural enough. Say one of them was a quiet little guy, big sad eyes. Say he was having a tough time, a writer maybe. She might have let him come up there when he had no place else to go. Possible?"

Liza looked at him. "Yeah. Possible and then some. Where'd you pick him up?"

"I haven't even met him. I'd like to. I don't even know his name."

"Sad Sack. That's what I called him."

"What did Dolly call him?"

"I'm telling you the truth. I don't know. Jim, or some easy name like that. Could be Tom, Dick or Harry. A hard name I'd remember maybe. He was sitting there one day when I went up. Shivering like a wet pup. She sent him out to the kitchen to make himself some coffee. 'You think we're in a tough racket,' she says to me…meaning show business. 'That kid's trying to sell poetry.' He didn't look like no kid to me, but he sure acted one. 'Poetry,' I says to her. 'I thought that went out with Shakespeare.' 'It sounds real pretty,' she says. 'I don't know what it means half the time, but

I figure it won't do me a bit of harm to know some poetry. It's like knowing French.' Dolly was going around with some mighty elegant people. She was always trying to improve herself, poor kid."

"Did you talk with the man at all, Liza?"

"Nope. The funny thing, he didn't come back in the room. I remember smelling the coffee after a while. I said I wouldn't mind if he'd bring us in a cup. 'Oh,' she says, 'he's gone. Comes and goes like a rainy day.'"

"And you never saw him again?"

"Never. I asked her about him a couple of times. 'He's around,' she says."

"How long ago was it that you met him, Liza?"

"A couple of years. More. It was when that silly song about Nature Boy was popular."*

"Liza, have you got any idea just what the relationship was between them?"

She looked at him a moment. "How do you mean?"

"Was he in love with her—attracted to her?"

She gave a vulgar laugh. "I get you. Lord, no. As far as I can figure it out, he was Dolly's pet charity. Maybe he read poetry at some fancy shindig. She went to the damnedest things."

Goldsmith pocketed his cigarettes. "Do you think he knew the business she was in?"

Liza thought about that. "I don't know. I'll tell you this, it wouldn't surprise me to find out that he didn't. I remember her saying once, 'that screwy kid wants me to go out with him listening to bird calls—at five in the morning.' Imagine. Five a.m. in Central Park. That's where I got the Nature Boy notion."

---

* "Nature Boy" was written by songwriter George Alexander Aberle—also known as eden ahbez and "ahbe"—an important figure in the California hippie movement in the 1940s to 1960s. The song was the first solo recording by Nat King Cole, recorded in 1947 and released in 1948. Quite popular, the song was inducted into the Grammy Hall of Fame in 1999.

Goldsmith laid a bill on the table and the waiter came for it immediately. "I'd offer you a nightcap, Liza…"

"I know," she said, sliding out of the booth. "I got another show and Simon Legree* tipped you off. That buzzard. He pinches my cheeks. 'You little tippler, you,' he says. Like it would make a difference in that flea trap. I'm going to be almost glad to get back where I belong. The smell of perfume in that place turns my stomach."

"I'm much obliged to you, Liza," Goldsmith said, collecting his change.

He walked her to the door of the club. "You were kind of down on your own luck when you met Dolly again, weren't you, Liza?"

She looked at him coldly. "Not that far down. See you around."

He watched her through the door and waited a few minutes on the street. Then he went down to the club again himself. The drunk was gone but the master of ceremonies was at the bar.

"Brought little Liza back on time, I see," he remarked. "She's a sweet kid."

"Yeah. Who's her agent, chum? I like her act."

The m.c. looked at him. Obviously he was trying to figure out who he was and whether or not he was on the level.

"I mean it," Goldsmith said. "Who's her agent?"

"Dave Albright. Ever hear of him?"

"Maybe. I'll find him. Thanks."

"Try right here after the midnight show tomorrow. That's when she gets paid off."

---

* The proverbially tyrannical slave owner in Harriet Beecher Stowe's *Uncle Tom's Cabin* (1852).

21

"And just like that, Mama, I got the job."

Katie Galli was happy. It was in her every movement that evening, her quick smile, her eyes, her sudden huggings of her mother.

"How much money?" Mrs. Galli asked.

She hesitated only an instant. "Fifteen dollars a week. That's to start."

"And that's what you couldn't wait all evening to tell me about. I thought it was fifty. I don't know, Katerina. I thought you were going to the city college?"

Katie realized her need for caution. "It can wait a year, Mama. I'm young."

"Young. When I was your age I was with the first child, your brother that died when he was a month old. What do you do for this fifteen dollars a week?"

"Answer the telephone. Typing. Just office work. It's a paint store."

"And what am I to do here? I can't hire somebody for fifteen dollars a week."

"I'll do my housework, Mama. I'll just do it at another time."

"Oh sure. You'll make the beds when the boarders are asleep in them. All right. Go to an office. The young ones don't want to stay home anymore. They don't want family business. Your brother, he can't live at home. He's got to have the room near his work. Four blocks he can't walk in the morning. And now he wants to give up the bakery. Your father killed himself paying for it. But not your brother. Your uncle will manage it by himself. Very well he will manage it. He'll make it big. But not Johnny. He wants to play in a band. Never a day's peace with him since he got the accordion."

"I thought you'd be pleased," Katie said.

"Pleased. Sorry. What's it matter? Did you ask me before you looked for the job?"

"I mightn't have gotten it. I wanted to see if I could first."

"Then be happy. You know how to get the job. When another one comes you can snap it. You're my little girl. I want good things for you."

That line of persuasion was more than Katie could resist for long. "Please, Mama, I'll need the experience to get a better one."

Mrs. Galli looked at her. "How much money will you give me?"

"How much do you think I should, Mama?"

"I'll buy your clothes. You keep a dollar to spend."

"A dollar isn't much."

"Fifteen dollars isn't much. When you make more, then you keep more. When do you start?"

"Monday."

"Oh?" Mrs. Galli turned from the clothes she was dampening and wiped her arms in her apron. "He knows when to pick an apple before it falls. Is he young or old, this owner of a paint store?"

"In-between."

"The in-between ones are the worst. Do you know how to take care of yourself, Katerina?"

"Of course, Mama. I'll finish the clothes if you're going to the movie."

Yes, of course she knew, Mrs. Galli thought. A girl didn't reach seventeen in their neighborhood without knowing that. She glanced at the clock.

"Don't you want to come with me, Katerina?"

"Not tonight. I'll take the fifty cents, though, Mama. Maybe I'll get some paper and go over to Nina's and practice typing."

"You don't have to be that good for fifteen dollars a week. If you're going to dampen those things, use lots of water. I don't want them dried out before morning."

She combed her hair then, and took her purse from a cupboard drawer. Opening it, she counted her change. "You can take your fifty cents from the coffee can, Katerina. Maybe I won't stay for the double feature. It's so hot when you come out."

"Thanks, Mama."

As her mother left the house, Katie began to sing. She flung the water over the clothes and rolled each piece quickly...five shirts for her brother, one for Tim. A silly thing to lose a shirt, she thought, but like Tim. Tim. Even the sound of his name was beautiful. It was like the fading sound of a bell. She laid the dampened clothes in the basket and covered them with a towel, shoving the basket under the table then.

She got a pencil and a scrap of paper from the drawer and wrote down several figures. Fifteen from twenty-two-fifty was seven-fifty and that times four equaled thirty. In a month she would have held out thirty dollars. The amount was frightening. Only for a moment did she permit herself to contemplate the gravity of her deception. The miracle was that she had gotten away with it. Her mother believed that she would start at fifteen dollars. It was not as though she didn't know that it was wrong. She intended restitution. Not that it was really stealing, anyway. She would earn the money and she would do her housework the same as ever. And her need for the money was so great.

Nevertheless the thought of doing it hurt. Something inside had plagued her since she had first conceived and nurtured the idea. She would never be the same again, having done it. The surge of happiness dissipated into depression, and then rose again because the joy of what the deed might bring was stronger. She crumpled the paper and threw it into the cardboard box under the stove.

Going to the cupboard, she took her fifty cents, and then because there was a great deal of change there, she took two more quarters, making a resolve to replace them some day. She gathered six cola bottles from the pantry and went out. At the delicatessen she turned them in and added twelve cents to her fund. From there she walked to her brother's bakery. She went into the back room where he was rolling dough.

"Johnny, can I have a dollar?"

"Johnny, can I have a dollar," he mimicked. "What did you do with the nickel I gave you yesterday?" He grinned and dusted his hands on his apron.

"It always smells so good in here," she said.

"Yeah. Sweat and sour milk." He gave her the dollar. "What are you going to do with it?"

"I'm saving up for a permanent."

"Give me back my buck. If you ever let them put a curling iron in that hair of yours…"

"They don't use curling irons anymore, silly."

"Mama does."

"She's old-fashioned."

"You think so? One of these days she's going to hook herself a nice fat widower with lots of moola. Then I'm going to kiss Uncle Ped and this whole damn bake oven goodbye. I'm going to buy me a little car, and if somebody says the word 'bread' to me, boy, am I going to let him have it. Right in the puss. Now get out of here, chicken, and let me go to work."

"Thanks, Johnny."

"Yeah. Count your change when you spend it."

She was almost skipping on her way home, a little dance rhythm fitting itself in her mind to her footsteps. At the corner of Twelfth a few boys loitering whistled. Tom Crosetti was among them. Katie hurried.

"Buy you a coke, Katie," one of them called after her.

"No thanks."

"Got a date?"

"Yes."

"You don't call him a date, do you?" That was Tom, she thought, hating him even more.

"Why don't you get a man, little girl?" another called.

"Why? Just to go to church with?"

Their laughter curled after her like the hissing of a steam engine. What did they know, she thought, what did they know... She almost collided with one of the boarders on the steps. "Watch it, kid. You'll get in trouble in a hurry like that."

She waited in the living room until she saw him pass the window on his way down the street. Then she went upstairs and knocked on Tim's door. He opened it almost the instant she knocked.

"Come down, Tim. There's no one home and it's cooler. We can talk and maybe play some records."

"Where's your mother?"

"She went to the movies. I've got something kind of important to tell you, Tim."

"And I've something to tell you," he said, permitting her to lead him from the room.

It was Katie who went back and turned out the light in his room. He looked very tired, she thought, glancing at the stack of papers on the card table, but she had never seen him happier or more at ease. His eyes were brimming with pleasure when she returned to him, and she had to rush ahead of him to conceal the response it quickened in her.

"What did you want to tell me, Katie?" he asked as soon as they reached the living room.

"It's nothing to get excited over. It's just that I got a job."

He seemed disappointed at the news. "You mean you'll be going away to work every day?"

His disappointment pleased her. "Yes. But I'll be home evenings. I never see you through the day, anyway."

"No. But it makes such a difference knowing you're in the house. It's like...I don't know what it's like, a happy bird maybe...that you hear singing off somewhere, and feel glad just to know that it's in the world with you."

"I feel that way too, Tim. When I know you're upstairs, it doesn't make any difference whether I see you or not. The house just seems different."

"Then why do you want to go to work?"

She saw then that she could not tell him directly. She would have to make him see the need for it first. "It's a good job and I'll be home Saturdays and Sundays, and by five-thirty every night," she said, attempting indifference. "Now tell me your news, Tim. That's what's important. It's about your work, isn't it?"

He began to walk back and forth across the room. "Yes. It's about my work. How can I tell you, Katie? It's pouring out of me like...like water down a cascade. Only it has shape. Shape as well as substance. Always before I used to get a great blob of color, as it were. Gushing." He clenched and unclenched his fists to demonstrate the splash. "Now I can contain it without losing it. I can hold it long enough to fashion the structure I want it to fit. And in the reading, it sounds like thunder, like the tumultuous rolling of storm clouds up to the very explosion of the heavens…and then it's quiet again. I'm doing that part now, and Katie, I can write the quiet parts now. And I've never been able to before. Did you ever hear a flower laughing?"

She giggled. "I've seen them laughing."

He smiled, looking at her and then away again as though at some picture he had conjured up. "How could you hear them in the bellowing of car horns and the choking of buses? Some day you'll hear them. I'll see to that."

"I want to, Tim. Very much."

"When I was a boy I used to sit in a field of daisies and I'd watch them rock back and forth, and if I'd listen very hard, I'd hear them chuckling. And the wind would come up a little stronger, and they would just seem to roll with laughter." He cocked his head, listening again for the sound. He turned to her. "I'm getting all that now, Katie. If only I can go on this way. I keep feeling that I must hurry before the storm breaks again."

"Don't hurry, Tim," she said very gently. "You don't have to hurry now."

"Bless you, my dear. If this is what I think it is, please God, it's you that it belongs to more than it does to me. You know that you're the flowers, don't you?"

"I hoped I was. I wanted to be part of it, I mean. I didn't dare to hope really."

"Always dare to hope, Katie. It's the least we can dare. There was an expression my mother used to use: we'll live in hope if we die in despair."

"That isn't very hopeful," she said.

"No, it isn't," he said thoughtfully. "It just happens to have the word hope in it."

"Did you love your mother very much, Tim?"

"No, I didn't," he said slowly. "She crushed me like a flower she was trying to save. She sucked all the life out of me. Why?"

"No reason especially. I was thinking of mama. She's like that too. When she's feeling affectionate she just loves you to death. Sometimes I wonder if I'm going to be like that some day."

"Women are like elephants," he said for no reason she understood. He began to move about the room.

"Tim, listen to me for a minute. Sit down and rest."

He hesitated.

"Please, Tim. This is such a good evening for us."

He did as she asked.

"Tim, you said that I'm the flowers. I'm very glad. It's more important to me than anything in the world. I'm not ashamed to say that. I've never been so happy in all my life. But if I'm the flowers, the way I see it, mama's the storm..."

His head jerked up, but she was studying her fingers as though the words she was trying to find were written on them.

"I mean, mama's a practical woman. She likes you, but she likes her rent and board money, too. We can coax her along for a while maybe. She likes music, and poetry is kind of like music. She'd like it if she knew. But she's got a quick temper. She's liable to flare up and say something nasty. Then it won't be quiet anymore for you..."

His sudden tension eased off. "Just a few more days, Katie. Then I'll go out and look for work."

"That isn't what I mean, Tim. You ought to have all the time you need. It isn't right that you shouldn't. Tim, that's why I got a job. Don't say anything. Just listen to me. I'll be able to give you eight dollars and fifty cents a week. I've got it all figured out. If you gave that to mama she'd be satisfied. I'm sure she would. It's just the idea of paying something. And you don't eat much. Then some day, if you wanted to, you could give it back without anyone ever knowing."

"Dear, dear Katie," he whispered after a moment, unable to speak aloud. The tears welled up in his eyes.

"Don't cry, Tim. Please don't. I don't ever want to see you cry again. This is fun. It isn't sad."

He sat where he was, his hands knotted in his pockets.

"There's always a way if you try hard enough. We're just lucky," she went on, tumbling over the words in her eagerness to get them out. "And I've got over two dollars now. Take them and tell her you'll make the rest up for this week some time."

"If all my lifetime were spent in it," he said then, "it wouldn't make up the rest for this week, Katie."

She got up and moved about the room, busy with ashtrays and doilies and the curtains. "Oh gosh," she said. "These last few days have been wonderful."

"Good days, Katie. Nothing dies but something lives..."* his voice trailed off with the words.

"What are you thinking, Tim?" she asked from the window.

It was a few seconds before he answered. "I almost went away that day when you came up at night and asked me to the party. I had enough money in my hand that night. But I knew it was money I could never touch. And I knew there must be no more of it—ever again." He smiled. "Don't look so serious, Katie. There are things that must be done. Evil that must be destroyed, for it corrupts the world. I know now, seeing how beautiful you are, that I was right."

---

* This is from Francis Thompson's "Ode to the Setting Sun"; see notes on pages 125 and 127.

Again she turned from him. "Tim, read something to me, please. Not what you wrote if you don't want to. But something that'll sound like it. Something you like."

He got up and went to his room for the books eagerly. Katie breathed deeply of the night air. There was a little smell of fish on it and a soft dampness. There were so many things he said that she did not understand but that she was content in his saying in her presence. When he returned and sat beneath the lamp turning the pages of the book until he found the passage he wanted, she chose a darker corner of the room from which she could watch him, her face in the shadows.

"We'll save Shelley for the flowers," he said, "or maybe Keats. But this is the stuff that storm is made on." His voice gained strength from the words, and she thought, while she listened to more words that she understood only to be beautiful, of the jeering cries on the street corner... "Why don't you get a man?" There would never be anyone more of a man to her than this dear, quiet one who loved her only with his eyes. Tim read:

> *Who lit the furnace of the mammoth's heart?*
> *Who shagged him like Pilatus' ribbed flanks?*
> *Who raised the columned ranks*
> *Of that old pre-deluvian forestry,*
> *Which like a continent torn oppressed the sea,*
> *When the ancient heavens did in rains depart,*
> *While the high-danced whirls*
> *Of the tossed scud made hiss thy drenched brood...**

---

* This is from Francis Thompson's "Ode to the Setting Sun," first published in *Merry England* in September 1889 and substantially revised for his collection titled *New Poems*, published in 1907. The version quoted by Tim is the revised poem.

He was still reading when Mrs. Galli returned two hours later and remarked that if she had known he was going to read aloud she would not have gone to the movies. "It sounds just like music," she announced, and Katie smiled happily.

22

It was not much later that evening that Sergeant Goldsmith was reading the same poem from the collection of Francis Thompson that he had taken from Dolly Gebhardt's apartment. He reread and marked a passage where the page bore the marks of much reading:

And so of all which form inheriteth
The fall doth pass the rise in worth;
For birth hath in itself the germ of death,
But death hath in itself the germ of birth.
It is the falling acorn buds the tree,
The falling rain that bears the greenery,
The fern-plants moulder when the ferns arise.
For there is nothing lives but something dies,
And there is nothing dies but something lives.
Till skies be fugitives,
Till Time, the hidden root of change, updries,
Are Birth and Death inseparable on earth;
For they are twain yet one, and Death is Birth. [*]

---

[*] This is the ending of "Ode to the Setting Sun."

Goldsmith laid the book aside and looked at his watch. Liza Tracy would be starting her midnight stint in a few minutes. He went into the kitchen and poured himself a cup of cold coffee. The place was already a mess although his wife had left only that morning for two weeks in the country. He was glad that the invitation had come when it had, he was home so little now. But he was also glad to get out of the empty house a few minutes later.

He timed himself to be in the club as Liza went off, but not where she would see him. He scanned the patrons at the bar and spotted one instantly he would have taken bets was Dave Albright. The man was sweating profusely—the sweat of an alcoholic in any temperature. His hand trembled as he reached for his glass and emptied it. He slouched off the bar stool and started for the dressing rooms. Goldsmith intercepted him.

"Albright?"

"Yeah."

"You handle Miss Tracy?"

"That's right."

"I've got a proposition for you."

Albright pulled himself together with visible effort. "Liza? Nice little routine she's got. That girl's coming. In a big way." He listed a little toward Goldsmith. "Did you see Weston's column yesterday? Something, huh?"

"Maybe. Got a few minutes?"

"I got to look in on Liza. Can you wait a couple of minutes?"

"I'll meet you at the Shamrock across the street."

He watched the agent's attempt at briskness down the passageway. He turned to find the m.c. beside him, smiling. "Hard guy to find, isn't he?"

"Maybe I don't look in the right places," Goldsmith said, starting to go.

"Why don't you book her out of here? We got prestige. Make a deal: we'll give her another week here to build..."

Goldsmith interrupted. "Build her another week. Then we'll talk." He broke away from the man, knowing the next question would be on his connections, his house. A deal, he thought, make a deal, everybody was making a deal, looking for another ten per cent from Liza's measly take.

Albright arrived at the Shamrock five minutes later, at best fifteen dollars richer. Goldsmith waved him back to where he was sitting, and showed him his identification.

"Homicide," the agent said. His wizened face turned a shade paler. "I thought..."

"I know what you thought," the detective said. "You've just got a one-track mind. Where did you find her, Albright?"

"Mahoney's Place. Eighth Avenue."

"You just happened by there, caught her act. The greatest little singer you ever heard. Just right for going places..."

"That's right."

"When did you sign her in here?"

"Six weeks ago."

"Why? She's gone as far as she's going and she knows it. So do you. Why did you bring her down here?"

"I needed dough. So did she. That's why."

"Maybe that's her reason. But it's not yours. You were doing somebody a favor, Albright, a big favor, somebody who had a great big heart and a friend going downhill. She liked doing things anonymously, and she knew a lot of anonymous people. You're one of them. Why you'd want to do her a favor—that's none of my business. Her murder is."

"I don't know what you're talking about."

"No? A ten per cent cut from Liza's legitimate. Maybe you get twenty. But the commission comes a lot higher in her friend's business. And it's smart to keep the talent happy, high-class talent like that. That's reason enough for a big favor."

"You shouldn't have any trouble proving that, Sergeant."

Goldsmith smiled. His voice softened. "I don't want to prove it. It's out of my line. Let the vice boys worry about it. I'm philosophical about the facts of life. And I know a good turn when I get one. I never forget it. Want a drink?"

Albright studied him a moment. "Okay."

"Bar whiskey?"

"Anything better would choke me."

The detective called out the order to the bartender. When they were set up he got the drinks himself and brought them to the table. He watched the trembling of Albright's hand as he lit a cigarette.

"The way I see it," Goldsmith said easily, "Liza's friend, Dolly, didn't understand the variety of agents there can be—theatre, literary, vaudeville—she didn't understand the distinction. To her, an agent knew the right people for any talent. Did she ever ask you to see what you could do for a poet?"

Albright sipped his drink. Each taste seemed to have a distinct flavor of its own. "I don't think I've got the right act for you, Sergeant."

Goldsmith lit a cigarette. Albright was not going to commit himself if he thought his information didn't weigh enough to guarantee the detective's silence on his pimping.

"Let me look at it. Even if I can't use it, I'll buy."

"Okay, if that's the way you want it. But I'm warning you, Sergeant, I don't look much maybe, but I got a lot of friends."

"I didn't threaten you, Albright. Let's not put it on such a low level." His words had an easy flow that belied his anger.

Albright shrugged. "It's over five years ago. She started working on me, working hard. She wanted me to read his stuff. What the hell would I know if I did read it? I didn't want any part of it. 'Meet him,' she says. 'Introduce him to somebody. You're always introducing me to somebody.' There was an answer to that one and I gave it to her. I never met the guy. I never read his stuff. I can't even tell you his name. Now do you see the pig in a poke you bought, Sergeant?"

"I've bought skinnier ones. Where was Dolly living then?"

"Right where she was last week."

"Where did she live before that?"

Albright shrugged. "I picked her up on Eighth Avenue."

"You do all right on Eighth Avenue."

"Gold dust and fool's gold, sometimes you find them side by side."

"Yeah," the detective said. "All you got to do is keep digging in the dirt."

The little man threw down the rest of his drink, curling in the last traces from his lips with his tongue. He grinned and looked for all the world like a bulldog trying to be coy. "Funny, you should say that, Sergeant."

"Why?"

"When she was trying to sell me on him—'he's a country kid,' she says. 'The city's killing him. He needs a break, Dave.' 'Look, baby,' I said, 'the best break you could give him is to send him back to the farm.' It turned out he didn't want to go. He was scared."

"Scared of what?"

Albright shrugged. "Maybe bulls," he giggled, "like the rest of us."

Goldsmith studied his cigarette. He detested that slang reference to police more than any other. "The stuff she wanted you to read," he said coldly, "had any of it been printed?"

Albright rubbed his chin. "Yeah. Wait a minute. Wait a

minute now. She had a handful of the stuff. All I saw was writing, but she took a page out of it. 'Look at this one,' she said. 'It's even printed. Like in a magazine. It's called *Mother*.' 'That's all, baby,' I said. 'You keep him. I've never been a mother myself. I wouldn't appreciate it.'"

23

"You gave me an awful start, Father, a terrible start seeing a priest."

"I'm awfully sorry. I should have called you before coming."

"I was afraid something happened to Mr. Grosvenor, my husband. Will you come in or sit here on the porch, Father?"

Father Duffy motioned to the porch chairs. A cat hopped from one of them and stretched. "Your husband is ill, Mrs. Grosvenor?"

"Not a day in his life. I wouldn't sit there if I was you, Father. The cat's shedding now and his hair's all over everything. It's the construction he works on is dangerous. Mr. Grosvenor's a carpenter. He's English, you know. A convert. He turned when he married me. A nicer man you never met for an Englishman."

Father Duffy smiled. "You met him in this country?"

"I did not. I met him in Dublin. He likes to say he had the pick of all the roses in Ireland and picked me hisself. We've no children, you see, and it makes us closer than some. I was the oldest of six girls, and glad I was to be picked. Some isn't picked yet and the youngest would have been better off not."

"As a matter of fact, Mrs. Grosvenor, it's one of your sisters I came to inquire about—Mary Brandon."

The woman did not speak for a moment. Her small blue eyes searched his face. "That's a queer thing for you to be asking me, Father," she said then.

She spoke as though by mere virtue of his being a priest he should know about her sister. Either that, or Mary Brandon had been so much in the news, she was common knowledge, he thought. In view of the event that had brought him halfway across the country to talk with this volatile, middle-aged woman, he suspected the latter reason. And yet there was no chagrin in her response. She was sitting, mild and comfortable, waiting for him to explain.

"Mrs. Grosvenor," he said, "I'll be frank with you. I'm trying to trace your sister. I can't tell you why. But I've come here from Marion City, Pennsylvania. When she left there over fifteen years ago, it was your address she gave to the parish housekeeper."

"She didn't give it," the woman said. "She sent it."

"Yes. I know that. She left Marion City after her husband's death. It was a year later that she sent it."

"Do you know why she sent it at all, Father?"

"Why?" he said, wanting to hear her version of it.

"Mary had a son. Not much of a one, to my thinking, but he was all she had. If you're coming from Marion City, I don't need to tell you what her husband was like. I'll never forgive our father for that. There's no woman needs marrying as much as to send her to the likes of him with the bargain made ahead of her. Mary was always delicate. Even in the old country she was ailing one day to the next. Her life was a misery…"

She rocked in her chair a moment thinking about it, and it occurred to Father Duffy that he was being prepared in her telling for some final tragedy that had befallen Mary Brandon.

"You were telling me why she sent your address to Marion City," he prompted gently.

"It was the son." She cocked her head at him, as with a sudden thought. "Is it the boy you're inquiring after, Father? Has he been found?"

"I didn't know he was lost," the priest said, avoiding her question.

"He came out to the preparatory school for the priesthood in Fort Grayson, Indiana. That was a year or two before Tim Brandon died. And never the word did his mother hear from him after the first year he was there, and after her giving her youth for him. She was pining so after him when she came here to me and Mr. Grosvenor, I took her to the parish priest. We thought maybe it was one of them cloistered orders. Well, our priest made inquiries. The boy just up and left the seminary where he was studying. He was working one day in the summer out in the fields with a team of horses, and when night came, the horses came home by theirselves. It near broke Mary's heart, hearing that, what was left of her heart for breaking, that is. From that day to this, there's been no word of the boy. It was her thought he might be lying dead in the fields, but the whole seminary had turned out looking for him when the horses came home."

"Didn't they send word to his mother?"

"They did, and the letter went back to them. She was gone then from Marion City, you see, and it was before she sent our address."

Father Duffy turned his hat around in his hands. He was no closer to Tim Brandon than when he had left Marion City. Indeed he had been closer to him in New York, for there it was a possibility that the man would seek him out again, having once found courage in his presence.

"And Mary Brandon, Mrs. Grosvenor?" he said, getting up.

"She took the blame for his failure on herself, Father. And

in the end it was right what she did according to her own lights."

"She's dead?"

"Indeed she's not. She joined the Holy Sisters of St. Clement ten years ago as a lay nun, and there's no one happier today this side of heaven."

24

Goldsmith paged through one magazine after another at the public library, some prominent and some obscure, religious and scientific journals, magazines flourishing and those now out of print. If poetry was a living art, as he had read in one caption, the publications bearing it often died in childbirth. He was reminded of the line from Thompson... "There is nothing lives but something dies." He left the library and began a weary search of the bookshops. It was late afternoon of his second day's searching that he found the Winter, 1944, issue of the *Young Poet.** He was sitting in the basement of a midtown shop, the sweat dropping from his nose onto the dusty cover. It was ironic that he caught the words "The Mother" shimmering under the drop of sweat. He turned to the poem then and read:

> *Who is this woman to be so adored?*
> *Her dress is torn and grimy at the thighs*
> *From hands that fumble there—young hands and old,*
> *No odds to her now which. She only stands and sighs.*

---

* A fictional magazine.

She'll scratch, and pat her hair back into place
And shift her weight, one foot to the other,
And let him have her hand across his face
If he keeps hollering with his—"Mother."

But still she is the only world he's heir to...
Except the God at night he cries his prayer to.

And it was signed: Timothy Brandon.

Goldsmith repeated the name to himself as he drove to headquarters, as though the sound of it were his reward. One thing was certain about the poem, it wasn't written to Mother with love. The *Young Poet* had gone out of business with the Spring issue, having been founded the year before. He wondered if the editor might not be as hard to find as Timothy Brandon.

At headquarters the detective began a simultaneous check of police records, selective service registration and social security. While he was trying to trace the sponsors of the *Young Poet*, Lieutenant Holden came in, listened a moment to the telephone conversation, shook his head and went on to his own desk. When Goldsmith got off the phone he took the magazine to his superior's desk and laid it open before him.

"That's our boy who wrote that," he said.

Holden read it through. "That's not Dolly he's describing," he said.

"No. Not exactly. But there's a connection, I think." Goldsmith picked up the magazine. "I'd give a lot to know what his own old lady was like."

"Now don't start that tack, Goldie. Just bring in this guy Brandon. Let his lawyer figure that angle."

"You know," the sergeant said thoughtfully, "I've got an idea that if we knocked on his door and said to him: 'Brandon, you're under arrest for the murder of Dolly Gebhardt,' he'd come in just as meek as a lamb and tell us all about it."

Holden pulled a cigarette from where it had stuck to his lip. He swore to himself. "Yeah, Goldie. Then on the way down here, he'd take out his hammer and beat your skull to a pulp, too. Don't get sentimental over him. He's a killer. I don't care what he did before or what he's doing now. I don't give a damn if he's scrubbing church steps somewhere or helping old ladies across the street. That Saturday night he did as brutal a job of murder as I've seen. Get him."

"Take it easy, chief. I want him, too. And I want him quick. Set him up the right circumstances, I think he'd have killed the woman he wrote this poem about."

"Then I hope he's writing lots of poetry these days," Holden said with some sarcasm, "if that's going to keep him happy till you get there."

"So do I," Goldsmith said. "It's occurred to you then that he might kill again?"

"Sure. That's why we've had a man on Mrs. Flaherty's back step ever since."

"Mrs. Flaherty," Goldsmith repeated. He took a cigarette from the package on Holden's desk. "There's a lot of neighborhoods this poem could have been written in. That's one of them."

Holden looked at him. "Is that the strongest hunch you got on where this guy is?"

"No. But I've fallen on my face chasing big ones before. That's an Irish neighborhood. He mentioned to her that she was Irish, and mentioned his mother in the same breath."

"But Flaherty never saw him before," Holden said.

"Did you ask her that specifically?"

"No, but hell, man, the way she was willing to talk, she'd have said it out."

"I wonder. She had her own notion of the kind of man who killed Dolly. It wasn't Brandon."

Holden ground out his cigarette. "Then ask her, Goldie. But I think you're wasting time, valuable time."

"Maybe I am, chief. But I'm going to risk it."

25

The detective fell into step with Mrs. Flaherty the next morning as she was going into the apartment hotel. He went into the laundry with her. "Do you remember the fellow you described to Lieutenant Holden, Mrs. Flaherty? You thought he might have been Miss Gebhardt's brother?"

"Are you coming to tell me he did it? I wouldn't believe it if he told me hisself."

"Well, that's not exactly what I came for," Goldsmith said. "You liked him, didn't you?"

"I don't know whether I liked him or no. I just liked his looks and the decent word he had for me."

"I was wondering if you'd ever seen him before, Mrs. Flaherty, not at Miss Gebhardt's, but maybe around your own neighborhood."

She looked up at him from where she was taking her apron from a laundry stack. "Do you think I wouldn't of told that to the officer if I had?"

"Well," the detective said, "I thought it might have slipped your mind. And there was no need to tell him when he didn't ask."

"No need, indeed. There was my own conscience. There's sins of omission as well as the kind you do in broad daylight."

Goldsmith smiled. "If only the world had your conscience. I won't keep you from your work."

"I would the Lord you could keep me from it this morning," she said. "I have to ready her place for new tenants today, and I'll have to go in there one day after the next, and looking every time and seeing her still lying there with her toes in the air. You've no idea the nightmares I've had since it happened. I'm always seeing someone after me."

"That could be a policeman," Goldsmith said.

"Could it now? Protecting me?"

He nodded.

"Isn't that thoughtful of them?" She unlocked the linen cupboard and then turned around. "Can you tell me something, officer? What do they do with her things in a case like this?"

"They're held by the property clerk to be put in evidence," he explained. "Then the family usually claims them. If not, they're sold."

She nodded. "I was arguing that with my Billy. He has the queer notion they're burned. Like murder was a disease, you know. Something catching."

"God forbid," Goldsmith said. He straightened up from where he had been leaning on one of the tubs. "If you ever should see that fellow again, Mrs. Flaherty, I wish you'd get in touch with us. Don't be alarmed about it. We just want to ask him some questions. But speak to us, not to him. Some people aren't as willing to talk to us as you are."

"You want to ask him the way you're asking me?"

He nodded.

"I'm glad that's all it is. A queer thing, the night I went home from here after I found her, Father Duffy, our assistant, came round when I was telling the story at home. He asked the same question as you—did I ever see the man around the church or in the neighborhood?"

"He was curious about that, too," Goldsmith said easily. "Well, it's a natural question. It was decent of the priest to come up and see you. Or was it an accident that he happened to come around that particular night?"

"It was no accident, though I was thinking then he was after something else. It came to me all of a sudden—he was going on a campaign to clean up...them kind of women. He's a sainted man, Father Duffy. But maybe you're right after all. He was curious about the little man."

"I wouldn't say that for sure, Mrs. Flaherty. I don't know Father Duffy at all."

"When you meet him you'll know him."

Goldsmith smiled. "I hope so. Thanks for talking to me, Mrs. Flaherty."

"Small thanks is due. I'm in no hurry this morning."

The detective paused at the door. "What parish are you in, Mrs. Flaherty?"

"St. Timothy. It's on..."

"I know it well," Goldsmith cut in. "Good luck to you."

26

Timothy, St. Timothy, Goldsmith thought, as he drove cross-town. He had already conceived the notion that Brandon was a religious man. It fitted with his idea of the circumstances of Dolly Gebhardt's murder. He could think of only one reason that the priest might have asked that question of Mrs. Flaherty: he too was looking for the man. Brandon might not be in the parish at all. Probably not or the priest would not have needed to question her. But St. Timothy was Brandon's patron saint. His name might account for the association entirely.

The detective parked some distance from the church and walked the intervening blocks. The doors to St. Timothy's were open. The great murky church seemed cool at first, but the air was heavy and humid. Goldsmith slipped into a back pew and sat down. Except for a nun moving with flowers between the sacristy and the altar, the church was empty. When his eyes became accustomed to the dull light, they perceived things in greater detail, the wordings on the stations of the cross, the names on the confessional boxes: Father Gonzales, Father Duffy...

Goldsmith had been in Catholic churches before, but never that he could recall alone. Partly out of curiosity and partly because Father Duffy's name was above it, the detective got up and went to the confessional. He looked about self-consciously and then opened the center door. He saw the little bench and the two small screened windows at either side. Closing the door softly, he drew one curtain and then the other apart, seeing the kneelers for the penitents, and in one the little ledge where they might rest their hands in prayer. He noticed the absence of the ledge in the other booth immediately for the wood was lighter where the two supporting arms had been taken away. And because he was trained to think of the likely places for finger-prints, he wondered at its absence. He tested his weight on the ledge at the opposite side. It would be unlikely to give under the full weight of a man, much less his quarter weight, leaning on it to rise from his knees.

Goldsmith stepped back and let the curtains fall into place. He left the church and went outdoors. Down the side street, a game of roller-skate hockey was in noisy progress. Among the spectators—a dozen girls and a few housewives with their baby buggies, hoods toward the game—was a priest. He was wear-ing his biretta* and cassock as though he had been attracted to the game on his way between the parish house and the church. Goldsmith ambled toward him. Two ashcans represented the goals at either end of the playing area, and the youngsters play-ing were streaked with sweat and dirt and played with a violent earnestness.

Goldsmith stood beside the priest. "Father Duffy?"

"Father Duffy's out of town for a few days. I'm Father Gonzales. Can I do anything for you?"

"No, thanks. I just thought I'd look him up." Goldsmith left it there purposely and pretended absorption in the game.

---

* A clerical hat with three peaks.

After a moment the priest looked at him as though trying to estimate his age. "Did you know him in the army?"

Goldsmith was saved from a direct answer by the roaring sweep of the players past them. "They're going to kill one another if they don't die of the heat," he said.

"You'd be surprised how well they survive. We get some of them off to camp for a while every year. Some of them like it better here. Which isn't to say they wouldn't change their minds, given half a chance."

"How long is Father Duffy going to be away?"

"A couple more days, I think. I got a postcard from him. 'Seeing America,' he wrote."

"There's a lot of it to see in a couple of days. How far away is he?"

The priest fumbled beneath his cassock and brought the card out. "Marion City, Pennsylvania."

"That part I never heard of," Goldsmith said.

"I don't think he did before, either. I never heard him mention it."

Goldsmith looked at his watch. "I'll drop around and see him one day when he gets back. Thank you, Father."

He was on his way when the priest called after him: "Shall I tell him you called?"

"I don't think he'd know me," the detective said. He hurried before an out-of-bounds puck, and heard the clang of hockey sticks on the fenders of the parked cars and the screech of roller skates on the hot brittle sidewalk in pursuit of the puck—the cry of "foul" and a spray of abuse on the one who had cried it… "What the hell, give us your stick if you can't take it…get an umbrella…what've we got to have a goddam creampuff on our side for?"

Which, Goldsmith thought, made up a kid's world in Hell's Kitchen.

27

"Of course I remember the boy. In my thirty-eight years as novice—master and superior, there is not one—not a single one, success or failure, scholar or dolt, whom I have forgotten. Sit down here beside me, Father."

Father Duffy took the chair the Superior indicated. Then, finding the sun glaring in his face, he got up and moved the chair back. Holes showed in the carpet from where he moved it. Many a tortuous hour had been spent here by novices, he thought, their faces to the window where their master might search their souls in God's sunlight.

"You find the sun disconcerting?" the old priest asked.

"Not disconcerting, Father. A nuisance. I like to see the person with whom I'm talking."

"So do I. Hence I have placed the chair there. Where did you take your orders?"

There was in the tone of his question the implication that he should not have received them under him without learning subordination. That he was severe was obvious. That he was more severe with himself than others might be a saving grace, one that would command respect as well as fear. But one thing Father

Duffy had learned early: an authoritarian has just so much authority, and if another human being stands up through the first brush
with it, he finds a man no stronger than himself, and perhaps
much weaker, needing the show of strength. How many times he
had met teachers and priests like this white-haired disciplinarian,
and how impatient he had grown with their show of strength.

"I received my orders in New York, Father. You were going to
tell me about Brandon."

The old man got up from his desk and drew another chair
near Father Duffy. "I remember taking him on the recommendation of his parish priest, himself a graduate of ours."

"Father McGohey," the young priest prompted.

"Yes. Father McGohey. And I remember at the time thinking young Brandon a strange sort for his recommendation. He
was an unlikely candidate for the priesthood from the beginning. Even if he had tried, I doubt that he should have made
the grade."

"Was he aware of his own inadequacies?" Father Duffy
asked, wanting more to ask if the novice-master had not made
them plain to him.

The Superior made a noise deep in his throat. "There were
times I was hard put to it to discover exactly what the boy was
aware of. He came from an unfortunate home—though some
of our best people have survived that. Brandon's father was a
drunkard, you know."

"And the mother?" It was a question Father Duffy asked
almost without being aware of asking it. For all that he intended
only to avoid the direct issue, he was learning duplicity.

"An unhealthy woman. She worshiped the boy. I use the
word advisedly. Her letters to him were..." the old man fingered
his lips while searching for the right words. "Well, I remember
thinking them at the time disgusting."

"They must have disturbed young Brandon," Father Duffy suggested.

"Oh, they did. We spoke about them often." Inadvertently, he nodded to his desk, and Father Duffy imagined how miserable the timid boy must have been during those sessions. "Finally, I wrote to her myself and suggested that she restrain her...remarks."

"Did he know that you wrote?"

"I don't recall now whether he did or not. That's a long time ago, but I think it unlikely that I should have told him. I don't think I've changed much."

Very little, Father Duffy thought. "Do you think they might account for his having run away, Father?"

"I doubt that. The business with the mother was very early. Besides, the devotion was all on her part. He was a much happier lad when she got hold of herself."

The Superior folded his hands and waited for questions. He would enjoy silences, Father Duffy thought. It was probably one of his many pat tests of a man: seeing if he could withstand scrutiny without words to cushion it. He took his time in framing a simple question.

"How long was he with you, Father?"

"About three years. I know that from the work he was permitted. Even his departure was characteristic: utterly irresponsible. Simply not equal to discipline. He left the horses at the plough. In the evening they came home."

"And no word from him after that?"

"No more than if he had been plucked off the face of the earth."

Father Duffy felt in his pocket for a cigarette and then thought better of it. The old priest watched him. "Just now you are reminding me of something else about the boy: he was forever denying himself things—milk on his oatmeal, sugar... He even fashioned himself a belt from a raspberry bush which he wore next to his skin. It was discovered when his skin became infected."

"That sounds like guilt," Father Duffy said. "It sounds like an adolescent punishing himself for being...an adolescent."

"Of course."

As matter of fact as that, the young priest thought. "It took a special kind of discipline to wear something long enough to cause infection," he persisted.

"I didn't say he was without self-discipline. Nor for that matter was he without devoutness. He merely could not abide authority. Nor was it that he deliberately defied authority. He simply failed to heed it. And there was no punishment he considered more than he deserved." After a moment the Superior added: "I like a boy with spunk."

There was the man, Father Duffy thought: even as an old man, he liked to be fought back. For all their service and devotion to God, this dean of the religious and the Father McGoheys reared boys much as they would tackle the breaking of so many colts. He shook off the thought and asked: "Do you remember his father's death while he was here?"

"Yes, I remember it," the Superior said after a moment. "He went home for a week."

Father Duffy kept his eyes on the floor. Wherever the boy had gone, it was not home to Marion City. "Was there any particular change in him after that?"

"Come now, Father Duffy. I have an excellent memory, but even mine has its limitations. All I can give is an over-all impression of the boy."

"The bramble belt," the young priest suggested. "Do you remember if that was before or after he returned from that week?"

"After. The belt affair was not very long before he disappeared."

Things that were suggestive, but that was all that he was to learn here of Little Tim, Father Duffy thought. Through the open window he could see the students stacking the shocks of grain, and from somewhere off he heard the whir of the reaper. There was something about it that gave him a sense of perpetuity. Without the sound of the machine the seminarians might have been young men of the middle ages reaping a hand-sown field while their brethren illuminated holy manuscripts. One of the boys straightened up and took off his straw hat to wipe the sweat from his forehead. He shaded his eyes from the sun and turned slowly to view the field from one direction and then another. There was adoration of God and gratitude for his own part in the harvest in that long look.

"He liked poetry," the Superior said abruptly, and somewhat as he might have said he liked cheese or buttermilk. "And he loved all ritual...the Mass, Tre Oré,* Benediction..." He was looking for characteristics, things he had drawn out of the strange boy in a weekly visit in this room.

"Yes?" Father Duffy said when the old man paused again.

"And he was very handy with a tool kit."

The young priest shuddered. He had all but forgotten that† in his sentimental musings about novices who toiled against the world and the flesh and prayed wordlessly in the open fields.

"The room is damp," the Superior said. "If you had sat in the sunlight you would not be uncomfortable. I am used to it."

"Did he receive special training in any trade, Father? I notice that you're self-supporting here."

"Not quite self-supporting these days. Of Brandon, I should

---

* The Tre Ore, or Three Hours, is part of the Good Friday service, commemorating Jesus's three hours on the cross.

† That is, the murder with the hammer.

have to say that he failed there also in discipline. He would be assigned to the fields and turn up, on inspection, in the tool sheds. Put him in the sheds and we might look for him in the fields."

"Were any of the priests here now friends with him, Father?"

"None who would know him better than I. We are not here for conviviality."

Clumsy, Father Duffy thought of himself. He asked: "His father's death—what do you remember of it?"

"It was I who told him of it. That is our custom. I remember it very well. I think it was probably then that I was certain he was not a proper candidate. He was unmoved when I told him. 'God is just,' were his only words. I asked him then if he presumed to sit in judgment on his father. 'Yes,' he said. 'My father sits in judgment of me.'"

Father Duffy got up and walked to the window. The sun upon his face heightened his sense of the coldness in the depth of the room. How abruptly he had changed his whole pattern of thinking...one little phrase had done it: "God is just."

Tim Brandon had passed yet another judgment. He had judged a prostitute in a New York apartment so many years later—so removed from the golden harvest where he, too, might have labored. But he had turned from it early, and the one germ nurtured within him was pride. From all his failures, and Father Duffy could now imagine a lifetime of them, he learned no more of himself than to be sorry for himself and to blame the world although he did penance. His penance was not for himself. He was sick in the shame of the world, even to murder. Father Duffy turned to the old priest.

"Did you give him the money to go home to his father's funeral?"

"His ticket would have been bought for him by the purser. The older seminarians are not permitted to go home, incidentally..."

"And money for his meals en route?"

"He would have been given enough."

"I am most grateful to you, Father," the young priest said. "I know you must be curious as to my interest in this man. And I cannot tell you."

The Superior leaned heavily on the arms of the chair, getting up. "I have always found curiosity the least of my temptations," he said. "By the way, Father, it occurs to me now that when he left he did not take so much as a change of clothes. If you are not in a hurry and think they might interest you, the custodian should be able to turn up his things."

"I'd like to see them," Father Duffy said.

28

Tim sat at the card table before the open window. The pages he had copied so neatly the day before were now so many sheets of broken, scratched-out lines. For each word he deleted, the one he added changed the meaning of the phrase, and sent him in wild search for another, brighter image. He was like a child catching snowflakes one at a time and seeing in each one passing a greater beauty than in the one he caught before.

Each word he selected was another name for Katie. But in his ecstatic pursuit he found himself at last exhausted and unsatisfied. Picking up the numbered pages he expected at least the pleasure of reliving the glorious lines to the point where he had bogged down. Until today that had sustained him in his failure to progress. There were many fragments in literature. Everything was a fragment in its making. His would comfort him another day.

But something had happened, something horrible and blasphemous. He could not even begin from the first clear lines he had written. The rhythm was broken, and words he had thought to have put down were missing. When he tried to remember them they flickered through his mind among others which he had rejected. The bad were good and the good bad. For an instant he glimpsed the distortion he had done to the very structure of his work.

He shook his head and turned the pages over. The distortion was in his own mind now, not on paper. He was tired. He got up stiffly and gradually stretched himself out of the cramped position his body had taken in its response to his mind's tension. He lay down and closed his eyes. For a few moments light splashed in the after-darkness. It took on color as he grew aware of it and tried to hold each changing swatch. He was aware of no particular shape or substance until he found himself imagining Katie's hair across his face, the strands of it a web over his eyes. He even sensed the smell of soap and lemon in it. His eyes open, he still held the illusion. He moistened his lips, examining their crevices with his tongue, half-expecting at least a single hair to have lingered there. Only the breeze from the open window sifted over him, but his whole body tingled with the excitement. He closed his eyes again and strained for a deeper identification. But the effort snapped the tendrils of fancy. The after-light was no longer sudden. It had a rolling motion, like flood, like running, slow-moving liquid.

He leaped from the bed in terror of what he anticipated, the darkening colors of that flow, an ugliness seeping through it and pouring over him. That had happened before, and this once he escaped it. A little dizzy, he stumbled about the room, putting his few books in order, straightening the spread, brushing the dust from the window sill.

He opened his door. The draft between the window and doorway cooled him. After a moment's indecision he went out. In the hall he listened to the sounds downstairs—singing. It was Mrs. Galli at her work, he knew, but from the distance he could imagine the voice to be Katie's. There was a likeness to their voices. Katie's, clear now with only an occasional tremble, would take on the vibrance of her mother's as she grew older. Moving from step to step soundlessly and listening for nuances in the voice that soothed him, he went downstairs and to the kitchen door.

Mrs. Galli was hanging curtains, her back to him. He watched her slip the rod through the hem and then climb up the small ladder. There was grace in her movements, and something in the way she tilted her head so like Katie when she was listening to him and trying to understand some special message in his words. Her arms seemed longer than he had thought them when she reached to hook the rod into its catch, strong arms, but round and soft as Katie's arms would some day be, or as indeed they might be now if he dared to touch his fingers to them. Her dress hung upon her like a veil, her body silhouetted against the light of day, a strong back with a little swelling beneath one arm as she turned slightly, the shadow of a breast. Her waist was slender as she stretched upward, or so he thought, and the thighs bulged out like molded clay. Flesh of my flesh, she had said of Katie…

As she descended the ladder she saw him, and she lifted her chin before speaking.

"It's queer," she said. "I thought you were there a minute ago, but I was afraid to look."

"Why?"

"I didn't want to see the empty place when I looked. I was thinking about you all morning. But I didn't come up." She took another set of curtains from the basket and laid them on the table.

"I shouldn't have minded," he said, standing in the doorway still.

"I do not interrupt poetry no more than music."

"I heard you singing."

"I have a good voice."

"Very good. It's like a cello."

"A good cello."

"Of course."

"Don't stand there. Come in by the table. There's a breeze today. I feel so good when the breeze comes up, I feel like I'm twenty years old maybe."

He came into the room and sat down at the table, but away from it, facing her as she put away the clothes basket and drew herself a glass of water at the sink. She glanced at him through the mirror there.

"It's foolish to feel twenty at my age, with a man for a son and a daughter almost a woman. But twenty is a good age to feel any time—even if you don't look it."

"You look thirty."

"Thirty is a good age, too," she shrugged. "I'm complimented." She dipped a washcloth beneath the faucet and wrung it out. With it she wiped her face and neck. "So nice," she said. "It makes me think of the nighttime."

As he watched her, he drew his hand across his forehead. Seeing the movement in the mirror, she rinsed out the cloth and brought it to him.

He did not lift his hand. "My forehead and neck," he said.

She brushed them gently and then laid the cloth on the table. With her cool hands, she massaged the tightened muscles first at the back of his neck. Her fingers plunged further down between his shoulders with each motion and spanned the width of his back, his shirt straining the top button at his throat until it gave and clinked on the porcelain-topped table. He let his head loll back, touching her breast.

Presently she stopped and let his head rest upon her for a

moment. Then she moved it away gently and picked up the cloth which she returned to the sink.

"I'm going upstairs now," she said, beside him once more. "I've got to hang the curtains in my room."

She picked them up and folded them over one arm. As she turned she extended her hand to him. He took it and followed her, waiting mutely while she threw the night-latch on the front door.

29

Lieutenant Holden examined the pencil portrait before him. He took his time, holding a blotter first over the mouth and then over the eyes, in each instance studying the feature separately. Goldsmith, watching him, lit a cigarette. A great deal hung upon his superior's decision. Nor was it an easy one for Holden to make. It was one thing for Goldsmith to want time to pursue Brandon in his own way, but quite another for Holden to go along with him. Should Brandon kill again, Holden would be under fire from the top, not the sergeant. Several times Goldsmith was tempted to say something, to try to influence him, but each time he held his tongue. If Holden came to his way of seeing it on his own, so much the better.

Finally the lieutenant slid the drawing across the desk to him. "Not good enough for you. Is that it, Goldie?"

"It's the best we can do, Lieutenant. We've given the artist every detail of his description we've got. We've shown it to Mrs. Flaherty three times. The same with Liza Tracy…"

"I'm assuming it's the best you could do," Holden interrupted. "I'm simply asking you if you're satisfied with it."

"No sir. I'm not. Change the chin a little, shade the

cheeks—almost any little deviation, and it resembles a dozen other guys, and maybe Brandon more than it does now."

Holden shook his head. "I don't like it a damned bit, but I agree with you. Keep looking, Goldie. But for God's sake, let's get something we can put our teeth into."

The sergeant put the sketch away gratefully. A general alarm had been forestalled a while longer. "I'm not the only one looking for him, by the way."

"That's nice. Who else is?"

"Mrs. Flaherty's parish priest. You were right that she'd never seen Brandon before or since. But it looks like the priest did. He's looking for him now."

"Where?"

"A little town in Pennsylvania, and then Chicago."

"Then he did skip town."

"No. I don't think so. I don't know what the priest's angle is, but I'm pretty sure he started out looking for his name like we did. The sheriff down there went over his moves. It could be that when he gets back here he'll lead us right to Brandon. It could even be Brandon will go to him again, maybe to confession."

"That's ticklish business, Goldie. I wouldn't count on the priest for help."

The phone was ringing on Goldsmith's desk. "I'm not counting on it," he said, going to answer it. "Just the opposite. I'm going to help him all I can." He picked up the phone. "Goldsmith speaking." He listened a moment and then said, "I'll be there within a half-hour."

Joshua G. Fabish, POETRY CONSULTANT, the detective read on the doorplate as he rang the bell. It was a walk-up apartment on Fifty-sixth Street just off Lexington. The building also housed consultants on beauty and Inca coinage. Nobody could be beautiful, poetic or rich without a consultant, he thought, waiting for the buzzer to release the door lock. As it sounded he thought of Fabish, ex-editor of the *Young Poet*. Magazines died, but editors transmigrated.

A bald, round-faced man opened the door to him. "Just eighteen minutes, Sergeant," he said smiling. "Only the fire department surpasses your efficiency." He led the way through ornate, wildly colored rooms. The odor of a sweet pipe tobacco permeated the place. Paisley shawls were spread over chairs, sofa and a grand piano that dwarfed the front room of the railroad apartment.*

"I have a passion for paisley shawls," Fabish explained as he faced the detective from behind a huge desk and saw him looking about the room. "They tell me my mother draped me in one when I was born."

Or dropped you in one, Goldsmith thought looking at the immaculate little man with a face as cold as salt. "Were you delivered by one of those?" He nodded toward one of many paintings of exotic birds with which the walls were hung.

"How clever of you to guess!" Fabish showed most of his teeth when he smiled.

Goldsmith resolved to keep his heavy humor to himself. "You said over the phone you'd found an address for Timothy Brandon."

"I did, and my dear man, you've no idea at all what I went through to find it."

"I appreciate it."

"How can you appreciate it if you don't understand it?"

"Look, Mr. Fabish, I'm just a cop—a dumb cop maybe. Thanks for any trouble you went to. Now can I have the address?"

---

* A "railroad apartment" has rooms laid out in a line, like a railroad car.

"I have a very good notion to send it back to the bank where all the estate of the *Young Poet* is in escrow, so to speak, and let you jolly well get a warrant or whatever..."

Goldsmith changed his tack. He needed all the time he could save. "I didn't realize how much trouble you had to go to."

"Bankruptcy complicates papers, you know. In this instance particularly. There was a check involved. The letter was returned to us unopened."

"I see."

Fabish opened a drawer and drew the envelope from it. He deliberately held it, turning it about in his hands and reminiscing all the while about the *Young Poet's* high aims and the sad state of the impoverished muse. How in the name of heaven anyone could work with this peevish, perverse character, the detective didn't know. And yet his desk, several chairs and the grand piano were piled with manuscripts. While he waited, his eyes on the man, the muscles of his jaws tight, he thought of how it must be to come to someone like this in the hope of guidance, looking for a way to success. Whatever help or encouragement he gave, the detective thought, was handed down like blessings from a god's shrine. It was given only to the worshipers and poetry became a cult. He extended his hand for the letter.

In his own good time, Fabish handed it over. "I'm going to write another check, my personal check," he said.

Goldsmith examined the envelope. Brandon had lived on East Eighteenth Street when he submitted the poem. He was gone from there by the time it was accepted. He drew the uncancelled check from the envelope and slid it back. It was for five dollars. Five lousy bucks.

Across from him, Fabish was putting the last flourish to his signature. "Now, if you find the young man, you might give him this. Morale, you know."

Goldsmith took the check and read it in front of Fabish. The poetry consultant had written: "For contribution to the *Young Poet*." The salt god was smiling in satisfaction of his benevolence. Poets don't grow old or die or steal or murder, the sergeant thought. On five dollars they live forever and write of spring and youth and love and beauty.

"This ought to fix him up," he said, pocketing the check. "So long, Fabish."

"It really wasn't a very good poem," Fabish said petulantly.

"No? I thought it was beautiful."

30

There was among Tim Brandon's things at the seminary only one clue to any contact beyond the school and home: a birthday card from someone signed "Teddy." The envelope bore an address in Cleveland, and it had been mailed to him a few weeks after the date of his father's death. Since Cleveland lay on the route Brandon would have taken to Marion City it was not too unlikely that there lay the story of his diversion from home and duty. Father Duffy arranged a few hours stopover in the city.

On the train, he drew the yellowing card from his pocket. Teddy might be man or woman. The handwriting was immature, but not necessarily that of a young person, he thought. Nor did the selection of the card tell much about the sender except that some pains were taken to be neither too personal nor too distant. It was "wishing a friend a happy birthday."

Putting the card back in his pocket, Father Duffy tried to reconstruct what might have been the young seminarian's journey when he started home for the funeral. He had not wanted to go, but he had been going because it was expected of him, perhaps because he had seen no way to avoid it. He was probably in dread of seeing his mother. He would have anticipated an overwhelming show of affection, a scene at his arrival and more of a one when the time came for his departure. And yet how great his need must have been in that period of his life for affection. Was Teddy someone he had met on the train? Or had he simply got off at Cleveland and wandered there much as he wandered away from an assignment at the seminary?

By the time he stepped from the train Father Duffy had decided that Teddy was a woman, and he found in himself a terrible dread of finding her. The boy had been here in the very depth of the depression with several days to spend and only enough money to buy food for one or two. He must have been in distress over the deception he intended on returning to the seminary, if he intended then to return at all. His ultimate return might have been an escape in itself. He might have expected his mother to communicate with them. It was curious indeed that she had not. But from what he had learned of her, Father Duffy decided that she probably thought the order had not permitted the boy to leave.

Glancing out of the window of the cab he took from the station, he saw in the distance the Cleveland Municipal Stadium, and the lineups at the ticket windows. That afternoon thousands of whiteshirted baseball fans would be cheering the Indians—men and women who had taken the day off from factory, store or office. They would go home to supper, their kids and a night on the back porch or a movie—healthy, ordinary people who never heard of the Big Tims or the Little Tims until the newspapers caught them into headlines or the radio scripters concocted them for a half-hour's distraction—and who could forget them with the turn of a dial and lie down to a quiet sleep. At that moment there was nothing the young priest would rather have done than pay off the cab and buy himself a ticket to the ball game. He longed for the smell of a cigar, peanuts, the sound of the rowdy cries for the home team and the feel of the warm clean sun on his back.

They drove out of the downtown area, through slums, at each block of which he expected the cab driver to flick off the meter. But on around the lake they drove, and he was wholly unprepared when the driver turned into a residential neighborhood of spacious and well-built homes and began to look for the house number. When the car stopped and Father Duffy read the number himself, he said, "You're sure this is right?"

"I know this town like I know my own teeth, Father."

Two little girls were playing in the yard. They stood at the walk and watched him pay the driver. When he turned, they chorused: "Good morning, Father."

He could remember no greeting that had given him so much pleasure. "Hello. Is your mother home?"

"I don't live here," one of them said. "I live across the street. We're not Catholics."

He smiled. "A lot of people aren't." He looked at the other girl.

"My mother's at the tennis matches, but grandma's home," she said. "I'll go tell her you want to see her."

"Thank you. My name is Father Duffy."

"I'm coming, too," the neighbor child said. "I want a drink of water."

He watched them run around the stone house to the back door. A cocker spaniel crawled out from beneath a clump of bushes and shook himself. He trotted a few feet after the youngsters and then stopped to look back. The priest whistled softly and the dog came to him, wriggling with friendliness.

A couple of minutes later a pleasant woman in her mid-forties came to the front porch and held the door open to him. "Won't you come in, Father?"

"Thank you," he said. "I'm afraid I don't even know your name."

"Benedict. Irene Benedict." She motioned him to a chair, and sat down beside him. The children returned to their play.

"Is there someone in the family called Teddy, Mrs. Benedict?"

"It's my daughter's nickname. Her name is Theodora, after her grandfather."

Father Duffy drew the birthday card from his pocket, feeling much relieved that he need not attempt to be circumspect here. Everything about the woman, the children, the dog, gave him a feeling of well-being, a security that would weather any trouble or intimation of trouble. It was a house where a family lived from one generation to the next. He showed the card to Mrs. Benedict. "I wonder if you happen to remember this boy?"

She took a pair of glasses from her pocket. Father Duffy watched her face: a look of puzzlement at first and then sudden remembrance, but no sign of disturbance at all. He felt an irrepressible surge of pleasure, a singing inside of him, which he knew had no relationship to the ultimate story at all, but which he accepted and enjoyed.

"Indeed I do remember him. We've often spoken of Tim and wondered what became of him."

Which somewhat dampened the priest's elation.

She gave back the card. "Teddy sent him that. She was twelve then, I think. Later, when he came back to us, he said it was the only birthday card he had ever received in the mail." Her voice grew serious. "I've often wondered if letting Teddy send that wasn't a mistake. He was such a sensitive boy. It may have been the one thing..." She lifted her hands in a gesture of inquiry. "Well, who can say? What became of him, Father?"

What indeed? "I don't know," the priest said flatly. "I'm trying to find that out myself. How did you happen to meet him, Mrs. Benedict?"

"It was at the old Union Station. That was in the mid-thirties, I think. A few women and myself had set up a canteen there for the C.C.C. boys.* Troops of them started out to their camps from there, and most of them were in need of a good meal. I can remember it just as plainly. I had noticed him during a lull—very thin, hungry-looking and dressed in his black suit. I motioned to him a couple of times, but when he caught me looking at him, he would turn away. To make a long story short, I finally coaxed him into eating something and drew out of him the fact that he was in a seminary preparatory school that he thought he had to run away from."

Mrs. Benedict took off her glasses and laid them on the railing. "It was obvious that he was a very disturbed young man. When I could, I called my husband and he consented to my bringing the boy home. He stayed for a week with us then. Most of it he spent in my husband's book room. Teddy was very fond of him. That little one, the hoyden†—that's Teddy's daughter."

Father Duffy looked at the children: happy, inquisitive, loud... They would run to meet their fathers and climb over them looking for presents... "My mother gave me a hammer for my tenth birthday, the only present..." The priest frowned at his recollection of the confessional... "The first birthday card I ever received in the mail..." A similar complaint.

"Do they disturb you, Father? I suspect they're showing off. They can play as well in the back." She leaned forward, about to call out.

"No, no. They don't disturb me, bless them. You should know what I'm used to: the west side of New York." He had not

* The CCC was the Civilian Conversation Corps, established in 1933 by President Franklin D. Roosevelt as part of the New Deal. It was intended to employ young men working in national parks and other public lands.

† A boisterous, rude, or ill-bred girl or woman.

intended to say that, but the picture of the tough, hard-humored kids of his parish swept before him. "You were telling me about the Brandon boy, Mrs. Benedict."

For an instant she looked at him, frankly inquisitive. When he met her eyes, hers fell away. There was an unspoken understanding between them then. "Yes," she said. "He was such a gentle boy. During those days I learned his story—or bits of it. Do you know that, Father?"

"Fragments."

She nodded. "I don't suppose I know more. Something I could never understand—his mother was very kind to him, he said, and his father cruel…but of the two, he liked the father better."

"I'm afraid that would be more accurate if you said that he disliked the father less."

"Yes, I suppose it would. Why?"

"The mother was a peculiar combination," the priest said, "inordinately affectionate toward the boy, and yet so religious she forced the idea of being a priest on him. Eventually, she entered a convent herself."

"I see."

Whether she saw or not, he could not tell, but the fact was no secret, and it suggested something of the spiritual tangle in the early pattern of the boy's life.

"Well," Mrs. Benedict proceeded, "he stopped with us in a real terror of going home. He was on his way to his father's funeral. My husband—he's gone now, which is why I live with the children—my husband with his good sense said that we shouldn't try to persuade the boy to go on. He reasoned that having stopped with us Tim might start on his way again, lose courage, and end up God only knew where. We did get him to send off a letter to his mother. And through that week we persuaded him to return to the seminary. He was very religiously disposed, Father. But I'm not sure now that wasn't a mistake."

"Do you happen to remember where he sent the letter, Mrs. Benedict?"

"I don't understand."

"From what I know, his mother didn't receive it. But I don't suppose that's important now."

"I do remember that he wouldn't let me mail it," she said. "I plainly remember offering to send it by special delivery. He was quite adamant. It never occurred to me that he might not have sent it..." her voice trailed off.

"He may have lost courage," he said.

"I suppose, but he might have been truthful about it. We were trying to help him."

How many people had tried to help Tim Brandon, the priest thought. "And then it may be that the letter itself went astray," he suggested, although he doubted it.

"That is possible, and he did go back to the seminary and make another try of it. That wasn't easy, having to explain to them that he had not gone home."

She wanted to believe the best of him. But there, too, Brandon had failed in courage. Was this failure accountable for his sense of guilt, the priest wondered. Was it sufficient to account for the belt of bramble he fashioned and wore?

"Or didn't he tell them where he had been at all?" she asked suddenly.

"It doesn't matter very much now," Father Duffy said quietly. "And when he ran away from the seminary he came back to you, didn't he?"

"Yes. That was a few months later. He said it was only a matter of time until they dismissed him."

"Did he tell you why he thought they intended to dismiss him?"

"That is a strange thing, Father. He said at first it was because he could not do the work they put him to. Then one day—oh, quite a while later—out of a clear sky he said it was because he got a birthday card from a girl."

Father Duffy looked at her. "Was it out of a clear sky?"

"Well, I wondered that myself. It was foolish, of course, the notion of their disapproving of that. For one thing, the name Teddy could be boy or girl. But what disturbed me, as you suggest, was its indication of what was going on in the boy's mind. He was seventeen or eighteen then—a late adolescent."

"How long did he stay with you?"

"Several weeks. My husband got him a part-time job at the branch library. Very little money. All this was before he made that remark about the birthday card. Teddy was in the eighth grade then, and not very good at English and composition. He helped her a good deal. He wrote very nicely—some excellent verses for a boy his age—delicate things, very much like him. I don't remember just when he said that, but after it I made a point of being nearby whenever they were together, and I watched him. You know how disturbing something like that can be to a mother. I'm certain there was nothing secret between them. I have always been very frank with my children. I have an older son, too. Tim occupied his room, in fact. He was in boarding school at the time. Well, about the time I started watching him, he took to staying out rather late at night. I thought that strange as he had no friends outside of ourselves that I knew of, except at the library. To make a long story short, Father, I was much relieved when he told me one day that he was leaving. I was very fond of the boy, please understand, but uneasy. I began to wonder if we really knew the truth about him."

"I suppose, when he came back, he again wrote a letter—this time to the seminary?"

"Yes. And again mailed it himself. I suppose that if he had not left us when he did, I should have taken it upon myself even at that late date to write the seminary about him."

"It might have been well," the priest said, thinking the words sententious as soon as he had spoken them. "I mean it's always well to know something of people you take into your home," he amended.

"Are you that careful, Father?"

She had faced him with the question and he felt the color rise to his cheeks. "No, I'm not. It was a stupid remark. Under the same circumstances I'd have done what you did."

"Tim was a good boy," she said. "I've always believed that. He may not have had much courage, but I don't think courage is the greatest of virtues. And I'm quite sure it was part of his innate decency that made him move from here. He understood my feelings—and his own, whatever they were. I know he was devoted to Teddy, and she to him. The amount of time she spent in the library after that was amazing. Then we let her go away to high school and that pretty much took care of it."

"Where did he go after he left you, Mrs. Benedict?"

"He used to come back to visit once in a while. He found a room over a shoemaker's shop where he could stay for cleaning up the shop. And he stayed on at the library for a year, perhaps. I don't know when it was that he stopped coming. There was a great scandal about then, a tragedy really. Mrs. Philips, I think her name was—the juveniles' librarian. She was beaten to death one night on her way home from the library."

Father Duffy felt a stiffening in his body, and a sort of helpless rolling in his head.

Mrs. Benedict was unaware of the effect of her words. "It was a shocking business. Her husband was arrested—a salesman. She had been seeing other men while he was on the road—young men."

The priest controlled his voice with effort. "I suppose, along with everybody else who worked in the library, Brandon was questioned?"

"I suppose he was asked some questions. The husband killed himself in jail the night of his arrest. But it probably affected the boy. The papers were full of it."

"Did you ever see him again?"

"Only once. I went around to the cobbler's shop, and he was mending shoes. The little Italian shoemaker had taken a liking to him. 'He's a good boy,' he told me. I remember his accent. 'Like my own son.' When I stopped by a month later, he was gone. He had walked out as I suppose he did from the seminary. The old man wept telling me. We never heard of Tim again."

In the afternoon Father Duffy canceled his railroad reservation and flew back to New York.

31

The house on East Eighteenth Street was not as bad as Goldsmith had expected when he got below Gramercy Park. The gray stone front was scrubbed clean and the window curtains were stiff with respectability. So was the ornate sign: MRS. MORAN'S THEATRICAL BOARDING HOUSE. It was the sort of place he imagined to have thrived before the Forty-second Street theatres converted to movies. When he rang the bell a small-voiced dog responded. It continued to bark until someone came and evidently picked it up, for he could hear mothering noises although the words were indistinguishable.

A large, handsome woman opened the door, the fuzzy dog under her arm, tail to the front.

"I'd like to speak to Mrs. Moran," Goldsmith said.

"I am Mrs. Moran." She said it in the grand manner and looked down at him graciously, for all the world as though he were a whole audience. She had been on the stage in her youth, he decided, and had retired from it to run a boarding house where she could "keep in touch." Her hair was a white mountained pompadour and her face elegantly powdered and rouged. Her pendulum earrings glittered in the morning sun.

On a sudden impulse he decided against asking her about Brandon directly. "I'm Ben Goldsmith, Mrs. Moran, homicide division of the police." He showed identification. "I'm working on the Dolly Gebhardt case. I wonder if you read about it in the papers?"

"Very little to read, I should say. Won't you come in?"

She led him through the vestibule into a large comfortable living room. There was a faded richness to it, the lace curtains and the doilies, the worn oriental rug on the floor. He could see the long mahogany table in the dining room and the circular windowed cabinet for dishes. Somewhere upstairs a soprano was warming up. Mrs. Moran set the poodle on the floor and gave his rump a shove with her hand that sent him almost to the dining room. "Run and play, Patsy. The gentleman and I wish to talk."

The dog gave a whimper of protest, shook himself, and went to the back of the house.

"Miss Gebhardt did live with you, didn't she?" Goldsmith asked.

"Yes. I think it was she." Mrs. Moran arranged her ample body in a chair and motioned him into one opposite her. "She was not Dolly then, however. Doris, and a respectable sort of person when she came. I have only respectable people in my house, Mr. Goldsmith."

The soprano chipped off a high note. "I believe you," he said, grinning.

"She does hit clinkers now and then. It's really a nice voice— when she sings, that is. She has an audition this afternoon for a new musical. So excited. Oh, my dear boy, the celebrations and the mournings I've been a party to in this house."

"You were in the theatre yourself, weren't you, Mrs. Moran?"

"How did you know?"

"Call it instinct—and the picture above the mantel." He nodded toward a well-corseted ingenue with a rich brown pompadour.

She smiled broadly. "I've changed a great deal but I've managed to keep young with young people about me." She sighed. "Though I sometimes wonder if anyone in the theatre stays young for long anymore."

"Dolly Gebhardt had a hard time doing it."

"Not as hard as some, I'm sure. She was a blonde in the days we knew her, by the way."

"That was in 1943, wasn't it?"

"Earlier. She came here before the war, I know that. The Sunday we heard about Pearl Harbor, I remember her sitting right here with us."

"Was she working then?"

"An occasional night club booking. She could have managed." Mrs. Moran insinuated her meaning into the words.

"But she didn't," Goldsmith said.

"Well, I'll say this, Mr. Goldsmith: she was no hypocrite. I'm not going to cast a stone. I'm not a fool. I've seen the scales in this business balanced by a lot of things. They say talent gets its reward. Well, I know where a lot of talent tests occur, and it's not behind footlights. I suppose it's the same in other professions. I just happen to know mine. Gebhardt wanted money. I don't know why. She wasn't greedy. She had no great notion of her ability as a dancer. I just don't know. I often said to her: 'Doris, if you had money, what would you do with it?'

"'I don't know,' she said. 'I'd like to have some fun. There's a lot of things I'd like to do. There's some people I could help...'

"'Don't sell your soul to buy peanuts for the monkeys,' I told her. That all came about because of a little fellow she was forever helping out, a nice enough boy, but scarcely worth a turn—well, you know, officer."

"I know," Goldsmith said. "Tell me something about the young man."

"Tim his name was. I can't even remember his last name. He came to the door one night and asked for her. She talked to him for a while and then she asked me to give him something to eat. 'A poet,' she said to me, 'down on his luck.' It's a very sad commentary on our world, but if there's anyone less in demand than an actor, it's a poet. Well, to make the short of it, my husband gave him a cot in the basement, and he stayed with us for quite some time—in fact, until after Gebhardt herself was gone."

"I wonder where she met him," Goldsmith said.

"I've no idea at all—except that I don't think it was in New York. But for the life of me, I can't tell you why I've got that impression."

"Maybe when he came to the house," he suggested, "when she first saw him that night..."

Mrs. Moran nodded her head emphatically. "That's it exactly. She was surprised to see him. 'What are you doing in New York?' That's precisely what she said. My, aren't you clever, Sergeant?"

"Not very," the detective said. "The first and last words are pretty handy keys. The trouble is, the last words aren't overheard very often. While they were both here, Mrs. Moran, how did they behave toward one another?"

"I'd say she tried to take care of him. He was like a friendly puppy, always looking for a hand to pet him. As a matter of fact, he rather looked for it from me after Doris left. But I have children of my own—four of them—and I was thirty-eight when the first one was born. Isn't that something?"

Goldsmith nodded that it was. "Why did Dolly leave?"

"To move uptown. She needed privacy, and, well, I needed

the room. She was getting so many calls—and no show. I didn't like it. I liked her, though. But on account of the children and all, I finally spoke to her. She had already set up the place for herself…where it happened. It was a sad day. I should have much preferred to see her take the bus back to Minnesota. How many kids go home after a try at it. Not Gebhardt. She had to beat it, one way or the other."

Mrs. Moran was growing emotional in her reminiscences. She fumbled about her breast for a handkerchief and then blew her nose. Why, Goldsmith wondered, did people think in terms of beat or be beaten. "And the little man," he prompted. "He stayed on with you?"

"For quite some time. In winter he stoked the furnace. When he wasn't busy, he'd sit down there scratching verses on wrapping paper."

"Tell me something, Mrs. Moran, did he know the occupation Dolly turned to?"

"It's funny that you should ask me that. I don't think he had any notion of it at all. But something strange: how I decided that Tim should go. I have a daughter—Sarah. She's married now but she was about fifteen then and sometimes I'd notice him looking at her. Then I found him saving her school papers from the waste basket. And if he was outdoors and she walked by, he would stop his work and look after her. Now that, you may say, can happen with any man when a pretty girl walks by, and my Sarah is pretty. But when a man who doesn't know a prostitute from a virgin starts looking at your daughter like that you do something about it."

"What did you do?"

"I sent him packing."

"It might have been a good idea to call the police."

"Why? He didn't touch her. Can you imagine what the cop

on the corner would have said if I'd told him? 'Lady, go wash your mind in a bird bath.' That's precisely what I'd have gotten."

"I guess you're right," Goldsmith admitted.

"If he'd come back, then I might have done something about it. But he went out of here with his tool kit as meek as a lamb."

"A tool kit?"

"Rolled up in sort of a canvas."

"Any idea where he came from, Mrs. Moran?"

"No more than I have where he went to. But I don't think he'd have had the strength to do a thing like—what happened to her."

Goldsmith looked at her.

"It was he you came to ask about, wasn't it?"

"Yes. I got the address from a letter to him you returned to the sender."

"From a poetry magazine. I remember it."

"I'd like to go back to when he first came here, Mrs. Moran. See if we can pin down the date."

"I've already pinned it down. It was during the first coal shortage of the war: winter of 1943."

"And you knew Dolly pretty well then—to take in someone like that on her recommendation?"

"Yes. She'd been here a couple of years. I know that summer she'd been away to some country clubs. She danced a little. But mostly, it was glamor. We kept her room for her."

"What country clubs?"

"I don't know. Upstate, I think. She got the jobs through an agent."

"Do you know his name?"

"I might if I heard it."

"Dave Albright?"

"That's the one."

"Tell me, Mrs. Moran, was Tim a religious sort?"

"He was. He was running to church every morning."

"How about Dolly? Was she a church-goer?"

"Not much. She had too much of it as a girl. Her father was the real old-fashioned revivalist. She would take a drink once in a while here—not so much. Sociability. And she would do her father getting saved on a Saturday night. 'The Lord God's bringing me down the aisle, brother. Make room on the sinners' bench. I'm in need of salvation.'" Mrs. Moran gave her own dramatic version. "Then he would go home and take his shaving strop to the children."

"Nice," Goldsmith said.

"Something happened one night that might interest you," Mrs. Moran said. "We had a nasty scene with Tim and her. She was higher than usual and the higher she got the more abusive she was of religion. She said something about what she thought of the Saturday night breast-beaters, the Sunday saints. Tim took issue with her. He started preaching about rising to fall to rise again. Gebhardt didn't care much about her language at times like that, and she said the word she had for it right out. Sarah happened to be there. Tim ordered the child to leave. Gebhardt needled him about protecting the innocent. He turned on her and slapped her across the face. She just looked up at him and smiled. 'Want the other cheek, honey? I need a lot of saving.' My husband finally took him from the room and I got her to bed. An ugly scene."

Goldsmith lit a cigarette and offered Mrs. Moran one. He lit them and studied the end of the match. "That looks like a beginning, doesn't it?"

"God help us, it does," she said. "I hadn't realized how significant it might be."

"No victims, no murderers," he said. "Got any more pretty things like that?"

"No. Another such scene and my husband would have put both of them out. They apologized in the morning, Tim most abjectly."

"I think that sounds like him, too," Goldsmith said, thinking of Father Duffy. "How did your daughter feel about him?"

"She thought he was wonderful. That was one more reason I wanted him out. Girls of that age are real suckers for poets. She was always getting him books on her library card."

Goldsmith took a notebook from his pocket and made a note. "Can you give me a description of him, Mrs. Moran?"

"I can do better than that. It's a group picture, but he came out very nicely in it. One of the boys took it one Christmas."

32

"Mr. Albright doesn't answer. Besides, we have instructions not to ring him before noon."

"This is Homicide," Goldsmith said. "Get him on the phone."

"Yes, sir. I'll keep ringing."

While he waited, the detective turned the group picture of Mrs. Moran's Christmas party over to the photography expert. He pointed to Brandon. "Can you blow him up and bring it out clear?"

"Sure. He'll come out nice and clean. Like Washington on a dollar bill—or is it Lincoln?"

"Just bring out this boy. How soon?"

"By tonight."

By tonight, Goldsmith thought, watching the lab man depart. Holden was apparently busy at his desk, but he wasn't missing a trick. Still seven years off Brandon[*] and by tonight—tomorrow morning at the latest—Holden would demand that a general alarm be put out with the picture. The papers would have it. He listened to the monotonous droning of the phone.

---

[*] Goldsmith means that the photo shows what Brandon looked like seven years earlier.

Suddenly the receiver was pushed off the hook at the other end. There was no sound at all. "Albright?" he said. He repeated the name several times.

The hotel operator came in. "Mr. Albright's taken the phone off the receiver…"

"Get him on that phone in five minutes or we'll bring him down to headquarters. Maybe that'll wake him up."

The fuzzy voice of Albright came on then. "What do you want from me?"

"I want to know what clubs you booked Dolly Gebhardt at in the summer of 1942."

"Oh, for Chris' sake."

It was some moments before Goldsmith coaxed and threatened him into coherence.

"It wasn't clubs anyway," he said at last. "I got her a hostess-entertainer job in a roadhouse—the Cabarino, a few miles this side of Albany."

"Okay. Thanks." Goldsmith sat for a few seconds, thinking about it.

"Want to put McCormick on that?" Holden said, glancing at him.

The sergeant was grateful for the suggestion. He had no time now for going back, however valuable the connection might be in tying Dolly and Brandon together. He made notes of the information he wanted. Waiting for McCormick, he called the librarian who had helped him in the first futile search for Brandon's "The Mother." He had not checked the possibility of a library card because when he was there he had not had Brandon's name.

Brandon without books was a beggar without a cup, he reasoned, and if he got a card of his own it was probably after his stay at Mrs. Moran's. That meant an address and a reference, a listed phone number. He hoped fervently that the idea was not a boomerang back to Dolly.

McCormick had come and gone, promising a preliminary report by that night, when the librarian finally called back. But the call was worth waiting for: a card had been issued to Timothy Brandon in June, 1944. His residence and reference were the same: care of Mrs. Gerald Fericci at an address on First Avenue.

33

New York had never seemed so small to Father Duffy as when he saw it from the sky—a child's model-city with squares and spheres poking upward—and never so large as when he drove through block after block of tenements on the way from the airport.

At St. Timothy's he stopped in the church for a few minutes to pray. This was home, he thought, and his place at his appointed altar of God. That he should have left it to seek someone who had already come to him there now seemed the folly of a vain man. What turns and twists the conscience took he thought. His own had urged him first to seek the man at his beginnings, and now it plagued him for not having waited where the murderer might have come again to him.

He wondered then if other priests in other parishes, perhaps in Cleveland, perhaps in New York, God knew where, had not suffered his same tortures, for there was something in the killer that made him feel righteous in his sin, arrogant in his humility. Somewhere in his warped mind, conscious of it or not, he took sadistic release in throwing the burden of his crime on the priest. Perhaps it was a vengeance for his own youth, his failures.

The first words of the Mass ran through Father Duffy's mind: "I will go unto the altar of God, to God who gives joy to my youth…" What must Brandon's thoughts be, he wondered, saying those words over and over? What a mockery he must make of them.

No. If that were so, he could not have persisted so long in his pursuit of God. It was no use trying to reason thus, the priest decided. He was judging the man, not finding him, nor helping him, and judging him by a behavior standard which was not applicable to him.

Leaving the church by the sacristy door, he met Father Gonzales. He was hurrying, about to go on a sick call and stopped only long enough to shake hands.

"Do you know if anyone was looking for me while I was gone?" Father Duffy asked, holding the door for the other priest.

"Yes. A man came by. He wouldn't give his name."

"Young? Old? What did he look like?"

"I haven't time now. Old Mrs. Pedrosa had a stroke. He was thirty-five or so. Rather slight. I'll see you tonight, Duffy…" As the door was swinging closed he turned: "He said he'd come back. I showed him the postcard you sent me."

Father Duffy murmured his thanks to God as he went to the rectory.

34

There was a hot damp smell in the hall. The one window at its end was veiled with the dust of many summers and the rough yellow walls mottled with grease and smoke. From Harlem to here, near the Bowery, this was the typical entry to a First Avenue walk-up. Goldsmith tapped on the door and waited. Downstairs a store—grocery, tavern, pawnshop, junkshop, army surplus, clothier or restaurant, and beneath that, a cellar of rats, old bottles and the debris of several bankruptcies. He knocked louder and heard a child within calling its mother. A warped laundry rack leaned against the wall beside him, several pairs of damp socks hung on it, and beneath it, a skooter with one wheel missing. The detective pounded on the door and loosened his collar. He breathed through his mouth to keep the smell from his nostrils. A moment more of waiting and he would stride to the end of the hall and get some air into it if he had to smash the window. The long patience of poverty, he thought, and the slow breeding of grudge, envy and despair— the wedding bed of want and get where crime is begotten with petty politicians and crooked cops waiting to act as midwives.

Someone was coming at last, and why should she hurry? Each

time an assignment took him into squalor, the bitterness came near to blinding him to the job. The door opened a couple of inches. A dark, thin-lipped woman looked out at him, her eyes angry.

"What do you want? You woke the baby."

"I want to talk to you, Mrs. Fericci. Sergeant Goldsmith, police department." He avoided "homicide," and added immediately, showing her Brandon's application for a library card through the door: "Do you remember this fellow?"

"No," she said, even before seeing the card.

At the back of the house the baby was screaming. Goldsmith pushed the door open a little wider. "Well, let's talk about Tim. Maybe it'll come back to you. You see, your name's on the card, too. I'll wait while you quiet the baby."

The woman gave ground before him. "My husband'll be here any minute. Please go."

"It would be better to talk to me now, Mrs. Fericci. I might have to come back when your husband is here."

She was a young woman, in her early thirties probably. Her face was a little drawn and sallow, but there was a suppleness to her body.

"Wait till I give the baby her bottle, then," she said. "I'll hurry."

"Take your time."

She started from the room, her hips quivering beneath the thin apron. At the door she turned. "If my husband comes, please don't say anything about Tim."

"All right," he said, although he wondered how else he should account for his presence.

A boy of seven or so met his mother at the door. "Go outside and play for a while," she said.

"I don't want to."

"Did you hear me?" she screamed.

Goldsmith went to the window, his back to them. He heard

the boy slam out and saw him on the street presently, kicking a bottle against a lamp post time and again until it smashed. A drunk watched him stupidly and then tried to clap him on the back. The kid yanked away from him and shouted something. The drunk drew his hand back clumsily as though to strike him. Instead, he scratched his neck. Two other youngsters joined the boy, and like so many little dogs they began to taunt the drunk, retreating when he swung clumsily on them, and charging his back as soon as he stumbled forward. Goldsmith lifted his eyes. The late sun was shining in the windows of the new housing projects, a scant few blocks away, complete with playgrounds. They were coming—a great slow tidal wave, but coming on. Stay young a while, kids, and the grass grows with you. At the back of the house, the baby was quiet now. The mother returned and the detective turned to meet her.

"What do you want to know?" she said.

"When you last saw Tim Brandon."

"Just after the war was over."

Goldsmith sat on the arm of an upholstered chair. His foot brushed the sofa. The room was overcrowded with furniture. "I wish you'd tell me how you met him."

She half-laughed. "I picked him up in the hall downstairs."

"Drunk?"

"Frozen. I was trying to get the baby buggy out. Tommy was a baby then."

"That was in 1944 maybe," Goldsmith said. "Was your husband in the army?"

"Yeah."

"I see."

"What do you mean, you see?"

"Am I jumping to conclusions? I think you asked me a minute ago not to mention him to your husband."

"That don't mean what you think. Gerald was sore because Tim wasn't in the army and he was."

"I've wondered about that myself," Goldsmith said. "Why wasn't Brandon in the army?"

"He didn't believe in killing."

Ironic, Goldsmith thought. "All right, Mrs. Fericci. You found him in the hall and brought him up here. You gave him a good meal. Then what?"

"Then nothing. I let him sleep on the sofa here that day. I went over to my mother's."

"You let a stranger sleep here? In this neighborhood you let a bum you picked up in the hall stay in your house? Come now, lady."

She went to the window and stayed there, looking down the street. "All right. Tim was no bum. You could tell that. And I was so damned lonesome when Gerald went away I thought I'd go crazy. I even hated the kid. He couldn't talk to me even, just squall at night and me almost scared to get up and look at him. I didn't know what was the matter. What did I know? Tim picked him up that first day when I let him come up and the kid stopped crying. He took to him like candy. I could've bawled. I never seen the kid smile before. After that I didn't care what people said. Let 'em live alone in hell a few months and see what they say then. He was the decentest guy I ever knew. And that goes for Gerry. He's all right but he ain't decent like Tim."

Thank God for that, Goldsmith thought.

She looked at him without turning her body. "What did he do, kill somebody?"

Goldsmith did not answer.

"You can bet your badge they deserved it if he did. He never had a chance. A good clean kid with a drunk for a father and an old lady who couldn't keep her hands off him. Then she sent him off to a monastery. A real cookie, she was."

She was watching the street again, straining for the first sight of her husband.

"Relax, Mrs. Fericci," the detective said. "If your husband comes in I'll say I'm a building inspector."

She gave an ugly laugh. "He'd drop dead. I've been trying to get somebody up here for two years. Maybe election time. Now we're training the rats. They don't care about elections."

There was no answer to that, Goldsmith thought, and he knew instantly he had no business trying to answer it, no business sitting here so maudlin at the miseries of the city. He was a cop on an assignment.

"I don't want to put you in bad with your husband," he said coldly, "but I do want every bit of information I can get on Brandon. If that means talking about him to your husband, I'll do it."

"Atta boy," she said. "Be yourself. I like it better that way. I don't like nice cops. Gerald doesn't know anything about him anyway. He thinks I was…being unfaithful with him. That's all he can understand."

"And you weren't?"

"No, I wasn't!"

The vehemence of her denial suggested to the detective that that particular circumstance was due less to her virtue than to Brandon. "Suppose you tell me where he was before he came to you."

"Tim?"

"Of course."

She shrugged. "Picking up whatever he could. That's all I know."

"Did he get any mail here?"

"He sent some poems away once. He wrote kind of nice. Real educated he was. But nobody cared. He got them back here, the poems. That's all."

"How old was he then?"

"Twenty-five maybe. I never asked him."

"Can you describe him?"

Her description was as vague as Mrs. Flaherty's and Dolly's friend's. Finally Goldsmith asked, "Do you remember any scars or birthmarks?"

"He had a funny mark, like a moth, almost purple."

"Where?"

The color rose to her face. "Here." She indicated the upper part of her hip. "He got a cold in his back. I rubbed it with Vicks."

"I see."

"What do you see?"

"That you were very kind to him. You were a mother to him."

"No-o," she said doubtfully, as though she weren't sure whether that was good or bad.

"Okay. A sister."

"Maybe."

"When did he leave here, Mrs. Fericci?"

"Gerry kicked him out his last leave home." She caught at the curtain. "There's Gerry getting out of the bus." She turned on him wildly. "Will you get out of here? I told you everything, honest I did. If Tim did something wrong, I don't want him to know about it. I'd never hear the end of it."

"I haven't said he did anything wrong, Mrs. Fericci."

"Then what are you here for? I never seen a cop come on anything good yet. What do you want from me? Five bucks, that's all I got..."

"I don't want your five bucks—or one buck or twenty bucks. And I'm not selling tickets." He got to his feet. "You were pretty gone on him, weren't you?"

"So what, for Christsake! He was clean. Do you know what it's like to meet a guy like that?"

"Sure. Did you look for him?"

"So what?"

"And you found him, didn't you?"

"Yes. I found him with her, the redhead, and if he killed her I'm glad. I wish I'd done it. She was no good. I tried to tell him. He wouldn't believe it. He wouldn't think bad of the devil in hell. Will you get out of here?"

Goldsmith brushed off her hands where she tried to push him. "But he wouldn't come back to you?"

"No."

He moved toward the door. "Where was he living? It wasn't with her."

"I don't know. I took his tool kit to him—a shop across town. I forget where. In the thirties. The Fixit it was called."

They could hear the heavy footfalls on the stairs.

"Tell your husband about it, Mrs. Fericci, just in case I have to come back." He opened the door as Fericci reached the hall. He bade him time of day and kept on going.

"Who the hell was that?" he heard the man say.

"They sent somebody to look at that rat hole, Gerry."

The door banged closed. And, Goldsmith thought, it was neither the first nor the last rat hole he would see in his business.

35

Katie was washing the supper dishes. She had been washing them for a long time, humming to herself at the chore, and holding each plate up for a special inspection. It was not the plate she was inspecting, her mother thought. It was her own face in it. Scarcely aware of what she wrote, Mrs. Galli added "soap" to her shopping list. The girl was filling out. And it was time. At Katerina's age she had already filled out. In America it was different, she told herself. Girls took their time. And here it was not such a disgrace not to be married altogether. Still, she preferred for her daughter to be in love. It was more natural. And there was no mistaking the signs…slow-motion, dreamy, blushing, taking a job…

"So," she said. "You've got a boyfriend."

Katie glanced at her over her shoulder. She smiled and shrugged, and then blushed, all without a word.

"It's nothing to blush about to your mother. Did I ever say you shouldn't?"

"No, Mama."

"I thought you were going to be an old maid. Some mothers have to worry their daughters go out too much. Mine, she never goes out. Then a boy or two comes to the house. Once, twice, three times altogether. Maybe Tom, I thought. He's all right. Noisy, but all right. Katerina don't talk much anyway."

"Oh, Mama. Stop teasing."

"Then that one Willy Doheny. That time I was worried. Irish. Irish and Italian. They don't mix good. Or maybe too good—like gasoline and matches. Still, I think it's better than oil and water. But Willy went and Deo gratia. Now tell your mother who it is."

"Who said it's anyone special?"

"I said it's somebody special. I know my little girl. Maybe you'll bring him around some evening? On a Saturday night you'll ask him. I'll get Johnny to bring a cake and his accordion and we'll ask…"

"Please, Mama. Not yet."

"Not yet but sometime. Ha! There is someone special. I knew. Is he bashful like you?"

Katie tossed her head. "Mama, I get paid tomorrow."

"You don't get paid enough to change the subject. When all of a sudden you got a job, I should've known. You're not lazy, but when you don't want to go to school, that's different. You're wasting soap."

"The bubbles are pretty. I've got a thousand faces."

"They don't taste pretty. Don't leave them on the cups." She got up and put away the pad and pencil. "I can remember the first time I was in love. Like yesterday."

"With papa?"

"No. But I didn't meet your papa yet."

"When you did meet him, Mama, were you in love with him right away?"

"He needed such a haircut. Maybe it was the next time I fell in love with him."

"And you knew then it was forever and ever, didn't you?"

"Yes, I knew." Mrs. Galli picked up a cup and turned it around and around in her hand. "Sometimes, when I like somebody I see your papa all over again after all these years."

"You've been terribly lonesome, haven't you, Mama?"

She put the cup back into the basin. "With not so much soap you would see the dirt. Lots of people are lonesome. Look at old Mrs. Gasperi. Two canaries. She talks to them like grandchildren. I heard her once. 'Eat your dinner, Tami. You won't grow big and strong if you don't.' Who ever heard of a canary growing big and strong?"

"Silly," Katie said.

"It's not silly if all you got left in the world is a canary. Give me the dish towel. Run upstairs and ask Tim if he would like a cup of coffee."

"I didn't know he was home."

"An hour ago I heard him. Back and forth again up there."

"He didn't even come down to supper. I'll go see."

"He don't eat enough for Mrs. Gasperi's canaries."

Katie was already at the door wiping her hands on her apron. She paused. "Mama, maybe it isn't fair to charge him as much as the others when he doesn't eat."

"You do the arithmetic for the big employer who pays you fifteen dollars a week for it. I'll do mine."

"All right, Mama."

She went up the stairs slowly, thinking about it. For the last couple of days Tim had seemed dejected again. He was proud, she thought. You couldn't just tell a man you were going to make money for him. Especially someone like Tim, no matter how right you tried to make it look. And it wasn't as though she were making enough anyway. With each step up the stairs, she was more convinced that she had spoiled things instead of helping them. Her boldness had shocked him, frightened him. A sudden shame in what she was doing overcame her. She could feel its telltale color in her face. She remembered other girls buying things for boys. She remembered a girl giving her brother Johnny a penknife, and him kidding about it with his friends. "She's gonna stick it in you, Johnny. She'll cut you up in little pieces with it." "The hell she will," and he had made her take back the knife and he didn't go to see her anymore. No, no, Katie thought. I'm not like that. This is different.

She went into her own room first and closed the door. But am I different? she asked the mirror. I want Tim for myself. She wanted Johnny. She wanted him to take her out, to buy things for her. I want to take care of Tim, and do things for him. If that's shameful, I should be ashamed. But it's not. He's good and decent. So am I. Or I try to be, anyway. She had almost convinced herself when she forced another question into the open: why didn't she admit the truth to her mother? Why didn't she say his name when her mother asked? Fear that because Tim was older she would object? Or because he had no money? Both of them were good reasons…but there was something else, something deeper that was more of a feeling than a reason—an instinctive dread of the issue. She tried to imagine Tim saying the things he said to her in front of her mother—to imagine him saying: "Katie is the beauty in my life, the flowers. I owe her whatever's good in my work." She conjured no picture at all. She could not even see Tim. He was afraid of her mother.

"But I'm not. I'm not afraid of anything," she said aloud and went out of her room.

She leaned down to see if there were a light beneath his door. The room was dark. "Tim," she called, knocking softly. Getting no answer, she opened the door a bit. The hall light fanned across the floor about her shadow. "Tim, are you here?"

There was a curious hollow sound to her voice, and even

in the fan of light she could see that his tool kit was gone from its usual place beneath the bed. She swung the door full open. His clothes were gone, the hangers stark in the empty corner.

"Oh Tim," she whispered, groping for the cord to the lamp. In its first light she saw the pin-neat emptiness—except for his books. He had stacked them on the dresser, and between the cover and the fly leaf of the volume of Francis Thompson was a single sheet of paper on which he had written four words: "Katie dear, for you."

That was all. No signature, no explanation. But that he was gone there was no doubt at all. Her own choked breathing was the only sound in the room. Why? Where? The questions whipped through her mind, uncalculated. There was only a knot of pain that would not be swallowed or dissolved.

"Katerina! What are you doing up there?"

She could only stand by the dresser dumbly, trying to rid herself of the choking lump.

"Come down. Do you hear me? Let Tim be if he wants to."

She went from the room slowly, carrying the books. Her mother was halfway up the stairs. "Why don't you answer me? You aren't so independent you don't answer your mother."

"He's gone," Katie said flatly.

"All right. But answer me when I speak to you. Did you take those books out of his room?"

"He left them for me, Mama. He's gone—left. Don't you understand?"

"He's moved out?" She started for the door to see for herself.

"Yes. His clothes, everything. Mama, did you nag him for his rent? Did you?" The tears had come, dissolving the lump.

"Don't speak to me in that voice." She looked from one corner of the room to the other. "Spit and polished." She gave a humorless laugh. "The little canary, the little half-a-man..."

"You drove him out, didn't you, Mama? You've got to have real men at your table, don't you? With hair all over them, coughing and belching and pinching your bottom. Yes! I've seen it. I'm not blind…"

"Shut up, Katerina."

"I won't shut up. You drove the only decent thing in this house since papa out of it. Just for a few lousy dollars."

Mrs. Galli stood with her hand on her hips and stared at her daughter.

"Oh my God! It was him! I thought maybe you like books with him. Once I thought…but I couldn't believe it. Look, Katerina. He's not for you. It's not right. He'll come back. I know as well as I'm your mother he'll come back. But you must get him out of your mind, little girl. He's no good for you."

"He is good. He's a saint."

"Then get yourself a sinner, Katerina. What do we know of him? A tramp who comes to the door for something to eat. 'Let me have a room,' he says. 'I'll pay you,' he says. He doesn't pay me fifty dollars in a whole year. When he makes money he gives it away. He even gave away the pipe when he fixed the plumbing downstairs. Pipe I was going to sell."

"You reminded him of that, didn't you, Mama? What do you know about the rest of them upstairs?"

"They pay their rent. That's all. And they don't look at you. I'm only trying to take care of you, Katerina. You don't know about these things. Can't you see?"

Katie's eyes met hers boldly, evenly, and then fell away. She went to her room and closed the door. Mrs. Galli went to the room where Tim had stayed. She flung the window up, and then turned off the light. Going downstairs she got the vacancy sign and hung it in the front window.

36

The Fixit shop was in the cellar of a West Thirty-third Street tenement. One thing sure, Goldsmith thought, Brandon wasn't getting up in the world. A bell tinkled on the door as he shoved it open, and he got the smell of cabbage and old clothes so strongly that it was like a warm spray in his face. The Fixit was a junkshop where the owner bought rubbish by the wagonload, sorted it on the floor of his living room in the back and found a use for every tack and string of it.

Goldsmith looked about while he waited. No need for Mr. Fixit to be in a hurry. There was nothing worth stealing, and no one wearing a suit of clothes like his was there for anything profitable to Mr. Fixit. There was a window between the store and the living quarters somewhere in the blankets, coats and horse collars, and Fixit was taking his measure. Insurance, he was probably thinking, or selling vest-pocket comptometers that counted everything but cockroaches.

Finally Goldsmith walked toward the rear. As he expected, Fixit met him squarely in the doorway. A whiskered man, he was bent almost in two from the practice of his trade. He had to cock his head, birdlike, to see his visitor's face.

"Your service isn't much good," the detective said.

"I don't sell service. What is it you want?"

Goldsmith showed him Brandon's picture. "Ever see him?"

The man fumbled for the glasses which hung from a string about his neck.

"Better take it to the light," Goldsmith suggested.

The Fixit man cocked his head. "What you miss in the daylight, I see in the dark."

Goldsmith smiled and waited. A tawny cat was washing itself on the table in the back room, surrounded by the supper dishes.

"Yes, I seen him. What about it?"

"When did you last see him?"

"Months ago—what is time?"

"In this case, quite a lot. I'm looking for him."

"Police?"

"That's right." He drew out his identification.

The man brushed it aside. "If you find him, I wish you'd find my horse at the same time. He took it out one day and came back later and said he'd lost it. I ask you, how can a man lose a horse in New York?"

"Are there such things as horse-pounds?"

"All I know, some peddler maybe got himself an animal just like that." He snapped his fingers. "Do you know how long I have to work to make the price of a horse?" He took an old raincoat from a rack. "For this I'll get two dollars, lucky maybe, and if I don't die before I sell it and if it don't rot before it gets bought. For this twenty-five cents." He picked up one rubber.

"You don't have to wait for a one-legged man to come along, do you?"

Fixit threw the two items on a packing box that served as a counter. "I have to wait for another rubber. How is it people always lose their right rubbers? Six right-footed rubbers I got."

"How did you happen to trust Brandon with the horse?"

"He knew where he could get me a load of lead pipe for nothing."

"Where?"

The old man shrugged. "That wasn't any of my business. I know he could walk it. When he lost the horse, he carried it himself. Three trips a day, two days. He said the pipe would make up for the horse. He was right. It had asthma bad. On its last legs. But I thought about the people in this world dragging around on their last legs. Why should horses die easy?"

Until then he had not smiled at all. But he seemed to feel that in this he had made a joke. His stooped shoulders quivered with laughter and his lips parted over crooked yellow teeth. He poked Goldsmith with his glasses.

"When he brought me the pipe and I got it weighed up I let him alone on the horse. Maybe he'll tell me, I thought. I got the idea, see, he just walked it over to the humane society and delivered it. All I wanted was the price of the hide. I'm entitled, ain't I? Oats, hay…"

Fresh air and water, Goldsmith thought. "Where did you pick up Brandon?"

"He came around, offered to do odd jobs. I had to give him something to put on his back—and in his stomach. Lord, God, he was a misery on two feet."

"All right," Goldsmith said. "Try and tell me the last time you saw him. Winter? Summer? Christmastime…spring house-cleaning, moving days…"

"Wait, wait, wait…"

The old man pushed by him and went to a rolltop desk in the corner of the shop. He lit an overhead lamp and adjusted his glasses. He glanced at the detective. "He was very handy fixing things. He put in this light for me. Did all the lights in the place."

He motioned toward the front of the shop. "There's some magazines up there. This is going to take a few minutes."

"I'm all right," Goldsmith said. He watched the man unlock one drawer and take a tin box from it. He unlocked that and drew out some papers. His tongue worked all around his mouth while he searched through them.

"I got it," he said at last. "Spring, 1949, he was still here, but not long after. He got himself a job for his room down a way's..."

"How far down a way's?"

"So far he could walk it in a half-hour. I remember him asking the time. Had to be there by three o'clock. He started two-thirty. You can see I forgave him the horse."

"I can see," Goldsmith said. A half-hour's walk downtown from here just over a year ago. "Thanks very much." As he reached the door he called back, "You're sure of that date?"

The Fixit proprietor nodded and showed his teeth in a smile. "I took a loss on the horse on my income tax."

37

At nine-thirty that night Father Duffy was in his room. He had brought the week's accumulation of newspapers up from the rectory basement and gone through them page by page. There was something terrifying in the fact that not one mention of the Gebhardt case appeared. Once more he experienced the sensation of unreality about the whole thing. Now in his own room with the grind and wheeze of the city beneath his window, the trip seemed a part of the dream from which he could not quite awaken. There was even a dizziness in his head as he straightened up at the sound of Father Gonzales' step outside his room. He half expected to spiral out of sleep and dress for a sick call.

The knock on his door sounded reality for him. "Come in."

"The man I told you about this afternoon is downstairs. Will you come down?"

"Will you bring him up? Give me a couple of minutes and then bring him up, please?"

"Up here?"

Father Duffy nodded, his heart pounding.

"Whatever you say."

In the instant Gonzales left him, he doubted the wisdom

of that decision. He had never felt so completely alone in his life. Once more he reminded himself of his duty to the man who came to seek his help. But over and beyond that, he was determined that Brandon this time should go with him to the police, or at least to some institution where attention would be paid him. That would be his key. The man wanted attention. He should have it. In the moment before his visitor's arrival the priest got out the ledge he had removed from the confessional box. He laid it in plain view on the bed. If need be, he would confront the man with the fact that his prints were on it. He arranged two chairs where they would sit opposite each other, the table between them.

"Your visitor, Father Duffy." Gonzales opened the door.

Father Duffy hesitated only a moment, seeing Goldsmith. "Sit down, please," he said mechanically. He sat down himself, stiffly erect, and waited. He had been living in a nightmare after all. This was normal, a stranger calling on him to talk of a mixed marriage, to take instruction, to enlist him in a citizen's committee, a veteran's committee...a complete stranger.

The detective sensed the situation instantly, glimpsing the newspapers and the oblong piece of dark wood. Although he had not quite planned it to this detail, he had intended to surprise Father Duffy, purposely withholding his identity from the other priest. Seeing the pale, sweating face opposite him, its muscles working in spite of great effort at control, he cursed himself and his job for its sometime cruelty to the innocent as well as the guilty. His greatest kindness now would be to ignore the priest's confusion.

"I've come to you for help, Father. Or maybe it's the other way around." He did not look at the priest after that. He spoke quietly, identifying himself and his job. "Sometimes I get an assignment because I like people. I give them a break if I can.

I'm careful and I can be trusted. So much for me. The reason I've come to you—I've got a notion we're looking for the same man. In fact, I'm downright positive of it—not through any indiscretion on your part...pure coincidence that I found out. I was trying to study the man. I came on a poem he wrote." Goldsmith shifted his position. "Came on isn't the right words. I spent three days looking for it."

He took the *Young Poet* from his pocket and opened it to "The Mother." He slid it along the table to the priest. Seeing an ashtray, he lit a cigarette while he waited. "He doesn't seem to think much of mothers," he said when Father Duffy returned the magazine.

"Not much." The priest accepted a cigarette.

"It struck me, reading it and talking to Mrs. Flaherty, that he could have been writing about someone in her neighborhood. I was fishing her for that when I pulled you in—quite by accident. By the way, she has the notion you're out to clean up the town's prostitutes."

"What?"

"She thinks there's no limits to the power you have."

"There'll be a very short limit if that gets to the Monsignor."

"I wasn't sure I'd be doing you a favor in suggesting to her that you were interested in only one prostitute. So I kept still." He saw the trace of a smile at the corners of Father Duffy's mouth, and knew then that his first estimate of the man was right. Under other circumstances, he was a regular—a right guy.

"I got to thinking about it, reading that poem, Father, and I thought maybe Brandon would come in of his own accord, if, say, a priest were to tell him something decent about his own mother—something that might change his notion about women. She's in a convent herself now, I think." He spoke easily, repeating information picked up for him first by the sheriff at

Marion City and then by the Chicago police following in Father Duffy's wake. "From all the other things I've found out about him, it seems to me that information should make him very happy. And Father…" He waited then for the priest's eyes to meet his. "It's very important to keep that man happy until we can bring him in."

"I see," Father Duffy said. The initial shock of seeing Goldsmith was spent now. It was foolish for him to have thought that he was acting in secret. For all that he fervently intended secrecy, he could not deny the comfort he took from this sure, easy man across the table.

"I don't say he intends to do murder again," the detective continued. "I'm pretty sure he didn't intend to then."

"Then?"

"Dolly Gebhardt," Goldsmith said without looking up, although he noted the question. "He used the hammer there first to try and force open a window. But whatever his intentions, I think he reaches certain points of crisis where murder or suicide is the only way he can find past them. Maybe he intends to get caught for murder, to give himself up and get the chair for it. I've known cases like that. And then, of course, I could be wrong altogether. He could be taking things into his own hands— righting the world. It could be some of both." He glanced at the priest to watch the effect of his next words: "He may have gone through this whole business before—even murder."

There was only a little quiver of the muscles about the priest's mouth. Goldsmith flicked the ash from his cigarette. "Whenever I get talking like this at headquarters they tell me to bring him in. Let the psychiatrists figure the angles like that. They're right. I'm just a cop. Would you like to hear the story as far as I have it?"

The priest nodded and Goldsmith recapitulated his

day-by-day pursuit of Tim Brandon. "You see, Father," he con-
cluded, "there's always been someone taking care of him. Some
women must want to be mothers awfully bad—or else he's got
charm of a kind I've never heard about. The chances are somebody's taking real good care of him right now. To be on the safe
side, I want to protect that person. That's one reason you don't
have this all over the papers."

He laid out his map of Manhattan on the table and traced
Brandon's movements as he knew them. Coming to the Fixit
address, he said: "That's as far as I go, Father. A year and a half
ago he was a half-hour's walk downtown from there. I have
people looking for his card number through every book of
poetry in every branch library in town. If he's done any reading lately, that might bring us home. Any little thing might
bring us home."

He folded the map and returned it to his pocket. He took out
a copy of Brandon's picture. "Here he is seven years ago. I don't
think he's changed much. You can have that. There'll probably
be a couple of thousand of them out in the morning. But only
for the police force. He's kind of shy, our nature boy. I don't want
to frighten him."

The priest picked up the picture. There was no doubt at all
now. Those were the wistful eyes that he would not forget ever.
The detective's voice droned on, a little hoarse now from so
much talking. He had had to carry all of it, and Father Duffy
thought that, for his own part, he had been trying to hide
Brandon in a glass house.

"...He's a religious sort," Goldsmith continued. "As a poet he
probably fancies himself another Francis Thompson. He might
even like to sit on the church steps scratching verses on sugar

bags—like Thompson.* There can't be so many churches a half-hour's distance from that shop."

"Not so many," the priest said.

Goldsmith picked up his hat. He motioned toward the bed. "I've collected pieces of wood like that myself—window sills, shelves...they're not much good if a lot of people handle them."

The priest stood up. "Am I being followed, Sergeant?"

"No. For a while you were being inquired after, let's say. Now maybe we're going to cross paths now and then, but I wouldn't call that following. I'd say we were traveling together. I tell you, Father, I like to get my man like any other cop—but I'd just as soon he'd come to me."

Father Duffy went downstairs with the detective and out into the street for a moment. Goldsmith extended his hand.

"Good luck and God be with you," the priest said.

"Thanks. You know, Father, looking for a murderer is a very lonesome business, even in a crowd. There's always the chance you're going to be the one to find him. Be careful."

---

* Before being "discovered" in 1888, Thompson spent several years living on the streets of London, addicted to laudanum. During this period, according to his biographer John Thomson, he sent his poetry to publishers on scraps of paper he found on the streets. *Francis Thompson the Preston-Born Poet*, 2nd ed. (London: Simpkin Marshall Hamilton Kent, 1913), 33. First published in 1912.

38

Goldsmith drove back to headquarters and sat a few moments in the car. He was beginning to feel the strain. Every effort he made to seem calm, easy and sure of himself drew the knot of his own nerves tighter. He rubbed the back of his neck to ease the aching tension there.

So many more things needed tying up. He had to have a report ready for Holden in the morning from which a directive might be drawn up to put out with the picture. He wanted to know what Father Duffy had learned beyond Chicago, the last report he had on the priest's movements. There was something in his attitude that had suggested some other pattern of violence in Brandon's background. That could wait, if necessary, until the complaint was prepared for the district attorney. Still, it was information that might precipitate a confession. Also, he would like to pace the distance from the Fixit himself. But time had run out on him.

He bought a carton of black coffee and took it into the station with him. McCormick was waiting.

"Maybe you don't sleep, Goldie. I like a few hours every night. It feels good."

"Sorry, Mac."

"I thought you'd like to know Brandon worked for the Cabarino while she was up there. Handyman."

Goldsmith nodded. "I'm not surprised. Get a cup if you want some of this."

McCormick didn't move. "Maybe this'll surprise you, then. There was a murder up there in his time he was never even questioned on: a girl about nineteen with lots of money, and she'd been around the Cabarino a lot."

"Why wasn't he questioned?"

"Let me tell it the way I got it. There's a girls' school a few miles from the place, a boarding school that takes day students, too…"

"Convent?"

McCormick nodded that it was. "The kids used to beat it away from the school whenever they got a car and they'd head for the Cabarino. All this got the soft pedal, of course. Anyway, it was a hangout of theirs. They were really living. Breaking loose. You know that kind of story from history. Brandon gave them holy hell one day. That's the only connection he has with the story at all.

"And Gebhardt tried to get them to go easy on the liquor. Had a fight with the management over it. Maybe that's how Gebhardt and him got together. Gebhardt quit the place in the fall.

"There was one girl that was the ringleader, the rich one with the car. She was going home one night after one of these escapades. Nobody saw her after she drove her friends back to the school. But about midnight a state trooper cruised past her car and stopped. He found her in the ditch, beaten to death. It was in the papers. But not much. The Cabarino never really figured in it at all. She didn't have her pocketbook and it looked like robbery. The car had a flat tire. Somebody started to fix it, and she was beaten with one of the tools. It was right there. No prints. Gloves probably. Her purse was found on the road near the school a couple of days later. The money was gone. My guess is she lost the purse when her friends got out of the car. Whoever found it took the money and left the purse there. In other words, whoever investigated put two and two together and made it fit where it didn't belong. That's it, Goldie, for what it's worth to you."

"When did it happen?"

"November 20, 1942."

"And that winter Brandon showed up in New York looking for Dolly Gebhardt. It figures, Mac. Maybe we won't prove it, but I'll bet the guy who couldn't stand to see a horse suffer could beat the pulp out of anyone who led the lambs away from the fold."

39

The shortest rookie cop in the station got the leg assignment—a night of marking the distance he could walk at varying clips southward from the *Fixit* in a half-hour. After three trips to the identical spot, he angled his direction by an east-west block, and repeated the pacing. By four in the morning, he was footsore and disgruntled. He was even growing confused about the pace he intended.

In the first damp mists of dawn, he tramped through Abingdon Square,* and saw the vagrants turn over on their benches and clutch the newspapers beneath their coats closer to them against the chill. A gust of wind picked up the dust and debris and swept it into his face as he walked. His eyes stung from it. He resented his job and envied the tramps their hard peace. To do his job, however, he clung to the pace he had set. But to vent his wrath, he drew his nightstick up and whacked the feet of the sleeping men as he passed.

Among those he roused, cursing and hawking the night's dust from their throats, was one who sat up quietly and rubbed the back of his head where it had grown numb after a night on a canvas tool kit.

---

* Abingdon Square Park dates to 1831 and is bounded by Eighth Avenue, Bank Street, Hudson Street, and West Twelfth Street in Greenwich Village.

40

At five o'clock that morning, the alarm clock on Katie Galli's window sill sounded. She had set it there that its ring might not carry through the house. It had no more than tinkled when she caught it and turned it off. She lay very still in the bed for a few moments listening for other sounds in the house. Sleep was heavy upon her, having come only a couple of hours before. She sat up, still listening and then satisfied that the alarm had awakened only her, she dressed in the semi-darkness. She went out the back door so that she would not pass beneath her mother's window. On the steps she put on her shoes and tied her shawl about her neck.

She went to the church first in hope that Tim might have gone to the early Mass. Only a dozen worshipers knelt beneath the one lowly lighted chandelier, all women, most of them in shawls, praying everlasting rest for some dearly beloved soul, and going forth themselves then with courage to face a day in which there was little rest for them. Katie remained through the Offertory,* offering the prayer that she might find Tim. A blue, green and purple light began to

---

* The portion of the Catholic mass in which the bread and the wine are offered to the congregation.

flow from the stained-glass windows as the sun edged near its rising.

Leaving the church, she watched the people who were familiar to the streets at that hour—workmen with their lunch buckets, a milkman, a janitor, a couple of drunken sailors, old men with gunny sacks slung over their shoulders, and women with shopping bags, these last hurrying toward the Eighth Avenue markets to pick up the freshest of the spoilage in vegetables and fruit.

She began to walk among them, block after block, peering into hallways and cluttered vacant spaces. The name Tim was often on her lips, whispered at moments of fear or hope. She looked for him as she might have sought a stray dog, coaxing gently at the rim of darknesses in which he might have taken refuge. At Mulberry Square she moved from bench to bench quickly. A grimy little man looked up brightly as she was abreast of him. He grinned toothlessly. "Looking for me, honey?"

She wove through the crazy patchwork of the Village streets and came then to Abingdon Square, not so very far from home. Even at the gate she recognized him, his knees drawn up beneath his chin, for all the world the shape of a small boy lost. At the sound of his name he unfolded and sprang to his feet. They met halfway across the park and clung to one another. A couple of tramps grunted as they watched the scene.

"Why did you go, Tim, why, why?" She led him by the hand to the nearest seat.

"I was going to watch for you going to work, Katie," he said. "And I was going to watch for you to come home."

"I was so lost, Tim. I need you terribly. Why did you go?"

His face was gray with the stubble of beard and there were deep hollows beneath his eyes. But the eyes were suddenly bright, burning bright.

"Say that again, Katie. Please?"

"What?"

"What you just said…about…" He faltered on the word. His fingers were like cold straps tightening and loosening about her hands.

"Needing you?" she prompted. He nodded gratefully.

"I need you more than anything in the world, Tim, more than home or job or mother. Sometimes when I think about it, it seems like I need you almost more than I do God."

The tears came to his eyes then, and he looked away quickly, knowing how it disturbed her. The men she knew didn't cry, and he wanted desperately to be strong before her.

She drew her hands away from him gently and got up. "I'm going to get a drink," she said.

He watched her to the fountain. The shape of loveliness and grace and even holiness, he thought. He brushed the tears on his sleeve and waited. He saw her need then. She did need him, someone who revered the pure beauty of her, and who would guard it against the filth of the world and the flesh. He was smiling in happy excitement when she returned. Drawing her down beside him on the bench, he folded his hand into hers.

"Nobody ever said that to me before, Katie. Until this moment I was never needed in the world."

"You were needed, Tim. You just didn't know it. Everybody's needed sometime."

"Perhaps," he said, trying to believe her.

"I can think of times mama needed me. And once when papa was sick he said he would have died if I hadn't been there beside him. You can think of times like that if you try."

He permitted his mind to obey her suggestion for an instant. "No," he said harshly. "I only used to think God needed me."

"He does," she said gently.

"Don't say that, Katie."

"I won't say it if you don't want me to, Tim. But I believe it. I believe He needs every good person in the world, and the bad ones need the good ones. That means everybody is needed."

He laughed then, a childish, gleeful laugh. And because it was good to see him laugh, Katie joined him. The two tramps glanced at one another. "Nuts," one of them muttered. "Goddam," the other one said. "On an empty stomach, too."

"What time is it?" Katie asked suddenly.

"A little after six. I heard the church bell…"

"Tim, we've got to talk serious. You've got to go home now. Listen to me, Tim. Mama expects you. She thinks you'll come back…"

"I don't want to go back, Katie. You don't understand…"

"I do. I know mama better than you think. She's either bullying you or smothering you. That's her way, Tim. All my life, I haven't known which one to expect. Johnny's that way, too. I mean he feels that way about mama. You've got to make allowances for her, Tim. She's lonesome, too. She was a young woman when papa died. Johnny and I didn't think so before. But I see it now. Look. I used to think thirty-four was awfully old. I don't now. Tim, sometimes I feel as old as you are."

"And sometimes I feel as young as you, dear Katie." He brushed the ends of her hair with the back of his hand.

"We've got to be practical, Tim."

"Yes," he sighed. "Why is it that we've always got to be practical? Do we want so much? A horse, a dog, a deer in the woods… I don't want any more than they do, Katie. I don't care about eating. A big meal makes me sick to my stomach. I don't want a heavy coat. I'd fall asleep in it. I just want to see the stars at night. I'd even like to go barefooted so I could feel the good warm soil.

Have you ever smelled the ground when it's just been turned over, Katie?"

"In a flower box I did. Mama transplanted a geranium once. I like the smell of geraniums."

"You've never smelled clover, have you? Or buttercups or even dandelions. You've never seen the worms wriggle deep when you've turned them out with the spade. I'll bet you've never seen a frog or a grasshopper, you've never seen the trail of baby pheasants after their mother, you've never seen a robin's egg or a lightning-bug. Have you ever seen an anthill?"

"We've got red ants in the basement."

He leaned back on the bench. "Oh, Katie. I loathe and despise the city. Every time I sit on a park bench I feel like I'm chained to it. My feet are stuck in the cement. Every time I go into a room I feel like there's bars on the windows and a padlock on the door. This time I was sure I was going to get away from it."

"Why didn't you go?" she asked, fearful of the answer and yet needing to know it.

He looked at her reproachfully. "You know why. I had to wait for one more sight of you this morning. Then I'd have had to wait until tonight. Your mother was right…" His words were bitter. "I'd have come back. I'm a coward and a fool and there's something wrong with me far beyond either one."

"Don't say that, Tim."

"It's the truth. I know it all the time, only I don't always understand it. What's in your own mind seems natural to you. Right. You say there's something terribly wrong, but when it's wrong with you, you don't really believe it's wrong. It's wrong for somebody else maybe, but right for you."

"Tim, we must go home. Mama will be getting up at a quarter to seven. She doesn't even know I'm out. I'd rather she didn't. Not right now."

"Good intentions aren't enough," he said not hearing her. "Maybe they're good enough for a person himself, but when he lives with another person they aren't enough at all. You've got to know yourself."

"Come on, Tim. I'll go as far as the back door with you. Then you'll go up to your room just the same as if you never went away. I'll go to church…"

"Know yourself. Know thyself…"

He got up and followed her through the square, turning over in his mind new hope, new resolution, new faith.

"We'll figure something out, Tim," she was saying. "But just now don't mention to mama I was looking for you. Just let her think you came back. We won't always have to stay in the city. But we need a little time right now. Just try and see that. I'd love the country. Don't you think I would, Tim? I'd like the flowers…"

"You are the flowers," he said then.

As Tim and Katie passed through the gate of the square, the two tramps got up and stretched, their eyes the eyes of scavengers. After a moment's wary subterfuge, they both sprinted for the bench on which Tim had spent the night. The more nimble of them got the tool kit.

41

Goldsmith showered and shaved at headquarters. He had spent the night there, catching a couple of hours sleep toward daybreak. When Holden arrived he was waiting for him, the map spread out.

The lieutenant looked at the shaded area. "He's in there, huh? Village poet. I thought those days were gone forever."

"I'm pretty sure of it, chief." He pointed to a mark on the map. "That's a branch library. He was borrowing books there a couple of months ago."

"There's a lot of city in there, Goldie. And he's committed murder since. And he did that outside your magic circle." He pointed to Gebhardt's apartment.

"I know. And probably confessed it to a priest on Ninth Avenue."

"On his way home, no doubt."

"I shouldn't be at all surprised."

"What else, Goldie?"

"I'd like you to read these two complaints, one McCormick dug up, and one I've sketched together this morning out of a couple of calls from Cleveland. They aren't full and documented by a long ways. But they're clear murder on the books."

Holden read the papers. "Can you pin these on him?"

"Maybe if he cooperates. But they tell his story, chief. He was saving souls by getting them out of the world."

"And Gebhardt? She came off pretty well in this upstate affair." He motioned to McCormick's paper.

"That was before she fell from virtue—in Brandon's eyes. But in the end the pattern fits her, too. Some time in there he got wise to her profession. Remember the hotel clerk's story—the young men she brought home with her now and then?"

Holden nodded.

"They're the ones Brandon was protecting. And that fine gentleman, Mr. Winters: on the phone that night she asked him how old he was. I think that was for Brandon's benefit. And when the old boy got playful with that 'over twenty-one' routine, I'm pretty sure he delivered Dolly to her death."

The lieutenant studied Goldsmith's face a moment. The sergeant was sure of himself and his way to the man he was after. His every faculty was keyed to it. "How do you want to do it, Goldie?"

"I'd like a few precinct men alerted, chief. Ready to move. But I'd like to go through there alone today."

"Why? Why take the chance?"

"Because he may have another sinner on his list. If he gets the idea we're closing in on him, he might want to take care of her while he has the chance."

Holden walked to the window and back before giving his answer.

"Don't move alone, Goldie. And check with us every hour. If you corner him, get help to bring him in."

Goldsmith grinned. "Don't worry. I'm no hero."

42

Mrs. Galli was getting breakfast when Katie returned from church. The girl set the table without speaking. Now and then her mother glanced at her. This was not like her daughter, she thought, this coldness and silence. She could think of no words to break it.

"You were at Mass?" she said finally.

"Yes, Mama. Six-thirty."

"So now you are praying for the special intention?"

"I often go to Mass in the morning."

"I'm not saying you don't. It's easier going to church than making the breakfast."

"How many times have I offered to make breakfast, Mama?"

"Water for coffee, eggs like stones. No wonder I have to get up. Who was at church?"

"I didn't look. Mrs. Fuselli. I met her coming out."

"She's getting old," Mrs. Galli said. "She used to go every morning at five o'clock."

Katie kept her eyes down. It might have been the earlier Mass at which she had seen the neighbor—when she went in to look for Tim... Her mother visited Mrs. Fuselli every day...

"You're spilling the milk," Mrs. Galli snapped.

Katie got the rag from the sink. Either her mother did not know yet that Tim had returned, or she was waiting to catch her off-guard with the information. The web of deception was growing thicker, and now it was becoming a film over her mind. She could think of nothing else. She wasn't any good at deception. She ached to be free of the fear and shame of it. You couldn't pray decently out of a lie. All you could do was make a resolution that if you got something you'd make up for the sin. It was almost like asking God to help you do something wrong. And it became harder all the time to face God. You began not even to want Him at all.

"He's back," her mother said.

"What Mama?" She did not look around.

"I said he's back. Your dime-store poet is back. I told you. Like a cur dog comes home when it's hungry."

Katie sunk her teeth into her lip. She would say nothing to provoke her mother. She would listen to the abuse and make no defense of Tim. Taking it out in talk on her, her mother would be easier on him. But this couldn't go on long. She would burst with it if she had to hold in her pride of him.

"Did you see him, Mama?"

"I heard him up there. Bumping around like a rat in a cage. I'll see him, don't mistake. He's going to the basement where he started. The first thing somebody comes looking for the room, they get it. Down he goes."

"Shall I beat up the eggs, Mama?"

"Beat them. Six of them. I'll put in the milk. You don't know how much to put in so they go further. Eggs, the price they are—oatmeal should be enough for them. And I'm warning you, Katerina. I'm watching you. Let me see one bit of fooling around making love—and he goes further than the basement."

Katie threw her chin up. "I don't want to make love with Tim, not the way you say it."

Her mother looked at her incredulously. "What do you want to do with him? Tell me. Wash his hair?"

Katie turned to her, near tears. "Mama, please stop teasing me."

Mrs. Galli came toward her. "I'm not teasing you, Katerina. Never in all my life was I so serious. I'm trying to figure out what kind of a girl are you?" She caught the girl's chin in her hand and forced her to look into her eyes. She let go then and shook her head. "The things a mother cannot tell to her own daughter." The words were more to herself than to Katie. "Leave the eggs and sit down to your breakfast. I'll make them."

Katie did as she was told, forcing down the tasteless lumps of oatmeal. While the boarders were at breakfast she made her own bed and her mother's, not even pausing outside Tim's closed door. Only on her way to work did she find relief from the oppression. And only then could she again begin to plan. This was to be her first payday.

43

Goldsmith cruised down one Village street after another, stopping at each Catholic church, waiting interminably and then showing Brandon's picture. Some of the priests thought they had seen Brandon, but they were not sure. When, near ten o'clock, he caught sight of Father Duffy in the rearview mirror entering a church the detective himself had just left, he decided to abandon that part of the search to the priest. For all the need for haste, there was no greater urgency now than there was each day since the Gebhardt murder. The chief pressure he had feared was from Holden, and that had been withheld.

He began a canvass of the area on foot. As he walked and made his guarded inquiries, he went over in his mind the kind of places Brandon might have worked. He stopped once and called the Building Service Employees' union. He expected nothing of the call, and got nothing. Brandon worked for his keep if he worked at all, and picked up an odd dollar handout.

The detective tried then once more to figure out the man's attitude toward his crime. He felt guilt toward it, part of the time at least. Otherwise he would not have gone to the priest. Being aware of guilt he must be aware of the consequences of the crime where the police were concerned. He must know that he is wanted, he reasoned. At such times, he would be cautious about looking for work. Suppose he needed a dollar? If he were desperate for it, what would he do? What did he have to sell besides his labor? Poems? The five-dollar check was in Goldsmith's pocket. Certainly not a quick buck. A handful of secondhand books? Possible. But Brandon would have to be absolutely desperate to sell his books. His tool kit. That would go first. Complete with hammer.

The detective called headquarters then to have every patrolman in the area check the pawn and junk shops on his beat.

44

Mrs. Galli ate her own breakfast after the boarders were gone. She sat over it a long while and then got up and piled the dishes in the sink. She went from one chore to another mechanically, wiping the oilcloth and folding it, cleaning the stove, the dust from the window sills. Upstairs Tim was pounding his heels on the floor as he moved back and forth across the room.

She needed advice now badly, desperately. If it weren't for her own guilt with him, she would go to the priest. Katerina was more important to her than anything in the world. She was the beautiful, sensitive child of her father. With a father in the house everything would have been different. Katerina was stubborn, secretive. But the hurt in her eyes that morning was not to be endured. And all this was her fault, the mother reasoned. She was a dirty old woman, looking for a man and her own lost youth. Stupid and full of lust, getting notions from alley-cats. Her stomach turned over with the thought of it.

She took the trash box from beneath the stove out to the refuse can at the basement door and emptied it. Bits of paper had stuck to the bottom through many emptyings. She plucked them loose with her fingers, grocery lists and coupons. She noticed figures on a scrap, and held it up to the sunlight. Fifteen had been subtracted from twenty-two dollars and fifty cents. The seven-fifty had been multiplied by four, coming to thirty dollars.

She put the paper in her pocket and went into the house. Katerina was supposed to be earning fifteen dollars a week.

Mrs. Galli washed her hands and face at the sink, not that she cared whether she was clean or dirty. But the water was cool and she could think better. Only once she glimpsed her face in the mirror, pale and hard and old-looking. No matter. She went upstairs, leaning on the railing with each step. Her breath was coming heavily. In her own room, she sat by the window for a few minutes, the breeze in her face. Now and then she glanced behind her at the dresser where her husband smiled confidently from his picture. Outdoors, a rag picker went by, a peddler with his fruit wagon. She had meant to buy some apples. No matter. A police car... If only she had renewed her license for the rooming house in July... No matter.

She got up and went to Katerina's room. Tim's books were still on the dresser. The room was no different than on other days. She opened one drawer and then another. Her daughter's clothes were neatly folded in their places, her knickknacks scattered in the top drawer, her rosary in a box at one corner. There was a letter from a girlfriend who had gone to Montreal for the summer, the dance program from her graduation night, a post-card from a boy with a picture of a steel mill: "Wish you were here to help me. Ha! Ha!"

The only sounds in the room were her own quick breathing and the ticking of the clock. She turned to see where it was. On the window sill. A foolish place for the clock. But Katerina probably slept with her head at the foot of the bed to get the breeze, and she had left it within reach to turn off the alarm. Mrs. Galli picked up the clock and looked at it. The alarm had been set for five o'clock. Katerina had gone to the six-thirty Mass.

45

While he walked back and forth across the narrow room, Tim tried to imagine himself scuffing up the dirt on a country road. He tried to pretend the wallpaper flowers were real, and for whole spans of pacing he succeeded. But each noise within the house brought him back to where he was. The noises themselves were not too bad. The distraction was only momentary, and after each one he could resume his flight. But when stillness settled on the house, his peace was gone completely, his peace and his dream. He listened at the door for the step of Mrs. Galli on the stairs. He had waited then, sitting on his bed. But she had not come to his door. She had gone into her own room and closed the door.

If only she had gone somewhere else, he thought, upstairs perhaps, he could have gone to her. Or if he had not waited. If he had gone down to her after he knew the boarders were gone. But he could never bear the sight of her room again.

He wiped the sweat from his face on his sleeve. His stubble of beard rasped across the cloth. If Katie had stopped before going to work, it would have made this waiting tolerable. A pulse was pounding in his head. He could almost hear it, and an ache was growing with its pounding. He could not tell then whether the sounds he imagined were in his own head or in the house. He went to the door on tiptoe and opened it a crack. Mrs. Galli's door was open. She had left the room. He saw her apron then, a flick of it, as she moved to the window in Katie's room.

He closed the door and went to his bed again. He plucked at the tufts of cloth on the spread. It occurred to him then that her slowness in coming was a good sign. She wasn't in a hurry to see him at all. Katie had said she expected him back. But she didn't care whether he came or not. She was going to leave him alone, after all. He could walk out into the hall and ask her what he could do around the house and she would give him a job. She wouldn't touch her hand to him. Otherwise, she'd have brought his breakfast up to him. She'd have come as soon as the door closed on the last boarder going out to his work.

He began to giggle with the relief, with the pleasure the thought gave him. He would never again have to be alone with her. Mrs. Galli swung his door open.

"The monkeys in the zoo laugh like that," she said. "I don't see anything funny. Maybe me. Am I funny?"

He had never seen her look so old, so sad. "I was laughing at myself, Mrs. Galli," he said.

"I wish I could laugh at you. Where did she find you?"

He remembered vaguely that Katie had asked him not to say that she had looked for him. "I came home."

"You couldn't find your way out of a floursack. Don't lie to me, Tim. There's already enough lies. I know she was out looking for you at five this morning. All right. I don't care where she found you. What I want to know: what's going on between you and her?"

"There is nothing going on, Mrs. Galli. Nothing you can't see with your own eyes."

"My eyes don't see at all what I know here." She pointed to her breast. "She can't think of nothing but you. She steals from her own mother for you. My Katerina was a good girl till you came."

"There is no better girl living than she is, Mrs. Galli. And I'll give my life to see that no evil comes to her."

"Your life isn't worth enough for that. What you've done with it, what good is it to her?"

"It's all I've got, and I'd give it to her."

"You'd give her a bag of moonbeams and fleas. I don't want you giving her anything, Tim Brandon. I don't know what you are, but you aren't a man. I don't want my girl spoiling her life with you. I don't care anymore who she takes up with. That Tommy, maybe. He's not so bad. He used to talk to me about her. I want her to marry him. He'll give her two rooms anyway, and kids."

The pulse had begun to pound again in Tim's head. He forced it still with his hand. "He'll give her dirty jokes," the words choked out. "And his big, fat hands all over her body."

"And there's something the matter with that when the time comes?"

Tim's eyes were wide upon her, incredulous and full of loathing. "You filthy slut," he said. He buried his hands in his face, pressing his fingers into his forehead.

Mrs. Galli crossed the room and yanked his head up by the hair. "Tell me, Mr. Angel, how do you think children get born?"

He only stared at her.

"To you just dirty people go to bed. You think of her and come to me to make believe you're a man…"

"Jesus, sweet Jesus," he whispered.

"Now you stay here. I want you to stay here a while. I don't know what else to do. I don't want her running away after you. But listen to me. If anything happens I don't like, if anything happens before I can talk sense to her, I'll talk the truth to her. I'll make her see. I'll tell her about you and me that day. Yes! You don't want that, do you? It would dirty her mind. It's better if her mind gets dirty. It's better she hates me, her own mother. Just so she hates you, too, Tim Brandon."

She flung him away from her and wiped her hands on her thighs. At the door she turned. "Think about that. Think good. And take those books out of her room. She don't need books for what she's got to learn now."

Tim pounded the calves of his legs against the iron railing of the bed, anything to distract him from the other pain. He could scarcely see with it, except the sworling yellows, browns, greens, oozing into one another. He took one hand from his head, and groped beneath the bed for his tool kit where it had lain for so many months.

46

From one rectory to another, Father Duffy worked his way downtown, inquiring in English and in his meager knowledge of Spanish which he had picked up from Father Gonzales. He came upon two priests who were fairly sure they had seen Brandon, and one who had given him a job the winter before. It was at a little church near the river called Mary, Refuge of the Sea. But the priest had no idea where the man had come from or where he went. "So many like him, Father. There aren't more fishes washed in from the ocean than men like him beached in New York."

At noon Father Duffy had to return to St. Timothy's. The Monsignor had insisted that he preside at a luncheon of the women's Altar and Rosary Society. It was late afternoon before he took a bus down Tenth Avenue and commenced again at Fourteenth Street near the river.

47

When Goldsmith called headquarters at four o'clock he received word of the tool kit. It had been sold to a secondhand store on Hudson Street that morning. He reached the store within ten minutes.

"That ain't the guy," the man said when Goldsmith showed him the picture of Brandon. "No sir. That ain't him. It was a big fellow. Big face with a nose like a piece of raw beef. I never seen a nose like it. He didn't get that smelling flowers. Not except there was a bee in them."

"A real tramp," Goldsmith said. "Is that it?"

"A Bowery bum if I ever seen one."

Goldsmith nodded. "Got a pair of pliers?"

The man got him one from the back room. Very gingerly, Goldsmith yanked open the strap with which the kit was fastened. It unfolded itself. He took a flashlight from his pocket and shone it on the hammer. Under the concentrated light little brown streaks were visible in the grain of the wood even to the naked eye. He waited at the store until a police car came for the kit to deliver it to the laboratory.

"How much did you give him for it?" he asked, while waiting.

"Seventy-five cents. That wouldn't last that baby till ten o'clock. Three, maybe four shots."

"If he had that kind of a nose, he could get a quart of his stuff for that money," Goldsmith said.

"Smoke?"*

"Yeah. Three-quarters kerosene."

The storekeeper shook his head. "Damn shame what people let happen to themselves."

"Yeah," Goldsmith said. He hadn't a chance in fifty of finding him. "He was here when you opened?"

"I wasn't in the place two minutes when he shuffled in."

He had found the tool kit, Goldsmith thought. That was even less consolation. It indicated Brandon was on the move. He had probably found it in a park. He might have snatched it when Brandon was asleep. There were two small parks and one large one within a few blocks. He ruled out Washington Square because it was the furthest. Besides which there were many more likely stores in its vicinity than this one. He decided against Sheridan Square also. Its route was zigzag through the Village. The tramp who got the kit would pick the straightest line to his money. Three blocks due north was Abingdon Square. It was no park, but a few scrawny trees poked out of it, and there were benches and a water fountain.

He checked his watch. He had less than three hours of daylight. He liked to work in daylight. Moving restlessly about the store waiting, he thought of Father Duffy. The priest might be closer to Brandon than he was. If Brandon had been turned out of where he stayed, he might go to a parish house for a handout in the morning. He called St. Timothy's then, and found that the

---

* Slang for "toxic, potentially fatal solvents used as substitutes for alcohol for the truly desperate." Tom Dalzell and Terry Victor, eds., *The New Partridge Dictionary of Slang and Unconventional English* (London: Routledge, 2006), 1792.

priest had left a few minutes before. He was not expected back until late evening.

He rode north two blocks in the car on its way to the laboratory and walked the rest of the way to Abingdon Square. No one had paid any attention to him as he got out of the prowl car. That was the way he wanted it.

Three youngsters were playing in the square, squirting one another from the weak spray of the drinking fountain. On one bench a woman sat fanning herself with a newspaper with one hand and rocking a baby buggy with the other. A couple of derelicts were stretched out on the ground, their backs to the fence in the only shade in the square. Goldsmith edged his way to the drinking fountain through the water fight. Neither of the two vagrants looked like the red-nosed customer. He was probably far, far away, crazy, mad-drunk, the detective thought. Leaving the fountain, he took off his hat and fanned himself with it. He sat down on a bench, his back to the tramps, and waited.

Presently, as he had anticipated, one of them scrambled to his feet and approached him. "Can you let me have a quarter, mister? I ain't had nothing to eat all day."

Goldsmith reached into his pocket. He let his hand rest there, promisingly. "You been around here all day?" he asked.

The tramp sneered. "I own the place. You're trespassing."

"I'm serious," Goldsmith said, drawing a dollar bill from his pocket. "I'm trying to check up on somebody. If you were around here maybe you saw them."

"I get it. Your wife, huh?"

"Maybe," Goldsmith said.

"A tall woman. Good looking. Not too tall maybe, not skinny, but kind of..." The tramp made futile gestures of improvisation.

"What kind of a woman is that?" Goldsmith said, grinning. "Here." He gave him the dollar. "You didn't happen to spend the night here, too, did you?"

"Me? I got a feather mattress and silk sheets. Never get out of it till noon. Thanks, bud." He slipped the bill in his pocket and motioned toward his partner. "Now there's a guy who's really got a lease on the place."

"Send him over," Goldsmith said.

He couldn't hear what went on between the two men, but he heard a long sigh and enough grunts to hoist an elephant. "Goddam," he heard. "I'm getting rheumatism."

"You giving away something?" the man asked, letting himself down easily on the bench.

"I'm buying, not giving. You spent the night here, right?"

"Maybe."

"You didn't happen to pick up a tool kit a fellow left here?"

"No sir. It wasn't me. I can't run that fast no more. The guy just went off and left it, anyway. Some kid came in and got him. Kid? Seventeen, maybe. Shawl over her head. God, it'd turn your stomach, them sitting there holding hands when she found him. Giggling like a couple of squirrels. Six o'clock in the morning. I ask you, is that civilized?"

"Not when somebody's trying to sleep," Goldsmith said. "What were they talking about?"

"Home. Home. That's the only word I got. Yeah, and something about flowers and birds. Hell, how do I know what they were talking about at that hour? But they sat there chattering like squirrels. Nuts, I'd say. Real gone. Then she leads him out of here like he was sleepwalking."

"Which way?"

The tramp nodded uptown. "They turned out of sight pretty soon. You see, we kind of had our eye on..."

"I know," Goldsmith interrupted. "Which way did they turn, east or west?"

The tramp scratched himself. He motioned with his right hand. "They went up that side of the street so I guess it was that way. East, ain't it?"

Goldsmith nodded. He had been just off the area, combing the mesh of the Village. He gave his informant a dollar and left the square.

48

It had been a slow day in the little office in the back of the paint store where Katie worked, slow in business, and slower for her because of her anxiety for Tim. Several times during the day she was tempted to call home, not that Tim would answer the phone if it were to ring the whole day through, but just to have some contact with the house. She resisted, not wanting to betray her anxiety to her mother.

At four o'clock she received her first pay envelope. The withholding tax jarred her. She had not calculated on it at all. Now and then through the day she had planned on changing the twenty-dollar bill into fives and singles on the way home, and when the envelope came there was not even twenty dollars in it.

Counting the money over, she despaired of saving enough to do anything for Tim in time. She knew from his nights and days of pacing that the little room in the back of the house was a prison to him, especially when he couldn't work. Now it seemed to her that he had not worked for months. She could not even remember seeing his papers. He had left her only his books, and he had come home with her that morning empty-handed. Either he had hidden them some place or he had lost them. Her hands were moist as she turned the pages of the catalogue, and copied the numbers of an order.

For an instant only could she concentrate on her work. She began to compute the amount she could hold out from her mother for the tax so that she would have something left. She was already sickened with the deception. Gradually she began to shape a desperate plan. There was enough money in the envelope to get them a few miles out of New York. They could sleep outdoors. Tim was used to it. He would love it, and with him near her, she would not mind. She could get a job as a waitress. They could manage. Tim would go without her if she waited. She was sure of that. He might not want to. But her mother would hound him, and he would have to run away. And now with her mother knowing how she felt about him...

Her boss came into the office, rolled down his sleeves and put on his coat. He looked over her shoulder a moment. Her fingers trembled as she turned a page.

"You scared of me, kid?"

"No sir."

"I hope not. I don't like nobody scared of me but my wife, and she won't scare easy."

Katie merely stared at the order book.

He flipped her chin with his forefinger. "That's a joke, honey. Look kid, get that order in the mail and knock off for the week-end. It's too damned hot around here for working." He took his hat from the hook. "The lock's set, but see that you slam the door. Happy weekend."

"Thank you Mr.——" she started, but he was already gone.

She managed a few moments' concentration and finished the order. She stamped it and laid it in the drawer on top of her purse. Friday night's supper was at five-thirty, she calculated, cold fish and hard-boiled eggs and salad. Every Friday night she did the dishes while her mother dressed and went to the Ferreros' to play pinochle. Ordinarily she was gone from the house by six-thirty. She did not return until almost midnight. In that time, surely she could persuade Tim to the rightness of her scheme. He could get his things and she could pack a few pieces of clothing...

Her heart was pounding and her mouth was dry. The thought of facing her mother in that long hour of waiting through supper was more than she could endure. She would betray them, breaking a dish, crying, laughing foolishly...

She went to the washroom and let the cold water run over her hands and wrists. She cupped the water in her hands and bathed her face. The first lines of prayers came to her but slipped away, unfinished. This was something in which, somehow, she could not ask God's help. Returning to her desk she called her mother and told her that she had to work late.

49

Working late, Mrs. Galli thought, hanging up the phone. Working late. Leave the dishes for me, mama. Don't worry. I got paid, don't worry. Go to Mrs. Ferrero's like every other Friday night. Don't worry. Leave them alone in the house to plot and scheme, to run off together maybe.

Panic began to overtake her. Was this to be her life from now on? Was she to have to watch one of them every minute? She picked up the phone and dialed the bakery. When her brother-in-law answered she asked for Johnny.

"Gone?" she said, after a moment. "He can't be gone. Ped, please run upstairs to his room. It's very important."

"I can't run upstairs. It won't do no good."

"Please, Ped, go anyway."

"I tell you, Lenore, he's gone. Monday he'll be back. I know. I'm all by myself. The ovens are killing me."

"But he didn't tell me," she said.

"He don't want to tell you. Him and another fellow they got the automobile. They go up to the country some place, play the concertina for a dance. I tell him he lose the business. What does he care?"

"What does he care," she repeated and hung up the phone.

She was still standing at it when her brother-in-law called back. "What's the matter, Lenore? Do you need something?"

"I need my children," she said almost in a whisper, and then loud enough for him to hear: "It's all right, Ped. Everything's going to be all right."

50

Father Duffy rang the doorbell of the parish house at St. Ambrose. While he waited, he turned idly on the steps and glanced down the street. A man standing on the corner was watching him. He tipped his hat and the priest recognized Goldsmith. This, then, was it, he thought. The trail was almost ended.

The housekeeper came, taking off her tea-apron. The rector and his assistant were at supper and they had guests, but on Father Duffy's insistence she took his message in. He watched Goldsmith from the parlor window while he waited. The detective turned away then, looked at his watch and went into a tavern on the corner. Straining to read the lettering on the window, the priest made out the name KREPIC'S. He watched the building for a time that seemed without beginning or end. From the rectory dining room came the sound of laughter. The pastor was in no hurry to leave the table.

"Sorry," he said when at last he came. "I have guests from the chancery office. What can I do for you, Father?"

Father Duffy turned and introduced himself. He drew Brandon's picture from his pocket.

"Yes, I've seen him," the pastor said, his impatience in his voice. "I don't know him well at all. Just by sight. A very fervent sort of fellow. Something about him suggestive of the seminary. I shouldn't be surprised…"

Father Duffy could not wait. "Do you know where he lives, Father?"

The pastor thought about it. "I shouldn't be surprised if he lives with Mrs. Galli. A boarding house down the street. I've seen him at Mass with her daughter."

"Her daughter?" Father Duffy repeated.

"Katerina. A beautiful girl. The two of them make a very devout couple."

"How old is the girl?"

The pastor straightened a picture on the wall while he thought about it. "Sixteen or seventeen. A bit young for that fellow. But it sometimes happens. These people marry young, you know. Marry young and raise large families."

"Can you give me their address, Father?"

"Not right off, I can't. You might try the phone book. The mother's name is Lenore. Keeps a boarding house. A widow. If they don't have a phone, I can look it up on the parish lists for you."

Father Duffy found the address in the phone book.

51

Katie watched the house from the doorway of a condemned building halfway up the block. She clutched her pocketbook until the buckle left its shape deep in the palm of her hand. As people passed she ducked to her knee and pretended to fix the strap on her shoe. No one must recognize her and talk to her now. She didn't think she could speak to anyone in the world at that moment except Tim. She heard the church bell ring at six o'clock. Every moment that passed after that was a labored hour. She tried to force herself to think of what she should do if her mother did not leave. She must think of that. She must think in terms of waiting, of persuading Tim to wait in some few secret moments snatched with him.

One of the boarders came out of the house. He had had his supper. She could see him working with the toothpick. He stood on the steps, shouting a conversation with someone across the street. He was dressed for an evening out, she could see, the sports collar outside his jacket. Why didn't he go? He waved as the person he was talking to moved on up the street. Which way? She listened for footsteps. In this place, her back against a boarded door, she had cut herself off from flight. The footsteps came. Desperately, she lowered her head and then lifted her skirt a little, fastening and unfastening a garter. A neighbor, seeing a girl do that, would glance away and keep on going.

The man walked on, not even seeing her in the semi-darkness. She could feel the perspiration running down between her breasts. The other boarder came out of the house then, and the two men walked up the street together. She took deep, shuddering breaths of relief.

Her mother came outdoors. She paused a moment on the steps. Although her head did not move and she seemed to be looking for something in her purse, Katie wondered if she were not looking up and down the street without letting on. She decided it was her nerves, her imagination, for Mrs. Galli had taken a hairpin from her purse and with it tucked a wisp of hair into its braid. She straightened the collar of her dress, and started up the street in the direction of the Ferreros'.

Katie hung back until her mother turned past Krepic's, and then waited no longer. Almost blindly she dashed from her hiding place across the street and into the house.

"Tim," she called, running up the stairs. "Tim, it's me, Katie."

He opened his bedroom door for the first time since Mrs. Galli had closed it behind her that morning. Katie stepped back involuntarily at the sight of him. His eyes were bloodshot and his face so gray that it was almost blue. He had gotten old since she had left him. He looked as though he had been beaten and tortured.

The veins stood out like welts on his forehead. And there was a close, sickly smell from the room.

"Oh, Tim." It was all she could say. She stood limp in front of him.

"I didn't think you were ever coming again," he said. "But I waited for you."

Behind him, the bedclothes had been torn from the bed. The sheets were twisted into ropes. At first she wondered if her mother had tried to lock him in the house. Then she realized the full horror of it: he had intended to kill himself.

"You're a Catholic, Tim." She pushed him back into the room and followed him. Something in saying the words gave her calm, strength. She could think straight.

"'If thy right eye scandalize thee, pluck it out...'" he started, his voice a thin chant.

She whirled on him. "Shut up, Tim! Stop it! Do you hear me, you're not to say that."

He stopped and watched her, his lips parted.

"What have you ever done in this life but kindness? Tell me that, Tim. What have you ever done that was wrong?"

He shook his head that he did not know.

"And has anybody ever been good to you for it?"

"Many, many people, Katie. But only you, really."

"Now listen to me, Tim. I've got everything planned." She watched him pluck at the ends of the dresser scarf. "Leave that alone. We don't have to be nervous. There's nobody home but us. Mama's gone out like she always does on Friday night. Remember? Are you listening, Tim?"

"You're like the voice of angels," he said.

"We're going to leave, Tim. You and me tonight. I've got enough money for a little while. It'll get us some place on a bus. We'll figure that out on the way. It's summertime. We can live outdoors. I'll get a job and you can write. What did you do with your poetry?"

"What?" he asked stupidly.

"Your poetry, your writing. Where is it?"

"I destroyed it. I burned it up piece by piece in a little can in the park."

"Why, Tim? What on earth made you do that?"

"It was like…like that." He pointed to the twisted bedsheet.

"Oh no. It was good. I know it was good."

"How do you know that?"

"Because you wrote it, dear stupid man." She met his eyes and forced him to look at her.

The tears came to his eyes and he turned away.

"Will you come, Tim?"

He nodded slowly that he would.

"Everything will work out. I know it will, Tim. Turn around and listen to me. We've got to hurry. The further we get away, the better. I don't know what mama will do. She doesn't know you like I do. She doesn't understand. Where's your clothes?"

"I don't know."

"You lost them. You lost your tool kit too, didn't you?" He nodded.

"Maybe we can buy another one if you get a job for a while. It might be easier for you to get a job than me. We'll see. I'll find some old shirts of Johnny's. Have you been in here since this morning?"

Again he nodded.

"You've got to go down to the icebox and get something to eat. You've got to do that, Tim. I haven't time. We've got to hurry."

"I'm not hungry."

"You're weak and we won't have time to eat. We've got to save our money. Tim…" She put her hand on his shoulder and turned him around. "Do you want to do this?"

"More than anything in the world," he whispered.

"Look at me. Look at my eyes."

He obeyed her.

"I love you, Tim."

She was gone from the room the instant after she had said the words. He fumbled about the bed, trying to unfold and smooth the twisted sheets.

52

"Take another look at him," Goldsmith said, the picture in his hand. "You've seen him. Think about it. Who was he with? A young girl, maybe?"

Krepic glanced at the picture again. "Sure I seen him. I know I seen him. Maybe yesterday, maybe last week. How many men go by here with young girls? I ask you, how many couples? It's summer. They go walking." He slapped his hand on the bar. "This I know. They don't come in here. Them what come in, I know."

Goldsmith turned around. He had been watching for the priest through the bar mirror. The glass was deceptive, murky. The priest might be quicker. And he could not follow him, anyway. Wherever the priest intended to go, he might pass up if he knew the police to be on his coattail. The detective glanced from the parish house to the police call box. Three patrol cars were waiting, their radios set. For what, he thought. The only course left to him now was canvassing, house by house.

While Goldsmith stood here, his back to the bar, Mrs. Galli made the turn at Krepic's. Stopping at the side of the window and turning back there to watch her own house from the shadow of Krepic's entrance, she was directly in the detective's line of vision. He watched her hand fumble for the side of the building to support herself. A distraught woman, he thought. He changed his position that he might see her better. Her face was distorted with rage or some other violent emotion, her mouth twisted almost into a grimace She was breathing hard.

"Who's this woman out here?" Goldsmith asked.

Krepic looked around. "Mrs. Galli. Lives up the street. A customer of mine. Every Saturday night, three quarts of wine…"

"Does she have a daughter?" Goldsmith snapped.

"Yeah, she does. Nice kid. Say, the old lady looks bad. What's the matter with her?"

"Why don't you get her in here and give her a drink?"

"I don't need orders from you for that. I take care of my friends." He was already around the bar.

"Don't pay any attention to me," Goldsmith called after him.

Krepic led the woman into the tavern as he might have persuaded a child from a window-ledge. "You don't look good, Mrs. Galli," he cajoled. "I fix you up. Krepic knows how to take care of you. Here." He pulled a chair from a table by the window and maneuvered it behind her. "Sit down. Easy does it."

She kicked the chair away. "I want to look by the window. Five minutes I want. I give them five minutes. Tell me then, Krepic."

Goldsmith looked at his watch. Surely in five minutes the priest would be out of the house. Or did he need him now? He waited. What a monstrous hoax this would be on him, if Mrs. Galli were watching a vagrant husband!

"A little wine," Krepic said. "I give you a little wine. It will fix you up like that." He went behind the bar to get it.

Goldsmith took Brandon's picture out. As soon as the wine was poured, he picked up the glass while Krepic was returning the bottle to the shelf. He carried it to the table and set it before the woman. He held the picture in front of her face.

"Ever see this man, Mrs. Galli?"

The woman's eyes darted from the window to his face and then to the picture. They rested on it only a moment. "No," she said. "Mind your own business."

"I want this man for murder," he said quietly. "I thought you might have seen him."

She spilled the wine in her agitation, but she did not speak.

"Do you want a policeman's help, Mrs. Galli?"

"I don't want help. What I have to do, I do myself. Leave me alone."

Krepic was around the bar. "Get out of here, whoever you are. Can't you leave the poor woman alone? Policeman? I gave you a drink. I give you a bottle to take home. Tell me what kind."

Goldsmith turned on his heel and went out. He walked to the call box and gave his location. The moment he left the tavern, Mrs. Galli ran from it and down the street, her big body rolling in her haste. Into the phone, he defined his area. As he turned from the box, he saw Father Duffy hurrying toward him. He saluted the priest and walked briskly toward the Galli house.

53

Mrs. Galli pushed open the front door and let it swing agape. She listened at the foot of the stairs, choking back her breath. There was movement upstairs. She pulled back into the living room doorway as her daughter crossed the landing.

"Johnny's shirts," she heard her say. "You'll look like a spook in them, Tim…"

The big woman started up the stairs, lumbering one step after the other. Katie, coming out of Tim's room, saw her. She stopped, unable to move backward or forward, her eyes and mouth open in horror at the look on her mother's face.

Mrs. Galli reached the top step. "Go to your room, Katerina. Go to your room and stay there."

"No, Mama…"

Mrs. Galli caught her daughter's wrist and pulled her after her. "My room. Better it is my room." With brute force she dragged the girl to the room at the front of the house. She held her with one arm while she took the key from the inside of the door and put it on the outside. Flinging Katie away from her, she lunged out and locked the door.

Tim was in the farthest corner of his room. His eyes were wild on her, the eyes of a trapped animal mad with fright.

"The police are coming for you," she said. "Get out of my house. I don't touch you. I don't dirty my hands. I go in with my daughter now. We wait till you're gone."

"Don't tell Katie," he whimpered. "Don't tell her. She's all goodness…a holy child."

"She's not that good," Mrs. Galli said. "What she has to know I'll tell her. It's better she knows the truth about her mother than she dreams about you."

Mrs. Galli had not passed the head of the stairway when Tim leaped from the corner to the window. He pulled it closed and then drove his fists through it, the splintering glass slashing his hands and wrists. Unaware of the pain or sharpness, he loosened a long spear of glass from the frame, clutched it in his bleeding hand and plunged into the hall after her.

54

At the sound of the glass smashing, Goldsmith drew his revolver and started up the stairs. He shouted at Tim to stop, but when the demented man did not even hesitate, the detective fired. He fired twice more before Tim fell. Goldsmith let the priest pass him on the stairway. Together, they turned Brandon over.

Goldsmith then took the key from Mrs. Galli's hand where she was moaning and fumbling at the door. Inside, Katie was beating her fists against it. Police sirens wailed their approach. Goldsmith unlocked the door and went inside with the big woman and her daughter, closing it quickly behind him.

55

"Remember when you came to me at St. Timothy's?" the priest said, close to Brandon's ear. "You asked for absolution."

Brandon opened his eyes. "How did you find me, Father?"

"From your boyhood at Marion City—all this long unhappy way. I found your mother, Tim. She's in a convent. Very happy."

"How could they take her? I don't believe it."

"You're dying, Tim. I wouldn't lie to you in any case."

"She didn't have the right…" His voice trailed off.

"Before God, who are you to say who has the right or who hasn't to do anything in this world, Brandon? God's mercy is greater than man's justice. Pray with me now that in His infinite mercy, He will forgive your most grievous sins…"

"Tell them for me, Father. I don't know."

"The greatest of them is pride. You have been proud even to murder, which you cried on heaven to witness."

Tim managed to focus his eyes on the priest's face. "Talk to Katie," he said, "so she'll know the truth forever."

"I'll talk to her."

"Bless me, Father, for I have sinned…" His head lolled over on the priest's arm.

READING GROUP GUIDE

1. Who should get credit for cracking the case here—Father Duffy or Ben Goldsmith?

2. Do you sympathize with Tim Brandon? Do you think that Dorothy Salisbury Davis intends the reader to feel sorry for him or to find him free of blame?

3. Is Tim evil?

4. Are the characters of Mrs. Galli and Katie dated? Or do you think that there are contemporary people like them?

5. Do you think that priests should be free to break the "seal of the confessional" to save lives? Attorney-client privilege may be broken, for example, if the attorney believes that someone is in danger.

6. Do you have a sense of what Dorothy Salisbury Davis thought of the Catholic Church?

FURTHER READING

BY DOROTHY SALISBURY DAVIS

Mrs. Norris and Jasper Tully Series:

Death of an Old Sinner. New York: Charles Scribner's Sons, 1957.

A Gentleman Called. New York: Charles Scribner's Sons, 1958.

Old Sinners Never Die. New York: Charles Scribner's Sons, 1959.

Julie Hayes Series:

A Death in the Life. New York: Charles Scribner's Sons, 1976.

Scarlet Night. New York: Charles Scribner's Sons, 1980.

Lullaby of Murder. New York: Charles Scribner's Sons, 1984.

The Habit of Fear. New York: Charles Scribner's Sons, 1987.

Standalone Novels:

The Judas Cat. New York: Charles Scribner's Sons, 1949.

The Clay Hand. New York: Charles Scribner's Sons, 1950.

A Town of Masks. New York: Charles Scribner's Sons, 1952.

Men of No Property. New York: Charles Scribner's Sons, 1956.
     Historical fiction.

The Evening of the Good Samaritan. New York: Charles Scribner's Sons, 1961. Historical fiction.

Black Sheep, White Lamb. New York: Charles Scribner's Sons, 1963.

The Pale Betrayer. New York: Charles Scribner's Sons, 1965.

Enemy and Brother. New York: Charles Scribner's Sons, 1967.

God Speed the Night (with Jerome Ross). New York: Charles Scribner's Sons, 1968. Historical fiction.

Where the Dark Streets Go. New York: Charles Scribner's Sons, 1969.

Shock Wave. New York: Charles Scribner's Sons, 1972.

The Little Brothers. New York: Charles Scribner's Sons, 1973.

Collections:

Tales for a Stormy Night. Woodstock, VT: Foul Play Press, 1984.

In the Still of the Night: Tales to Lock Your Doors By. Unity, ME: Five Star, 2001.

CLERICAL NOVELS BY OTHER WRITERS

Chesterton, G. K. *The Innocence of Father Brown.* London: Cassell, 1911.

———. *Father Brown Omnibus.* New York: Dodd Mead, 1951. Includes fifty-one stories, including those in *The Innocence of Father Brown.*

Herr, Dann, and Joel Wells, eds. *Bodies and Souls.* New York: Doubleday, 1963. An anthology of clerical mysteries.

Kemelman, Harry. *Friday the Rabbi Slept Late.* New York: Crown, 1964.

McInery, Ralph. *Her Death of Cold.* New York: Vanguard, 1977.

CRITICAL STUDIES

Freeman, Lucy. "Gently into the Darkness: An Interview with Dorothy Salisbury Davis, Grandmaster of the '84 Edgars." *The Armchair Detective* 20, no. 3 (Summer 1987): 267–72, 274, 276–78.

Hays, R. W. "Religion and the Detective Story." *The Armchair Detective* 8, no. 1 (November 1974): 24–26.

Lachman, Marvin. "Religion and Detection: Sunday the Rabbi Met Father Brown." *The Armchair Detective* 1, no. 1 (October 1967): 19–24.

Paul, Robert S. "Realism Turns to Religion." In *Whatever Happened to Sherlock Holmes: Detective Fiction, Popular Theology, and Society,* 195–226. Carbondale: Southern Illinois University Press, 1991.

Spencer, William David. *Mysterium and Mystery: The Clerical Crime Novel.* Ann Arbor, MI: UMI Research Press, 1989.

ABOUT THE AUTHOR

Dorothy Salisbury Davis (1916–2014) was born in Chicago and adopted as a baby by Adolph J. and Margaret Greer Salisbury. Raised on farms throughout the Midwest, Dorothy knew hunger throughout her childhood, growing up during the Great Depression. She attended Holy Child High School in Waukegan, Illinois, and graduated from Barat College in nearby Lake Forest in 1938.

Her father was, she recalled, a cheerful man and an optimist. They shared a love of history and politics. Her mother, whom she described as more an Irish Jansenist than a Catholic, tried to raise her as a "little lady." Her father, a convert to Catholicism and "certainly more devout than his wife," in Davis's words, encouraged her to be an active person, with a love of animals. She later remembered the most traumatic event of her youth, when she discovered a baptismal certificate revealing that she had been adopted. It took her a year to confront her parents with this knowledge. "It was the only time I remember seeing

* Lucy Freeman, "Gently into the Darkness: An Interview with Dorothy Salisbury Davis, Grandmaster of the '84 Edgars," *The Armchair Detective* 20, no. 3 (Summer 1987): 274.

[my mother] cry," Davis wrote in 1984. "That whole room tilted over on its side and then somehow fell back into place again. I put everything back the way I found it. Except me.""

First employed after college as a magician's assistant, then by meat-packers Swift & Co. as a technical writer, she soon moved to *The Merchandiser* magazine as a research librarian and editor. In 1944, on a blind date, she met the Canadian actor Harry Davis, whom she wed in 1946. They remained married until his death in 1993.

Dorothy credited Harry for her career as a writer. Describing the development of her writing career in a 1984 essay, she wrote:

> *The hardest thing for me to account for as a writer is why I am a crime writer. It does not hold to say I am giving vent to suppressed anger. I could kick the cats or pound bumps on Harry. I think it goes more to craft, to the nature of the mystery form itself; more bluntly, to the demands the medium relieves the writer of having to put on herself, both psychological and technical.*
>
> *When I married I left the church—or again, left to take it with me, and one of the first things my husband gave me was the urge to write. I did not want, nor was I able, to write about myself. I got around that monumental problem by writing about something else of which I knew virtually nothing, murder. No matter where the writer starts in the murder mystery, the game is already afoot, and it concerns the ultimate in human misbehavior.†*

---

* Dorothy Salisbury Davis, *Tales for a Stormy Night: The Collected Crime Stories* (Woodstock, VT: Foul Play Press, 1984), xiii. Davis eventually identified her birth parents but decided not to seek them out. "I was losing the feeling for the deep parental attachment of my life—to the Salisburys." Freeman, "Gently into the Darkness," 274.

† Davis, *Tales for a Stormy Night*, xi.

Once Davis began to write—using her life experiences extensively in her work—it was as if a dam had broken. She produced twenty novels between 1949 and 1987, along with a torrent of short stories that continued until 2009. These won her five Edgar nominations for Best Novel and three for Best Short Story, as well as the Grand Master Award from the Mystery Writers of America in 1985. *A Gentle Murderer* was designated the "Haycraft-Queen Cornerstone" for 1951, as part of a list of 125 books devised by Ellery Queen and Howard Haycraft that highlighted the best from two hundred years of mystery fiction. Davis was also deeply involved in the writing community: she served several times as the executive vice president of the Mystery Writers of America (its working head) and once as its (honorary) president; she was also on the steering committee of Sisters in Crime at its founding in 1986.

While women writers had achieved success in the mystery field before 1949, including luminaries like Anna Katharine Green, Agatha Christie, Daphne du Maurier, Ngaio Marsh, Dorothy L. Sayers, and Mary Roberts Rinehart, Davis found herself part of the first generation of women writers to succeed with tales of domestic suspense. These included Charlotte Jay (1952 winner of the first Edgar awarded for Best Novel), Margaret Millar, Charlotte Armstrong, Dorothy B. Hughes, and Celia Fremlin, all of whom flourished in the late 1940s, 1950s, and early 1960s.[*] As the pendulum swung in the direction of women's liberation and equality for women writers, however, those authors were eclipsed by writers such as Helen McCloy, Barbara Mertz, Mary Higgins Clark, Ruth Rendell, Marcia Muller, Margaret Maron, Sue Grafton, and Martha Grimes, whose work featured spies, private investigators, and police instead of stories of homelife.

---

[*] Hughes and Millar were also recognized by MWA as Grand Masters.

When Davis died on August 3, 2014, at the age of ninety-eight, Sara Paretsky, another Grand Master and cofounder of Sisters in Crime, said, "[Davis] focuses on people's interior struggles much more than other thriller or crime writers do. She doesn't see some people as wicked and some as good. She sees people as having both qualities within them and circumstances, ambition or insecurity as leading you to do more of one than the other."[*] Davis herself explained this interest:

> *Nothing a writer can say about the villain or the suspected villain, or even the unknowing villain, is too terrible. It is only unsuitable if it is unbelievable. And that is where craft enters and where, by the back door, this writer, almost unbeknownst to herself, began to probe the darker possibilities of her own nature. I don't think that I have written a villain in whom I am not present… The best I can do for them is to make them, too, fallible, potential villains perhaps, and then urge them to proceed upwards.*[†]

Davis's tragicomic sense of humans and her awareness that people are not wholly heroes nor wholly villains informed her writing and her fascination with religion. Clergy and detectives need to plumb the human soul, and in pairing the two, Davis's writing successfully combined entertaining fiction with deep psychological insights.

---

[*] Quoted in Davis's obituary by Elaine Woo in the *Los Angeles Times* on August 10, 2014.

[†] Davis, *Tales for a Stormy Night*, xi–xii.